KYIV TRANCE

Gus Gresham

This novel is a work of fiction set in Ukraine during the Orange Revolution.

Copyright © 2022 Gus Gresham
All Rights Reserved.

ISBN: 979-8-8371-2467-9

First published in serialised form (2022) on Medium.com

Acknowledgements

For their valuable input and their unwavering support and kindness during the serialisation of this novel on Medium.com, a big thank you to my many writer-reader friends.

With special thanks to Martyn Waites & Emma Dunford for their fantastic encouragement with an earlier draft in 2007.

for Laurie

prologue

April, 2005

In a stupor, Richard had been haunting the metro system for weeks. Today, like other days, he rode the improbably long escalators. From deep down behind, he could still hear the accordion music and husky voice of the old busker in the strains of a Slavic folksong.

It wasn't necessary to understand Ukrainian to know that the song was about tragedy and loss.

He watched the descending commuters falling away to his left. A man with a forest of beard. A teenaged couple kissing, eyes closed. A statuesque woman with overdone make-up, smothered in mink, a Siamese cat placid in the crook of an arm and a lapdog nestled in the other. Two police officers, the ear-flaps of their hats in the fair-weather, *up* position, their gazes lingering on Richard a moment too long for comfort.

And suddenly there — *there*.

He recognised the set of her shoulders and her threadbare mackintosh the colour of mushrooms. Her dark bobbed hair and perfect face in profile. Her slender hand on the grab-rail.

For five seconds, he didn't move or breathe. Simply watched as she was carried further and further down, the dry ruminating groan of the escalators increasing her distance from him.

"Nadya!" he called. "Nadya!"

Some people looked back, but not her.

He began to clamber on the no-man's-land separating the escalators. It was a dangerous, crazy stunt, and he only abandoned it because he realised how close he was to the top. He pushed by the last few people and swung around and onto the downward escalator.

Nadya had joined the "fast lane". She was overtaking the stationery riders. Passing the police officers. Passing the woman in mink, who was so broad that Nadya had to twist sideways to squeeze through.

Richard's heart hammered. His breathing grew fast and sweat broke out on his forehead.

Where space allowed, he leaped two steps at a time. Where space did not allow, he barged and elbowed, ignoring the angry glares and remarks, the scandalised shriek from the woman in mink with her exotic pets.

What's with all the fur anyway?
Doesn't she know it's April?
Down, down, down.
Arsenalna.
Deepest underground station in the world.

Near the bottom, he glanced back at the sound of a fresh disturbance. The uniforms — forging their own aggressive way down.

He jumped the last three steps, stumbled and nearly fell as he hit solid, unmoving ground. He looked frantically about. Over the heads and hats. Between the packed bodies.

Where is she?

The old busker pumped his accordion and sang. Commuters streamed around Richard, all making for the arched entrances leading to the platforms.

Eastbound. Westbound.

A hand gripped his arm. Tightly. An unhappy face with compelling eyes loomed close. Cigarette breath and words Richard did not understand. It was the younger of the uniforms, ahead of his partner.

He pushed Richard against the wall.

From the westbound platform, Richard heard the familiar clatter and hum of an arriving metro train.

He tried to barge the officer aside. No good. He head-butted the officer. It was pure instinct. He had no idea he'd do such a thing until it was all over. The officer staggered away, blood slicking the lower half of his face. There was a nearby shout. The partner.

Richard ran for the westbound archway, battling though the crowd. He burst onto the platform and glimpsed Nadya getting on the crammed train. There wasn't time to reach her carriage. The doors were closing and more passengers were trying to wedge themselves in. He fought his way to the nearest door. Got a firm grip on the rubber-trimmed edge and hauled himself aboard. The doors rattled and hissed and finally shut.

The train lurched into motion.

Among the dozens left behind on the platform, he saw the uniforms. The one he hadn't head-butted was speaking into a radio.

one

February, 2000. London

Richard can almost believe the promise of the early sunshine. Almost deny the scene of horror laid out at his back. It's a winter morning. The sky is blue and the countryside glistens from last night's rain.
Don't look behind, he tells himself.
Why ruin such a nice day?
He could step into the meadow and enjoy the February sun. He could take off his boots and socks and feel the wet grass flatten beneath his feet. Could walk away and keep on walking, as innocent as the sleeping oaks. But he turns and looks.
There's a smell like freshly washed knives coming off the river. Such a pleasing smell. Or is it just pollution from the catheter factory? Trixie lies close by, half in the reeds, half in the water. Her face is turned towards the opposite bank, her long dark hair fanning out in the slow current.

The scene was a work of morbid fantasy, and many variations had shaped his nightmares. He didn't discover Trixie's body. She was discovered by a dog walker. And — as Richard told the police — he wasn't there when Trixie died seven hours earlier on that rain-streaked night in the first February of the new millennium.
She'd been making her way home along the river path, back towards the flat after meeting friends in the pub.
During the first interview, Detective Sergeant Dwyer was mostly on his feet, striking poses to the left and right. Sometimes he'd even stand behind Richard for particular

questions. Detective Inspector Maugham sat opposite, sucking her teeth and doodling notes.

"The dog walker," said Richard. "The one who found her. Are you planning to interview him?"

"It's a her," said DS Dwyer. "She's currently receiving trauma counselling."

"Trixie was a counsellor ... A student counsellor."

"Pity she didn't do some on *herself* then, and counsel herself into leaving you before it was too late."

Richard frowned.

"*Trauma* counselling?" he said. "Does that mean the dog woman was shocked at the sight of ... ? Does it mean Trixie was ... hurt in some way?"

"Hurt?" growled Dwyer. "Of course she was fucking hurt. She's dead. And you killed her."

"No ... no. I meant was she attacked? With a knife or something?"

"Why would you say that?" said Dwyer, though he sounded disappointed. "One way or another, we think you killed her and dumped her in the river."

"No."

"You argued before she went out. The neighbours heard you. Did she tell you it was over and you couldn't take it? Did you make sure it was over for good so that you were still in control?"

"No. No. No."

2000 — 2004. London

Some experiences change you utterly. It's not possible to go back to being who you were before.

Richard was never charged.

At the nadir of the ensuing grief, his philosophy to anybody who cared to listen was, "Shakespeare had it right. 'Life is a tale, told by a fool' ... *etcetera*. Most people blunder through their days in a series of hypnotic trances. Barely conscious. Never taking the blinkers off for more than a few moments at a time. Blindly following some hackneyed script laid down in childhood, no matter what torment it brings."

There was a little bar he visited every night, called Marrakech, where they served cloudy designer lager in frost-coated glasses. It went down well with tequila chasers. They had a reasonable lunch menu, too, and the bar was only a ten-minute walk from the university.

Because he was such a good English language and literature tutor, showing up at work half drunk was overlooked for a long time.

At some point in the dark early years of the new millennium, he was invited to resign. It was a comfort that he had substantial savings — once meant as capital on a house before Trixie's death.

Autumn, 2004. London

Never grasping where all the time had gone, Richard lay on the sofa reading a broadsheet newspaper one evening in late November 2004 when he saw the advert.

Kyiv School of English ... Come and teach at our brand new facility ... Immediate vacancies ... Visas and flights arranged ... contact Alexei Koval ...

At the same moment, the TV news cut to images live from Kyiv, where the "Orange Revolution" had been gathering pace. Furious crowds filled Independence Square amid allegations of vote rigging.

Richard looked at the impassioned protesters waving their bright orange flags and banners. They *cared* about something. They looked *alive*.

He sat up straighter and read the job advert again.

November, 2004. Kyiv

A second-storey window of the apartment building was a blackened hole open to the falling snow. Above the hole was a pattern of charring that resembled a twisted black crown, and all that remained of the balcony was a soot-caked ledge.

It was about four in the afternoon, local time, the light failing. Alexei parked the BMW and together they unloaded Richard's bags. Wind and snow whipped about their heads as they hurried to the entrance.

The interior was dimly lit and the walls were daubed with graffiti. A crude sign in Cyrillic was taped across the lift doors.

"Out of order," said Alexei, starting up the stairs.

"Which floor am I on?" called Richard.

"The tenth," he called back cheerfully.

"I hope there's not another fire, then."

Alexei stopped, turned and smiled. He had a broad face, intelligent eyes and silvery hair.

"Ah, yes, the fire," he said. "Don't worry, Richard. It wasn't an accident."

"*Wasn't* an accident?"

"I mean, for example, you don't have to worry about careless neighbours leaving burning candles next to the curtains. The fire was deliberate."

"Right. That's ... still worse."

"Business rivals," Alexei said with a shrug.

"Did the occupant get out safely?"

"No. He was burned to death."

Richard nearly said he'd check into a hotel until somewhere else could be found, but — perhaps in a very English way — he said nothing.

There was a smell of damp stone. Fainter smells of cleaning fluid. More graffiti. He couldn't be sure under the poor lighting, but the doors of the apartments they passed looked as if they were made of steel-plate.

On the tenth floor, a woman came out of the apartment to the far left. She wore furry boots, a big shapeless coat and a black beret with a gleaming spider-brooch on the front. Alexei spoke to her and waved a hand in Richard's direction. The woman looked Richard over as if assessing, with doubt, the suitability of a side of mutton on the market. She pursed her lips, gave a grudging nod and made for the stairs.

Alexei produced keys.

Richard watched in fascination as first a steel door was unlocked and then a conventional wooden door.

"Uh, this seems pretty secure," he said, fingering the thick steel-plate of the outer door.

"Yes," said Alexei, the sarcasm lost on him. "You will be safe. They're all like this. So far, the KSE — the Kyiv School of English — owns three apartments for the use of non-local staff and academics. I insisted that you came to this building. The others are in quite a rough area."

Richard strangled a burst of laughter.

This *wasn't* a rough area?

The bedroom had a king-sized bed and an *en suite* bathroom. The living-room had a television, an armchair, a sofa, a dining table. Through a curtain at the back, the kitchen was so small it almost wasn't there.

Alexei stood at the main window.

The snow fell faster, thicker.

"Are you checking that you've still got wheels on your car?" said Richard.

"Sorry?"

Richard joined him at the window.

"The weather," he said. "Is this normal?"

"Yes. Soon, the Dnipro will be so frozen over that you will be able to walk on its surface."

"It's too warm in here." Richard had already taken his coat and jumper off. "How do I turn the heating down?"

"You can't. It's state controlled. A legacy from the Soviet era. Okay, meet me at noon tomorrow, as we arranged. Take the metro for five stops. Get off at Maidan Nezalezhnosti — Independence Square. If you need anything here in Dniprovskyi, there's a shop at the crossroads. It sells groceries, vodka, most things."

When Alexei had gone, Richard dozed on the sofa for a few hours. Then he stood at the window again, watching the snow falling in the dusky light. Grey, run-down apartment buildings marched into the visible distance.

On the way from the airport, he'd seen tower-cranes at high-rise construction sites, the colourful advertising of luxury goods, plenty of modern Japanese and European vehicles on the roads. But there was nothing like that here. It seemed a part of Kyiv where the trusty old Lada ruled — built in the Fifties or Sixties, then forgotten and left to crumble.

Outside, a blizzard was raging.

It would be madness ...

Richard reached for his coat.

two

Snow blanketed the ground, making pot-holes hazardous. He nearly twisted his ankle twice before he began looking out for the giveaway indentations. Across a scrubby park at the end of the road, the approach to the metro station was cluttered with kiosks and stalls selling "groceries, vodka, most things".

He followed stone steps underground.

In a line, down one side of the steps, plump old women sat bundled up in coats and headscarves, their wares set out before them. One had potatoes spread on a piece of cloth. Another had eggs — sold singly if required, judging by the half-empty box.

Who would buy a single egg on the way to or from the metro? Wouldn't it get broken? Did these *babushki* make enough to sit here in sub-zero temperatures? Or were they so poor that they had no choice?

In a gloomy passage, more *babushki* and other vendors sold goods direct from the ground or from makeshift stalls.

Richard entered the concourse.

Commuters milled and queued, many wearing oranges scarves. Alexei had provided some plastic tokens for the security barriers, along with a metro plan.

There were system plans on the walls, too, but it took Richard a while to match up the Cyrillic characters and choose the right platform.

When the train clanked in, it brought with it an acrid smell of brakes. It was flat-nosed and ancient-looking, blue with yellow trim — the colours of the Ukrainian flag.

The journey offered standing-room only, but wasn't too crowded. He noticed that everybody held themselves upright and that any accidental eye-contact was soon broken. Despite the run-down appearance of the city's built world and its infrastructures, everything was impeccably clean. His overriding impression was of a culture that had its dignity.

Stations came and went. Carriage doors opened and closed. Five stops to Khreshchatyk, Alexei had said. The doors opened again. *Is this the fourth or fifth stop?* There wasn't time to compare the Cyrillic on his metro plan with the Cyrillic on the station wall.

He jumped off before the doors closed, then followed some orange-scarved teenagers up two of the longest escalators he'd ridden in his life.

The street was badly lit but the blizzard had abated. He trailed the teenagers as they pushed into the darker distance. Between railings and trees he saw statues and a fountain, lent spectral visibility by their coatings of snow.

At some shouted cue from the leader, the teenagers crossed over and went tearing down a side street. He hurried after them, the sting of cold air in his nostrils and the feel of blood quickening to his face.

Another couple of turnings and he'd lost them.

A car with one working headlamp sputtered past. Then stillness and silence returned, disturbed only by the pluming vapour of his breath and the dull crunch of his boots in the snow.

But on this street — flanked by partly lit five-storey buildings — was a little bar, set below ground, the sign over its window level with the pavement.

Café Oasis, it said in English.

Richard turned into the open gateway of the railing and went down the steps with two ideas in mind — a drink, and a confirmation that this dead, dark street somehow delivered itself into the centre of a capital city.

Inside, it was olive green walls and grey linoleum. Little tables with menus. A naked bulb hanging from a ceiling wire. Smells of coffee and cigar smoke. A window onto the sunken yard. No customers.

Richard judged the woman behind the counter to be about thirty. Giving him a blank look, she raised an index finger and drew it across her throat in a slashing motion, then returned her gaze to a wall-mounted television.

He wondered if the throat-slash gesture meant that the place was closed, or was about to close. He went to the counter anyway and placed his hands on the hammered-copper surface.

She now offered him a welcoming smile.

Before leaving England, he'd crash-coursed himself in basic Russian, imagining somehow that Ukraine would be a stopping-off point on a teaching tour of Eastern Europe, and that basic Russian might be useful.

"*Pivo, pazhalsta?*" he said.

She took a glass from a shelf.

A minute later, he sat at a table drinking beer.

The woman reminded him of Trixie. She had the same dark eyes and dark hair, a creamy complexion, high cheekbones. The way she blinked, too, was like Trixie — though it wasn't really blinking at all — more a closing and opening of her eyes in a slow, long-lashed manner.

As he finished his drink, she turned her head, smiled, lifted the counter flap and came over. She wore a simple black jumper with a crew neck and long sleeves. She smelled faintly of a musky perfume.

Richard watched her slender hand picking up the empty glass. She gestured. Another? He nodded.

Almost apologetically, she slid the menu towards him. Alongside the Cyrillic were the English translations. And there'd been the English sign outside ...

"*Vi gavoritye po angliyski?*" he asked.

"*Nyet,*" she said.

He pointed to an aubergine dish.

The woman frowned, but quickly flashed a smile.

She went back behind the counter and through a door to what was presumably the kitchen.
Richard heard muffled voices.
The woman reappeared, poured another beer and brought it over to him. Next thing, she was at the coat-stand by the door, putting on a threadbare mackintosh the colour of mushrooms.
Then she went out into the night.
Was it her knocking-off time? Would the dish now be prepared and served by somebody else?
Richard almost followed her. The thought of her going out into those cold dark empty streets disturbed him.
Anything could happen. Take Trixie ...
He steadily sank his beer.
At one point, a man came though a door in the back wall at the far end of the counter. He had a broad, square, clean-shaven face. He was tall and powerfully built and wore a blue shirt and a dark suit.
"*Zdrastvoytye,*" said Richard, offering the formal Russian greeting.
"*Zdraas,*" he drawled, not interested.
He gathered a sheaf of papers from beside the till and left by the same door. There were footfalls ascending a staircase, a rattle of keys.
The woman came back. She began to cross the room, keeping her hands in the pockets of her mackintosh — a poor woman's coat, Richard decided. The idea that she was poor and stuck in a shitty job only increased her appeal. But he was wondering now — as she crossed the room, avoiding his gaze — why she hadn't returned her coat to the coat-stand by the door.
Suddenly, he was on his feet, blocking her way.
She searched his face. Her eyes were wide. Rapidly melting snowflakes glistened in her dark hair.
Richard reached down and gently prised her left hand from her pocket. She became docile, as if hypnotised. He

thrust his hand in the pocket of her coat and could feel something firm, leathery, rounded.
He brought it out.
An aubergine.
He smiled. Or did he laugh?
The woman stared at him. She looked embarrassed and vulnerable. Very beautiful.

Richard left the café as soon as he'd eaten. Since the aubergine episode, the waitress had served him food and drink wordlessly, and otherwise stayed away.
He didn't attempt to find the city centre that night.
By the time he'd taken the four stops to Darnistya Metro Station, the temperature had plummeted. He was lost, too. He doubled back, doubled forward, but just couldn't find the apartment block.
There were no street numbers, not that that would have helped. He didn't know the address.
The picture was the same in both directions — spindly trees lining the quiet road, stark buildings looming in the darkness, a few shadowy figures shuffling about the snowy ground.
Fixed to the wall beside a closed shop was a blue telephone in a transparent head-and-shoulders cowling. But Alexei's contact details were in the apartment. Richard could visualise the silver lettering on the ivory-white business card — *Alexei Koval, Director of Studies, Kyiv School of English* — but he could not visualise the phone numbers.
His bones were frozen and his teeth were chattering like crazy. He whacked his arms against his body. Stamped his feet.
He started back towards the metro station. Nothing was familiar. He ducked into entrances checking for a crude sign on lift doors. At the fourth attempt, he found one, but the words were printed rather than hand-

written. Finally, a few buildings further on, he spotted the fire-damaged second-floor apartment.

Out the front, a man in a leather cap and navy boiler-suit was hard at work with a shovel that looked as old as he did. Snow was piled either side of the footpath. A caretaker? An overzealous resident? There was something grim and indomitable about the way he worked. He radiated a kind of old-guard Soviet attitude that would no doubt follow him to the grave.

"*Dobray vecher*," said Richard.

The man growled a similar greeting.

Richard went inside and trekked up the stairs to the tenth floor. The apartments weren't numbered, which, again, would not have helped anyway. It wasn't the one by the stairwell, he knew. Nor the one on the far left, because that was where the spider-brooch woman lived.

Of the two remaining, he approached the nearest and pushed his key in the lock. It wouldn't turn. Then it got stuck. With a yank, it came free, but the jolt made the steel-plate door judder and clang in its frame.

From inside, bolts were shot and lock mechanisms clunked. He had to back away as the door swung outwards. Then he was being eyeballed by a burly, cobble-faced man in vest and braces.

"*Dobray vecher*," said Richard. "Sorry, I ..."

The man came forward aggressively.

Richard backed off.

"Don't worry," he said. "I wasn't trying to break in. I'm staying here."

He raised his keys as evidence, but the man kept coming. Exerted his bodyweight against Richard. He was like a bulldozer. Richard backed up again and caught the iron stair-rail in his ribs.

He went down a few of the steps.

"*Vi gavoritye po angliyski?*" he said.

Something registered in the man's eyes, but it was fleeting. He advanced, bouncing Richard with his gut. Richard stumbled backwards down the rest of the stairs to the first landing.

"Wait," he said with a nervous laugh. "This is crazy."

The bulldozer man kept coming. He wouldn't speak and he wouldn't stop. He barged Richard towards the next flight of stairs — he was in it for the long haul, prepared to shepherd the "intruder" down the entire ten floors and out of the building.

Unless Richard wanted to fight, he'd have to retreat.

He began a rapid, dignified descent.

In a glance back, he saw that the man was now staying put, arms folded, legs spread.

Outside, the old-guard snow-clearer was resting a foot on the shoulder of his shovel and gazing up into the dark, starless sky.

Excited voices drew Richard's attention across the road, where a tall woman with long red hair ran ahead of a man who appeared to be chasing her. The man wore a shirt, light trousers and no coat. The woman was in a long fur coat and high heels. Her steps were surprisingly deft and nimble as she skipped through the snow.

Richard stood beside the old man with the shovel.

The woman was twirling round and round. Her red hair flew about her and the open coat showed that she wore only black underwear beneath. The young man caught up with her, and she laughed as she held her coat wide open and carried on twirling. Then she spotted Richard and the old man across the road, smiled and folded the coat about her. The young man put his arm round her shoulders and they laughed together as they approached a nearby apartment block.

The snow clearer drew on a cigarette, blew smoke from his nostrils and muttered a few phrases. Richard didn't understand the words, but speculated from context that it might be something like, "Young people today, eh?"

He gave the old man a nod and went inside to make another attempt at "getting home". He laboured up the stairs. Thankfully, the bulldozer man had abandoned his defence of the tenth floor.

Richard stood at the window of his apartment looking down into the quiet street. The couple had seemed genuinely happy. It was good that they were happy.

It was good ...

He thought about the woman at Café Oasis again. And he thought about how he had to meet Alexei in Independence Square at noon tomorrow.

What the fuck am I even doing here? he thought. *What am I doing with my life? I'm forty next May. What have I got?*

The snowy street swayed in his vision. He felt nauseous. He had the impression of being a hundred floors up instead of ten.

Some words of Marcus Aurelius came to him:

It is not death that a man should fear, but he should fear never beginning to live.

three

Late morning, and the train from Darnitsya Metro Station was packed. Many commuters were wearing orange scarves and talking excitedly.

At the next stop, a *babushka* with a wicker basket that reeked of fish squeezed in beside Richard. As the train moved on, he kept getting jostled against her. Once, his hand was stroked wetly and coldly by a tail protruding from beneath the cloth. The fish had to be dead, he supposed. But he wasn't sure if his hand or the tail had done the stroking.

By day, the sluggish Dnipro looked wider. In places, fat shoulders of dirty-looking ice jettied out from the banks. The bridge spanning the river in a series of stretched arches doubled as a road bridge, carrying traffic at a lower level. On the approaching hillsides, some of the golden domes of the monasteries and churches were visible. Under a harsh light that stabbed at the eyes, everything had a pale, washed-out quality.

Voices from a nearby group were raised in anger over a front-page news story. Accompanying the bold Cyrillic headline and columns of text was a picture of an attractive dark-haired woman.

On the other side of the river, the train stopped at Dnipro Station. The junction below was comprised of a wide road, a tram-stop and a transport-style café. It was here that the *babushka* with the fish disembarked.

Beyond Dnipro Station, the train plunged through tunnels threading deep beneath the city's wooded hills.

***

"Maidan Nezalezhnosti — Independence Square," said Alexei, meeting Richard by the entrance to the post office, as they'd arranged.

The crowds numbered perhaps several hundred thousand. A sea of orange flags and banners undulated all across the vast square. Legends on banners were Cyrillic, but one in English said, *'Stop Vote Corruption'*.

"We hope to overturn the election result," said Alexei.

"I did my homework," said Richard. "Allegations that the Russian-backed Yanukovych only won because of vote-rigging."

"Facts, Richard, facts. Not allegations. An independent report has identified three million fraudulent votes." He produced an orange scarf and offered it.

"Thank you," said Richard, draping the scarf round his neck. "It's ... a really big protest. Is it likely to get violent, do you think?"

But his words were drowned by a short loud burst of rock music from the amplifiers at the podium. Then somebody was speaking into a microphone and the crowd took up the chant on cue.

"*Razom nas bahato! Nas ne podolaty!*"

"Together we are many," Alexei translated. "We cannot be defeated."

"Is that a politician on the mic?"

"No. Just somebody. It's impromptu. The opposition leader Viktor Yushchenko may speak later."

"Right. What's that high monument over there?"

It was a tall column with a statue on a plinth. The sky was bright and hazy, and he had to squint to make out a robed and possibly winged figure with raised arms.

"Built three years ago in 2001," said Alexei, "to mark our first ten years of independence."

Richard had to lean close so that they could hear one another over the chanting.

"And what's up that hill, past the digital screen?"

As he watched, the giant screen flickering with images of dolphins underwater changed to an advert for Toyotas. The compass in his head was telling him that Café Oasis – and the waitress from last night – were somewhere in that direction.

"There is nothing up that hill," said Alexei.

"Nothing? Are there any cafés? Bars?"

"I believe maybe one small bar, yes."

"And a metro station?"

"Yes," said Alexei. "Arsenalna Metro Station is in that direction. I can tell you that it is 105.5 metres deep, the deepest underground station anywhere in the world."

Richard remembered the long, long escalators.

"Arsenalna is a good stop for Marinsky Park," said Alexei. He considered for a moment and added, "But there is nothing else there for you, Richard. Unhappy People. Dead Streets. Nothing."

He led them away from the square and along a wide curving boulevard flanked by stately buildings with ornate stonework around windows and doorways. At ground level, restaurants and shops flourished. Richard imagined the blind-windowed storeys above being home to governmental and civic functions.

"Khreshchatyk," said Alexei, waving a hand before him. "Constructed after the Second World War. The Red Army rigged the original buildings to blow up when the Nazis arrived. What you see today — these monumental edifices, this sweep of Stalinist architecture ..." He paused to check that Richard was impressed with his English. "It's the result of a frenzy of post-war reconstruction."

Even away from Independence Square, the main boulevard was home to a vast encampment. Thousands had erected tents and appeared to be living temporarily on the streets.

"The Russian influence in our architecture and our politics is undeniable. But we are moving into a new era.

The aim is to align ourselves more closely with Europe, with the West. Okay, enough dawdling and tour-guiding — your students are waiting. They are excited to have a tutor who is one hundred per cent English."

"Er, not exactly true," said Richard. "My grandfather was Russian."

Alexei gave him a look.

"I see."

"He's been dead a long time," said Richard.

"Of course. Now ... Your first group is already at a good level. They just need finishing off. Not literally. With an AK47, for example. Or a machete."

Richard laughed.

They passed a newspaper display-stand beside a kiosk. Three different dailies carried the same photo of a dark-haired young woman.

"The latest on last night's murder," said Alexei.

"Murder?"

"A semi-professional Ukrainian ballet dancer. Actually it happened near where you are staying. She was a guest at Hotel Yalta, which in relation to you is on the opposite side of the metro line. A taxi dropped her at the hotel around midnight, but she was found dead in bushes near the car park. Early this morning. Her throat slashed."

"That's shocking ... I ..."

Alexei scanned the newspapers again, then gave Richard a hard stare.

"It seems the police believe their man could be from out of town. Possibly even a foreign visitor. What do you think to that?"

"What? I ... I don't think anything. I mean — "

"A foreign visitor," Alexei repeated, his eyes gleaming.

"*What?* You think ..."

Alexei laughed and punched Richard on the arm.

"A joke! It doesn't say that at all."

Richard kept his expression deadpan.

"I may as well tell you," he said. "It *was* me. I teach English in a different European city each year and kill women. Last year, it was Naples. This year, Kyiv. Next year, Prague."

There was a micro-flicker of uncertainty in Alexei's face, then he roared with laughter.

"Ah. Very good, Richard. I see we both like to joke a little. It is terrible, however — the murder of an innocent young woman."

They walked under an arch in the high stonework and came out on a long narrow street where the buildings towered and threw down heavy shadows. The other end of the street was similarly walled in and arched, permitting only single-file traffic.

"Passazh," said Alexei. "In English, Passage. You see? And the KSE is here, above the photographic studio."

They entered a small foyer and took the lift up to the next floor.

"I spent some time with your group this morning," said Alexei, "and set them a task to start you off. I like to keep my hand in with teaching now and then. They'll like you, Richard. I'm sure of it. However, watch out for Lola Tismenetsky. Early twenties. Short red hair. She has been upset by the murder. She knew the young woman. Not closely. But they were at university together."

The high-ceilinged room smelled of polythene and perfume. It had peach-coloured walls. At the front were a whiteboard and a big, glossy, phonetics chart. The workstations were all occupied: nine men, seven women.

"Hello. My name is Richard Farr."

A few friendly smiles and hellos.

Most were in business suits. One blonde woman wore a fitted jacket of lime-green leather. Another wore a black diaphanous garment that looked like a negligée.

My name is Richard Farr. I'm thirty-nine years old. For some time now my life has been unravelling and spiralling in what I can only acknowledge as a terminal descent. You can see through the sham, can't you? Right through to the poisoned core?

"As you know I'll be your tutor until next spring."

One mature woman, a man of about eighteen — the rest between early twenties and early thirties. The men all clean-shaven, the women with impeccable make-up. All of them bright-eyed and eager.

"It's a big room. I'd like you to leave your workstations, bring your chairs forward and make a semi-circle. Then ... oh, that's great, thank you."

He waited while they finished getting into position.

"Thank you. So ... Alexei asked each of you to write fifty words about yourself, so that I can begin to know you and ... No, don't hand them in. I'd like everybody to read out what they've written."

An immaculate young man jumped to his feet.

"I am Sergiy Dralo. I am black hair and black eyes. I wearing very smart clothes and for work I am manager in the big company selling computers. I am twenty-eight years. I drive company car, the good Volvo with power engine. In bed my girlfriend likes me to ... Finish. Fifty words. Thank you."

It raised a storm of laughter and Richard doubted he could have planned a better ice-breaker. *Always good to have a joker in a group.*

"Well done, Sergiy. Who's next?"

The blonde in lime-green leather raised her hand. She had a prettily plump face, extra-full lips and eyes of liquid green ice. Richard thought that her origins had to be from much further east.

"My name is Annushka Yaremenko," she said, reading straight from her laptop. "I am twenty-five. My parents are from Siberia. We came to Kyiv when I was little. I work as manager in a book shop. I would like to start my own business. I am single girl. Romantical and homely. I have a poodle dog. I would like one day to meet a gentleman, sensitive and kind, and likes the children and animals. Possibly a man from Italy or America. Or from England ..."

"Ooh, Mr Farr!" said Sergiy. "How can you say no?"

The trouble with having a joker in a group ...

A man with gelled hair and a suit and tie stood up.

"Yvan Shevchenko. I am same family name of famous Ukraine football player, Andriy Shevchenko. He is play for Milan Italy now. I like football. I like my job. Importing shoes from Italy. Thirty-four years my age. I have one children, beautiful wife. I am born Sevastopol. Beautiful place."

A woman with short red hair stood up.

"My name is Lola Tismenetsky. I think that men who kill innocent women must be killed themself!"

She paused and looked around, eyes blazing.

"But maybe killing is too good for them. Yes. This man must be chained to the wall and tortured. Yes, tortured! With the very hot metal pressed on his skin. Open up his body with the sharp knife and bring out the stomach. Fingernails — yes, bring these out using the special tool I don't know the name of it. Pour acid on top of his eyes. Make him eat his own liver. Torture this fucking man for one year and he will die very slow and with pain."

The room was silent.

Sergiy Dralo had slouched down in his chair by now. He had his hands clasped behind his head and his legs stretched out, ankles crossed. A cocky, amused smile played over his lips.

"More than fifty words," he said.

Some of the other men laughed.

"Fuck you," said Lola.

"Er, right," said Richard. "A good speaking voice, Lola, and good pronunciation. Some vivid descriptions, too. Well done. Who's next?"

"Yes," said a woman of around fifty. "I am Galyna. I am happy to see you Mr Richard with an orange scarf. We need election fairness in Ukraine and we need peace. Not corruption. The news today, there were some people with hammers attacking Viktor Yushchenko supporters in Luhansk. Why should we have this violence in the east of country from Yanukovych voters? Orange Revolution is peaceful. After class I join my brothers and sisters protesting in the Maidan ..."

four

Richard took two more groups then went through some administrative procedures with Alexei. For the first week, he was to teach only in the afternoons.

It was dusk by the time he left the Kyiv School of English, the KSE. The boulevard of Khreshchatyk was festival-like in the dusk, with tents everywhere, rock music blasting and people boiling up water for hot drinks on camp-cookers. Independence Square was still packed with orange-flag-and-banner waving demonstrators. As he pressed closer into the square, he realised that different rock music was being pumped through amps on the temporary podium.

The atmosphere was friendly and vibrant — all the more impressive given the icy temperature. He thought again about Café Oasis, but he was cold, tired, hungry, and just wanted to get back to the apartment.

All evening it snowed.

It was snowing when he left the apartment the next morning. He jumped on the metro and got off at Arsenalna. It wasn't difficult finding his way back past Marinsky Park; down through the winter-white streets; past the five-storey tenements with their flaking facades, iron balconies and arched traffic entrances.

Café Oasis was the only business in the area. It was set in a deep yard. Along the front was a waist-high railing, the bars buckled inwards, as if from the sometime impact of a wayward vehicle.

He went down the steps and entered. A short, stout, woman served him coffee. She had a wrinkled face, grey hair in a bun at the nape of her neck, and wore a dark-blue print dress with white flowers.

Richard was the only customer.

There were no signs of the younger woman from two nights ago who'd reminded him of Trixie. No threadbare mackintosh on the coat-stand.

Before disappearing into the kitchen, the old woman switched on the wall-mounted TV. The programme was a Ukrainian chat-show of the Jerry Springer variety.

Richard sipped his coffee and watched the snow falling into the sunken yard. A heavy truck rumbled by, causing the window panes to rattle in their frames.

It was a worm's-eye view of the outside world.

She arrived at ten. Although she didn't look his way, her cheeks coloured slightly as she hung up her coat.

"*Dobray ootra,*" said Richard.

"Good morning," she said, eyes lowered.

Interesting, the English response ...

She went into the kitchen and came out a minute later wearing a name badge on her white shirt. He couldn't remember her wearing it last night, and he indulged the fantasy that it was it for his benefit, fished from the back of a drawer somewhere.

He got up and asked for another coffee.

The name badge was in English. It said *Nadya*.

"It's okay," she said, half turning from the coffee machine. "I can bring it to your table."

Richard stayed where he was.

"You *do* speak English, then?"

"Yes. Some."

Nadya placed his coffee on the counter.

"Come out with me," he blurted. "Tonight. A bar, a restaurant, a club. Anything you like."

She laughed and said, "I will be working."

"Tomorrow then. Or another day. Yes? No? Maybe?"

"No to everything," said Nadya.

He noticed that her hand was flat on the counter, palm down, fingers spread, mirroring the position of his own.

She looked him in the face. Her eyes were so dark that it was impossible to distinguish her irises from her pupils.

"How about at the weekend?" he said.

"No to everything," she repeated, closing and opening her eyes in that slow, long-lashed manner.

"*Nadya!*" came a gruff voice.

The man from the night before stood in the doorway that led onto the stairs. His square jaw jutted and his face muscles twitched.

Richard imagined himself storming over and — in the words of his ex-commando uncle — "decking the twat".

Nadya turned to Richard, smiled and said, "Sorry. Book-keeping."

He watched her go. In his thoughts, he replayed the simple transactions that had passed between them. He thought about the way she'd smiled and laughed, the grace of her movements.

No to everything.

December, 2004. Kyiv

Richard had never seen an uglier human, and he had to make a conscious effort not to stare. A beak of a nose stuck out from the squashed and haggard face. Eyes like bruised grapes swivelled this way and that. Beneath an open overcoat, he wore gold-trimmed purple livery.

He belonged in a fairytale — a footman for Cinderella's pumpkin coach.

It was Wednesday evening. Only Richard's third full day in the country. But it already felt like weeks – so swamped had his senses been with new experiences.

Deep beneath Khreshchatyk, he was waiting for the next train with about thirty other commuters. Some were in industrial gear or office clothes. Others were in evening suits and furs, ready for a restaurant or show.

And now he'd been busted. He looked away, but was aware that the man was strolling over. Closer, closer ... Richard pretended to look out for the train. Pretended to study the metro scheme on the marble wall.

"American?" came a bronchial voice.

Richard tried to ignore him, but the man persisted.

"American?"

He was less than five foot tall.

"English," said Richard.

"Same same," said the man. He laughed energetically and his breath smelled like an open drain. "Tony Blair. Charlotte Church."

"Yeah, *you're* clever," said Richard.

The man smiled. He went down on one knee, took Richard's hand and kissed it. Some of the nearest commuters laughed. The man sneered as he spoke now, loudly and at length, in Russian. More laughter from a few commuters. The man spoke in English again.

"Fuck your Big Ben and your bangers-and-mash."

A rush of warm air blew through the metro tunnel and there was a metallic clanking that grew nearer. Looking up at Richard, the man made a hacking, burbling sound in his throat. Then he spat a great gob of spittle and mucus into Richard's face.

Richard was too shocked to move or say anything.

The train hove into view. When it was only twenty metres away, he had a brief fantasy about pushing the man into its path.

Then it halted, the doors opened and people were getting off and on. The man winked theatrically and sauntered to a carriage, supremely confident that there'd be no challenge.

Richard found an old tissue in his pocket and wiped his face. And stood by as the train left without him.

Back in his corner of Dniprovskyi district, between the metro station and the apartment block, he stopped at the only local shop. It straddled two corner premises and its windows had a sea-green tint that reached halfway up the panes. He remembered Alexei advising him that it sold "groceries, vodka, most things".

Snow was covering him like an extra garment, so he stamped his feet and brushed himself off in the recessed doorway.

He stopped short, just inside, blinking in the sudden fluorescent glare. Despite the wall racks and aisle racks loaded with pre-packed goods, and the glass cabinets displaying meat and dairy products, he seriously wondered if Alexei had set him up.

Behind the long counter were three girls in their late teens or early twenties. Two held make-up mirrors and were applying lipstick. On Richard's entrance, they abandoned their beauty aids and adopted provocative poses. One even ran her fingers through her hair while giving him smouldering glances. She was wearing a leopard-print dress.

The place looked like a knocking-shop pedalling groceries as a front. Alexei's "most things" took on a whole new meaning.

"You are English?" said the one in leopard print, her accent heavy.

The customers were ordinary enough — a middle-aged couple handling and discussing a bottle of wine, a bent old man squinting at canned goods, a *babushka* shovelling handfuls of leafy vegetables into a basket.

The girls all smiled at Richard, flirting like crazy. Yet there was a disarming innocence to it as well.

"Yes, English," he said, stepping forward.

"Okay," said Leopard Print, "You want vodka, beer, cigarettes? You want tea, coffee, sausages, eggs, cheese, milk, bread, butter, biscuits?"

"Yes," he said.

She laughed, her bright red lips stretching back across perfect white teeth, her eyes half closing.

"All these things?" she said. "You want all?"

"No. Some milk. Some bread and butter. And cheese." She pointed to blocks of cheese in the display cabinet below the counter.

"This? This? This?"

The other two sashayed off to different parts of the shop. He couldn't help noticing how short their skirts were. They returned with his items and set them on the counter with little flourishes and happy curious smiles.

"I'm Bella," said Leopard Print, after the goods had been bagged up and he'd handed over some *hryvnia* currency notes. "Come back soon, okay?"

He'd had worse retail experiences.

The girls were too young anyway — even assuming he hadn't made a cultural misinterpretation of their flirty behaviour. But as he trekked home through the snow, he felt light-headed and was grinning like a lunatic.

On the Friday afternoon of his first week at the KSE, he went with Alexei to Independence Square. A few students tagged along. Orange flags and banners surged like a tide above the gathering. The KSE's administrator, Oleg Skarshevsky — a brooding, shaven-headed man — forged a path to the front.

In fur hat, overcoat and orange scarf, Alexei looked proud and vital and happy. He nudged Richard as — amid loud applause — the podium microphone was approached by an attractive woman with blonde hair in a long plait wound about her head.

"This is our Yulia Tymoshenko now," said Alexei. "She wants to be Yushchenko's prime minister when he wins. They are old allies in cracking down on crony capitalism."

"*Yulia! Yulia! Yulia! Yulia!*" chanted the crowd.

"She is nicknamed 'the Gas Princess'," laughed Alexei. "It's from her success as a businesswoman and energy mogul. But then she saw the problem of obscene wealth being siphoned off by Ukraine's oligarchs, and she fell out of favour with the Kuchma regime."

The crowd grew hushed as Yulia began speaking.

Alexei provided Richard with translated cherry-picks.

"Ah, yes, she jokes about the pro-Russian Yanukovych and how he dared to offer Viktor Yushchenko the role of prime minister. Yushchenko refused. Our whole point of being here in Maidan is that Yanukovych is kicked out and Yushchenko becomes president. Following that, Yulia as PM is pretty much a done deal."

"Intriguing," said Richard, only partly listening.

To his right, six or seven people away, stood Nadya.

He recognised the profile of her face, her dark hair in its long bob, the pale mackintosh. She wore an orange scarf today, too, and seemed to be with another woman.

"... and she recalls her conversation with Russian journalists from yesterday," Alexei continued. "How she said Mr Putin should set things right in his own country. Maybe introduce some Orange-style reforms himself. Instead of sticking his unwanted nose into Ukraine's internal affairs. Ah, yes, the media love Yulia. They also liken her to some kind of Slavic Joan of Arc."

"Excellent," said Richard.

When Yulia left the podium, Oleg and Alexei threaded back through the crowd. Others filtered out, too — including Nadya, Richard noticed.

He pushed forward, trying to influence the direction of his own group. At the edge of the crowd, he caught her up and said, "Nadya! It's Richard."

She looked flustered.

"Café Oasis," he said. "Remember?"

"Yes ..." she said. "I think so."

"*No to everything!*" he joked.

She lowered her eyes and smiled.

The woman she was with regarded Richard with suspicion. She was shorter than Nadya, and she had a ruddy complexion and a broad forehead.

"This is Alla," said Nadya. "She doesn't speak English. So, Richard ... You support our Orange Revolution?"

"Yes."

"And I am Richard's boss," laughed Alexei, beside them suddenly.

Oleg and three students hovered nearby.

"This is Nadya," said Richard. "Nadya, Alexei."

"Ah. *Nadya. Vi Ukrayinets?*"

"*Tak*," she said.

Then they were chatting. Richard felt happy. It was good to see the barriers coming down. Good to see her at ease in company.

"But the eyes of the world are on us," said Alexei, switching to English and gesturing an apology to Richard. "Poland's president Kwaśniewski is coming to Kyiv in a mediation role. Lithuania's president comes tomorrow. The West is watching, too. America, France, Germany — "

"We will be like our brothers and sisters in Georgia," said Nadya, "with their Rose Revolution. The reasons and circumstances are even similar."

A familiar chant had started up in the Square: *"Razom nas bahato! Nas ne podolaty!"* Together we are many. We cannot be defeated.

"It was nice meeting you, Alexei," said Nadya. "And nice to see you again, Richard. Alla and I will go now."

"No," said Alexei. "Please. We are having coffee in Passazh. My treat."

Nadya frowned. "It is kind of you, but — "

"You must come. It's my very special place. Just along past the revolution's Tent City. A few doors from the Kyiv School of English where your friend Richard is teaching. Okay? We are all going?"

five

The café on Passazh was itself called Passazh. It had turquoise ceilings and salmon-pink walls. Modern jazz. A smell of fresh pastries. Clientele who looked wealthy. Waiters and waitresses in white shirts, black bowties, black aprons, black trousers.

All the tables were occupied, but Alexei was greeted with joy and a large table by a window was "located".

As everybody's coats were whisked away by staff, Richard noticed that Nadya and Alla refused to give up theirs. They both appeared awkward as they sat down.

Coffee, pastries and vodka materialised in short minutes. Alla's eyes widened. She grabbed two pastries and began eating.

Oleg watched her from beneath hooded eyelids.

Nadya kept her hands in her lap and fended off questions from Richard's student Sergiy, who'd somehow ended up next to her.

"So," he said. "You are Mr Farr's girlfriend? Yes?"

"No," she said. "Is it compulsory to call him Mr Farr when he is your tutor?"

"Hah!" said Sergiy. "We can to call him Richard, but I am sucking up to him so I am get good marks."

Alexei had poured vodka into shot glasses for everybody. Now he rapped his own glass on the table and fired the vodka down his throat.

"*Slava Ukrayiniy!* Glory to Ukraine!"

Richard reciprocated along with the others.

"I should not be telling anybody this," said Alexei, lowering his voice, "but I have a contact inside the Supreme Court. You know ... the delays on their decision ... But later today, *they will announce their findings that the election second-round results are invalid.* We will get our re-vote."

"That would be very good news," said Nadya.

Oleg looked scandalised, but Richard guessed it was to do with Alexei's causal disseminating of confidences rather than anything else.

"Once Yushchenko is in power," said Alexei, "he will push for closer ties with the West. And for membership of the World Trade Organisation, NATO, the European Union — "

"It will not be so simple," said Nadya. "Russia's influence is ... There are the separatists in the east and the south of the country. The Rostov Cossacks are ready to get involved. Perhaps take power in Ukraine by force. They want the east and south to be part of Russia."

"You are right," said Alexei. "Although — "

"Nadya, your English is gooder than mine," said Sergiy, cutting across the conversation and looking her up and down. "And yet ... well, you ..."

Nadya blinked. Her cheeks flushed. She covered a frayed mackintosh-cuff with her hand and winced as Alla reached for another pastry.

Sergiy didn't finish what he going to say, seemed embarrassed and repentant, but Richard now terminally disliked him. He wished that Nadya had taken her coat off on arrival. He could see that she was wearing a good, black, polo-neck jumper underneath.

Alexei coughed and poured more vodka.

"Nadya is right," he repeated. "Although I understand that Ukraine's military is more than ready to prevent any violence during the protests. And I believe that they are in solidarity with the Yushchenko camp ..."

Richard wasn't completely sure if it was here — or at an earlier meeting — that he decided he needed to save Nadya. To rescue her. Protect her.

From what, he wasn't sure either.

But it was another moment of vulnerability for her.
And Richard's heart pounded.

Later that Friday afternoon, the Supreme Court made the announcement Alexei had predicted — the second round of the November elections was declared invalid. Now talks would focus on re-vote criteria.

Richard read about it on Saturday in the *Kyiv Post*, an English-language newspaper he bought from a kiosk at Darnitsya Metro Station. Sharing the front-page was a story about how the police were questioning a man in connection with the murder of the ballet dancer Maryna Petrenko. There were no details about the suspect.

After taking the metro to Arsenalna Station and following the familiar route, Richard was on his way down the hill towards the café when a black Land Cruiser with tinted windows pulled up outside. Three men got out and filed down to the sunken yard.

The two youngest were clean-shaven and gel-haired. They wore stylish black leather jackets. The man in the middle was about sixty. He walked with quiet authority, wore dark glasses and had grey hair in a pony-tail.

When Richard entered the café, the men were sitting at a corner table amid a fug of cigarette smoke, drinking vodka with Nadya's boss.

"*Pivo?*" said Nadya when Richard reached the counter.

"Yes, please. How are you, Nadya? It was good seeing you at ..."

She turned away to pour his beer.

"I will ... bring to your table," she said over her shoulder in a halting, stiff way, as if trying out school English for the first time in many years.

Richard sat by the window. From the corner, Nadya's boss looked over and made brief eye-contact with him. The three other men were laughing about something on a mobile phone.

Nadya opened the flap in the counter and brought Richard's beer to his table. She wore black trousers and a black jumper. No name badge.

"What time do you work until this evening?" he said.

She glanced towards the corner table, back at Richard, and said, "*Shto?*"

Then she busied herself straightening the menu and mopping up a tiny amount of spilled beer. He watched the dance of her slender hands.

"Why aren't you speaking English today?"

She half turned away, half lingered, smelling faintly of musk. Her left arm trailed behind her. Floated there. Almost invitingly. Richard reached out and gently closed his hand around her wrist.

She turned her head, eyes bright. He released her.

"Sorry," he said.

Nadya went back behind the counter and through the door to the kitchen. He could hear her talking with the old woman. Their talk was punctuated with muffled laughter. When she came back out, she didn't look in Richard's direction but was smiling to herself.

The men in the corner got up to leave. Nadya's boss let them file out, then went to the counter and slapped a sheaf of paperwork down. Nadya went rigid as he spat a chain of invective at her.

Then he saw Richard watching.

With a smile, he crossed to the table. He was six foot six and built like a mechanical loader. Richard shrank back a little in his chair. The man jutted his face forward, let out a bellow, and laughed because Richard jumped.

He waved a hand, inviting Nadya to laugh too, but she lowered her eyes.

A car horn sounded. Looking up through the window, Richard saw that the Land Cruiser was still outside, its rear door hanging open.

Nadya's boss left, got in, and the car pulled away.

"Don't worry about Pavlo," she said.

Richard nodded. He got up and set his empty glass on the counter.

"Another beer?" she said.

"Er, coffee this time. Pavlo ... *He's* a piece of work. Nadya, what are you doing in this place? You're bright, clever. You could do ... *anything* else maybe. And your English is outstanding. Where and how did you learn?"

"It's ... complicated. Everything is complicated."

"Come out with me sometime."

She smiled and began to make his coffee.

"Any day that's best for you," he said. "I've got lots of spare time from the KSE. Long lunches. Early finishes. Weekends."

"So," she said. "You have time to kill?"

"Yes," he said. "I have time to kill."

For the remainder of Saturday, he took it easy in the apartment, mostly reading and marking up written work he'd set for his students.

Late that night, he jumped on the metro back to Arsenalna. He stood in a doorway across the road from Café Oasis, huddling and shivering in his inadequate coat. It was ten past midnight before the lights went off.

Some minutes later, a classic grey Mercedes nosed out from the nearest of the arched entryways in the tenement buildings. Pavlo was driving. Nadya sat beside him, statue-still and achingly beautiful.

August, 1999. London

The man who got on the bus had difficulty paying his fare. He had money, but it seemed that his fingers had a life of their own. Coins spilled over the pay-trough and down into the driver's cab. Some fell onto the metal floor of the passenger deck. An old woman got up from her seat at the front to help. The only seat available for the man, once he'd got his ticket, was on the side-facing bench, putting him in full view of everyone.

He was a hive of tics, twitches and vocalisations. His hands flew about uncontrollably. His head swivelled and jerked. His tongue kept shooting from his mouth, curling and uncurling like a butterfly's.

At the time, Richard was reading *The Man Who Mistook His Wife for a Hat* by Oliver Sacks. In one section, there were case studies of people with extreme Tourette's. Oliver Sacks described them as "super Touretters", and Richard wondered if the man on the bus fell into that category.

A woman in her late twenties sat in an aisle seat diagonally opposite and about five rows back from the Tourette man. She was pretty, had long dark hair and wore a long leather coat despite the August heat.

She was crying — moved to tears by the Tourette man.

Richard was further back in the bus, diagonally opposite to *her*.

When she got off, he followed. It was long before his own stop, but he got off anyway.

"Excuse me," he said. "I ... noticed you were upset."

She was still upset, and tried to hide it by putting on sunglasses. She looked at Richard warily.

"Uh ... thanks," she said. "It's been a bad day."

"The man on the bus," he said. "It's not fair, is it?"

"How did you ...? No. It's not fucking fair."

A soft summer rain began to fall.

There was an electronic beep.

She produced a cheap-looking mobile phone and checked a text message. Richard looked at her in her Police sunglasses and ankle-length leather coat.

"Can't afford the flip-top Nokia yet then?" he said.

She put her phone away and peered at him over her shades. Then she laughed.

"Oh ... *The Matrix*. Yeah. You seen it yet?"

"Of course. And I'm thirty-four, but the only way to describe it is by getting down with the kids. Wicked, awesome, ace."

The rain got heavier.

"Look, we're getting wet here. Could I walk you somewhere? Or there's a coffee place further along ..."

Lame enough pick-up lines, but she accepted.

It turned out that "Trixie" was also reading *The Man Who Mistook His Wife for a Hat*. Richard thought it was an interesting coincidence, nothing more; but Trixie was a big believer in synchronicity and fate.

In the early days, when they met each other's friends, she delighted in telling everybody the story of "the book, the bus and the super Touretter".

She told him that she used to have an amphetamine habit and a tendency to harm herself — the former involving white lines on a mirror and a rolled-up ten-pound note, the latter involving a Stanley blade and an inner thigh. She didn't do those things any longer.

There was so much more in her life. The appointment as student counsellor. Her sister's invitation to stay in Paris anytime she wished. Italian cookery. Spanish film. Nick Cave (his CDs anyway). And now Richard.

Within a week of them being together, she admitted to the "very occasional slips" with speed at parties. He quickly assessed that her friends were a bunch of losers and degenerates who encouraged her to get as wasted as possible, when ever possible.

Then she told him, "To be honest, I've still got a medium-sized problem with speed *and* self-harming."

He wasn't surprised or put off by this.

In a way, he was relieved. Because he already knew that he wanted to save her ... or something.

six

December, 2004. Kyiv

He looked out from the tenth-floor apartment window, watching the falling snow. Thinking about coincidences and synchronicity. About a chance encounter on a bus and about getting off a metro train at the wrong stop.
 He didn't believe in fate. He believed that life is like Robert Frost's poem 'The Road Not Taken'.
 In the poem, a traveller stands at a diverging path in a wood, undecided over which direction to choose, but takes the less-travelled path, the good path – the path that leads to happiness.
 And yet how can we ever really know, thought Richard, *if the less-travelled path will lead to happiness or to darkness?*

Lesson plans for his second week at the KSE fell through his hands like dust. Even though he focussed on the Orange Revolution — the main topic in town — events were unfolding at break-neck speed.
 "I thought we'd look at the bigger picture today," he said. "I've been reading the *Kyiv Post* and accessing the Internet from the computer in Oleg's office. Key points for discussion and written exercises ... As you all know, there's to be a re-run of the election's second round in less than three weeks on the twenty-sixth of December; observers from the international community are monitoring; the West *and* Russia are in support of a fair process. In fact, I understand that Putin has told press he'll work with *any* Ukrainian president who is freely elected by the Ukrainian people — "

"Hah!" said Sergiy.

Galnya and Lola folded their arms.

"And," said Richard, "he's confirmed that Moscow will not involve itself in local conflicts in old Soviet-bloc countries. He will accept the choices of these new nations in determining their political fates."

"Hah!" said Sergiy.

"I am sad," said Galnya. "We wrote a long letter to Mr Putin on sixty metres of orange cloth. We presented it at the Russian embassy and they refused to accept it. We are asking him to please love Ukraine and respect us. Not to gobble us up like some dish of caviar with his vodka. Not to interfere in the election."

"But he's said he won't interfere," said Richard.

"You think we can *trust* these statements?" said Lola.

For the next few days, it was gruelling – beginner groups back-to-back. He was expecting an easier time of it with his advanced group on Wednesday's last session ...

"No, no, no, no!" Lola said within minutes. "I am sorry, Richard, but the subject we need to be discussing about today is this!"

She had a newspaper open in front of her and kept slapping it as she spoke.

Next to her, Sergiy was chuckling.

Richard hadn't seen any papers yet. He'd travelled in on the metro bleary-eyed and semi-conscious following last night's consumption of a bottle of unexpectedly potent wine from his local grocery store.

"They printed a picture of the killer," said Annushka. "The man that the police have been asking questions to."

"Ah, ah!" said Sergiy. "Questions. But I am wonder if he is ... *not* the killer. I am wonder if he is ... impotent."

"Impotent!" said Lola. "You mean *innocent*!"

"Yes."

"*He is not innocent! Look at him!*"

"Er, right, Lola," said Richard. "A discussion means that we talk calmly. No shouting."

"I am sorry. But look at this animal. Look at this Nikolai Gaidak. He looks like one of those I don't know the name of it some kind of monster."

Her newspaper was open at a small picture of a man accompanied by two columns of text. For the first time, Richard looked closely at the picture ...

Cold sweat slicked his brow. He felt as if his guts were being sucked into a vacuum.

"Excuse me a moment," he said, already on his way to the door.

He made it along the corridor, into the toilet and into a cubicle before the vomit gushed from his throat. He spat and hacked. Leaned against the wall. Exited the cubicle and stood swaying in the middle of the floor.

The pristine whiteness of the urinals and sinks, the gleaming blue of the wall tiles — everything was too bright, too sharp. Cruel on the eyes.

He went to a sink, gripped the edges of the porcelain bowl and looked in the mirror. He was deathly pale. Beads of sweat stood out on his forehead like rivets. He ran the cold tap. Splashed water into this face. Rinsed his mouth. Spat. Drank deeply.

Back in the corridor, he walked straight by the classroom. Just before he reached the stairs, Alexei came to the door of his office.

"Richard. Richard? Not trying to escape my *gulag* already, are you?"

"No, I ... No."

"But you look terrible! Are you ill?"

"Er ... possibly."

Alexei beckoned him into the office, pushed some documents aside on the desk and produced a small square-section bottle of vodka and shot glasses.

"You strike me as a man of integrity, Richard. And isn't that all we have in the end? Personal integrity?"

They drank while Alexei *precis'd* his life. Born in Kyiv. Happily married with three children at university. A professor of Ukrainian language. Also fluent in English, Russian, French and Italian.

In his head, Richard added "wannabe politician". Alexei was charismatic and likeable — the sort of person to be emulated. He struck Richard as a big, clever, benevolent spider at the centre of a web.

"I'm feeling a bit better. I should get back."

Alexei smiled. He unfolded a newspaper on the desk.

Nikolai Gaidak. His squashed face had deep-set eyes and a large misshapen nose. His thin lips were curled in a sneer. He wore a gold-trimmed purple cap and a gold-trimmed livery jacket.

Alexei said, "The headline says 'Is this the face of a murderer?' Tell me, Richard, have you ever seen such an ugly human being?"

"Yes. I saw him on a metro platform last week."

"You saw him? What was he doing? Did he say anything to you?"

"No, I ..." *Memories of the troll kissing his hand, spitting in his face ...* "No. He was just there. Like any other commuter."

Back with his group, he said, "Okay, Lola. I understand from the news story that Gaidak is being questioned. He's a night doorman at Hotel Yalta, so he was in the right place at the right time. But we don't know if he's guilty. He hasn't been charged."

"You only have to look at him," said Lola.

"Hmm ... let me ask you — do you think someone is more likely to be guilty because they are ugly?"

"Ah ah ah!" said Sergiy.

"Who says he's ugly?" said Lola. "Please, Richard, do not treat me like some stupid person or I don't what. It is not just how he looks. *I see something in his eyes.*"

"Sorry to interrupt," said Alexei, entering. "I just this moment heard on the radio. Nikolai Gaidak has been released. In fact the police had already decided to release him as the newspapers were being printed."

"Well ... " said Richard.

"Also," said Alexei. "Please, everybody find your coats and come quickly. Viktor Yushchenko is about to speak in the Maidan."

Although crowds had thinned since the announcement of the re-election, there was still a huge presence.

"This is Viktor Yushchenko now," said Alexei.

Richard saw a proud and dignified man of about fifty at the podium microphone.

"They will not poison us," Alexei translated. "They will not poison us."

"With propaganda?" said Richard.

"That, too," said Alexei. "But he is talking about ... Ah, he reminds us that we have paid a price for freedom. *He* has paid *his* price. If we were closer, you would see the scarring on his face. A side-effect of the poisoning."

"What? Actual poison?"

"They think it happened at a dinner with Ukraine's security services back in September. He was ahead in the polls and they tried to kill him. He was very ill, but he has survived."

Cheers erupted from every direction.

"He speaks out against corrupt local governments in the Donetsk, Kharkiv and Luhansk regions. They should not be implicit in the separatist movements. When he is president, he says, he will continue fighting corruption and cronyism, continue to promote democracy and economic reform. He says that the Orange Revolution is a victory. And, for now, it is time to stop blockading governmental offices. But he asks protesters to stay in the Maidan right up until the election has been won."

Richard had arrived first, as agreed, and Nadya would arrive ten minutes after him. The Marquise de Chocolat — an upstairs place on Prorizna, off Khreshchatyk — was like a kinky boudoir.
    It had red velvet sofas in the shape of lips. Puckered, dusky-pink fabric lined the ceiling. The textured walls were hung with photos — back-lit and mounted in red box-frames — showing a young woman dripping with chocolate. In some pictures, her eyes were closed as her tongue licked at the chocolate that melted down from her hair. In the only one showing more than her face, chocolate ran down her neck towards her breasts.
    Richard sat by a big, semi-circular window. The music was quirky and ambient. Judging by the dual-language menu, the place specialised in cocktails, coffees and desserts. Except for a small group in one corner, it was empty, and he was struck again by his impression of a clean but stark ex-Soviet city bejewelled with random pockets of wealth and colour.
    Clearly *not* one of Kyiv's *nouveau riche* elite, Nadya arrived. She undid the belt and buttons of her old mackintosh and hung it on a hook inside the door.
    He smiled as she joined him.
    A waitress appeared, took their orders and went.
    In a land where women often went heavy on the make-up, Nadya had used only a touch of eyeliner and mascara; no lipstick. Her bobbed dark hair was neat and lustrous. She wore black trousers and a cream-coloured woollen jumper.
    "So, Richard," she said, "why did you want me to come out with you?"
    "Why do you think?"

"Oh, I really don't know," she said casually. "Because you want to fuck me?"

He laughed and fidgeted with his placemat. She watched him with calm curiosity. In every direction Richard looked, he saw pictures of the girl covered in melted chocolate.

Since Trixie's death, he'd been prone to intrusive, unwanted thoughts. What he was thinking now — while simultaneously hating himself for it — was that he'd been set up. This venue had been *her* suggestion. And even though *he'd* done all the chasing, and *she'd* played so hard-to-get, he had the crazy idea that Nadya was a sex-worker.

"Your English," he said. "It's very good."

"You mean good for a common girl who works in a backstreet bar?"

She was less like Trixie now. Trixie could often be straightforward, but not so prickly or defensive ...

"That look ..." said Nadya. "Why do you look at me that way?"

"What way?"

"Like I'm an insect in your laboratory."

Richard laughed, but failed to hide his discomfort either from himself or from her.

The coffees arrived, along with a chocolate sundae in a tall, fluted glass.

Nadya became absorbed in the sundae, then her cheeks flushed as she realised he was watching her.

He sipped his coffee and feigned interest in the chocolate-brown wall. The irregular folds of the surface were rigid to the touch. The effect must have been achieved with paint-soaked, bunched-up fabric, fixed in place before it dried. It was as if a giant Cadbury Flake had been unravelled.

"I'd be interested to know about you, Nadya," he said.

She didn't answer him, so he added, "Your life, your family, anything you want to tell me."

"This is a very nice dessert," she said.

Then she smiled at him, her dark eyes sparkling with the pleasure of teasing him. He liked it that she was relaxing, and he grinned.

"So you won't tell me about yourself?" he said.

"Why are you in Kyiv, Richard?"

"I told you. I'm an English tutor at the KSE."

"For how long will you do this?"

"At least until the term break in February. But Alexei says he could offer something longer."

"And you were teaching in London?" she said. "At a school? A college?"

"University."

"And ... what? Why did you leave? Or were you fired?"

He laughed, but he remembered his slippery days of hiding the drinking, remembered the faculty's invitation for him to resign.

"Why would you think I was fired?"

"So you weren't fired," she concluded. "But why would you come to Ukraine? It is strange that you would come here and not to somewhere warmer and without political upheaval. You were curious about the east of Europe?"

"Yes," he said, still feeling off balance from her potluck question and about his own apparent need to lie, even if only by omission. "Something like that."

"But not exactly that?"

Richard sighed. Her intuition, her logic, the probing questions — was she even aware of how she came across? He smiled and shook his head.

"I have made a joke?" she said.

"No. Not really."

"It must be so boring for you here," she said. "You can't find anything you want to have. You try to eat at Café Oasis and there are so few things on the menu. You want an aubergine dish and there are no aubergines. The girl is sent out to find some. Then you have to ask her six times before she will meet you for a coffee."

The sparkle in her eyes was back.

"You would like to know about me, Richard? All right. I'll tell you ..."

seven

"I live with my mother and sister. My father was Russian. He grew up in Volgograd but came as a young man to Kyiv — or Kiev, as he insisted. When Ukraine was newly independent in 1991, he took us to Volgograd. We stayed for eight years, until he left us. He is in Moscow now.

"When we came back to Kyiv in 1999, the economy was bad. Much worse than now. Although now it is still bad for most people. My mother worked days and nights as a cleaner at the hospital. She wanted a better life for us and she ... *encouraged* me, paid for me to go to an English tutor. It was very much money for us.

"She dreamed, and I dreamed, to live in London. How things were changing in Ukraine, it was getting easier to travel and even to work in other countries. *If* you had money. Maybe we were only having fantasies."

There was an intensity in her eyes — a refection on how hard she and her family had struggled, Richard thought, but something else too.

"And did you ever get to London?" he asked.

"It was a dream. And then the dream ended."

She shrugged it off as unimportant.

More evasiveness. Has she been to England or not?

"You could work as an interpreter," he said. "Or, I don't know, maybe a tutor at the KSE. Alexei liked you."

She smiled.

"And you, Richard? I have noticed that you sometimes speak a little Russian. But no Ukrainian?"

"Not all Ukrainians speak Ukrainian," he said, "but everybody speaks Russian."

"That is not correct. Many Ukrainians speak *only* Ukrainian. Particularly in the west of the country."

"At the KSE, a lot of students are local. Some are from Lviv, Odessa, the Crimea. Some from different countries. Moldova, Belarus. They all seem to speak Russian."

Nadya looked angry. So he stopped, thinking, *We're almost having an argument on our first date — even assuming it's a date.*

He introduced topics from music to literature. Told her that, at seventeen, he read *Crime and Punishment*, then devoured the rest of Dostoyevsky's novels.

"A Russian," she said. "He was brilliant. I agree."

"My grandfather was Russian," said Richard. "I was given all his books. Chekov, Bulgakov, Gogol."

"That's interesting. Iryna Vilde maybe?"

"I don't — "

"A classic Ukrainian woman writer. Do you read any female writers?"

"Jane Austen, Emily Dickinson, Toni Morrison."

Nadya smiled.

"I like very much Emily Dickinson's poems."

"Yes. She's — "

"I must go now though, Richard. It has been very nice. But I must take the metro and the tram."

"The metro *and* the tram?" he said. "That sounds like a hassle. We could go by taxi? I'll pay."

"*We?* No. I told you, when I agreed to come."

"I understand," he said. "You don't want me to know where you live, for now, and for whatever reasons ... but ... I'm thinking about your safety."

"I will be safe."

He took a wad of notes from his pocket.

"You could still get a taxi."

"You are very kind, but no. And, please, remember ... you will stay here for ten minutes before leaving?"

He nodded.

"There's more to you, isn't there?" he said. "I mean, a lot more to know about you?"

"Of course. Did you think you would know everything on the first date?"

He watched her go.

It *was* a first date then.

Later, in a little antiquarian bookshop, he found a gift for her — a collection of Emily Dickinson poems in both English and Ukrainian.

She'd claimed not to have a mobile phone, and although Richard didn't have one either, Alexei kept offering him one on expenses. Anyway, he decided to play it cool with Nadya. Maybe let some days go by and then call in at Café Oasis with the gift.

By Monday, Viktor Yushchenko was back in Kyiv following a two-day visit to a clinic in Vienna, where doctors had confirmed that his facial disfigurement and illness were consistent with having been poisoned with dioxin. In the *Kyiv Post,* Vladimir Putin was reported as saying that he would not interfere, or have any reservations, if Ukraine wanted to join the European Union. There was another article, citing *The Washington Post*, to the effect that former US ambassador Richard Holbrooke was appealing for Ukraine to be given NATO membership within three years.

At the KSE, Alexei said, "I'm not being critical of you, Richard, but your advanced group in particular have been requesting that you include more business English in their lessons."

Although the students lapped it up, Richard cringed as he disseminated terms like "blue sky", "brainstorm", "think outside the box", "find a window", "roll out", "head up", "ramp up", and even "*sex up*" — gleaned from the British government's 2003 sexed-up-documents debacle over alleged Iraqi WMDs.

Meanwhile, election campaigning was at fever pitch.

"We're only ten days from the ballot boxes," said Richard near the end of the week. "What does anybody think about this Ukrainian language bill that Yulia Tymoshenko submitted to the acting parliament?"

"It was thrown into the rubbish bin," said Lola. "So it doesn't mater."

"It's embarrassing," said Sergiy. "Yulia, she should not to try this."

"Is language a part of our identity?" said Richard. "Is it partly what makes us who we are?"

"Yes, of course," said Galnya. "And Sergiy is correct. Yulia Tymoshenko wants to be Yushchenko's prime minister, so she is not, should not behave like a little dictator. It was wrong putting this idea, this bill to say all state officials must only use Ukrainian language when they are doing their jobs. Orange Ukraine must be fair. We have different languages here."

"Respect for different languages and different cultural identities?"

"Yes, Mr Richard, but the biggest worry now still is how we will get fair vote. Russia and the West, they accuse one each other of interference. Now there are I think more than six thousand foreign observers here. And Ukraine police and army, many thousands are ready for action. Kyiv is like one of those pressure saucepan lid cookers. It may explode!"

Bella laughed as she bagged up Richard's grocery items. She wore her leopard-print dress again and was in her usual ebullient mood.

"Okay, Richard. Nice doing business with you. You come in here and teach us English for free one day, yes?"

"Yes," he said. "I will. It's a promise. Good night."

"Good night," said Bella. "You come back soon."

Four hours later, she was dead.

***

For the second time since meeting Nadya at the Marquise de Chocolat, Richard dropped by her place of work, Café Oasis, only to find it closed and in darkness — strange for a Saturday evening. He copied down the Cyrillic of a notice in the window.

On a trip to the grocery shop on Sunday, he discovered that it, too, was closed when it would usually be open.

The channels he had access to on the apartment TV were all in Ukrainian, but he intuited that something different was happening in the news. Orange Revolution coverage was interspersed with to-cameras of police spokespeople and repeated shots of what looked like a crime-scene tent in a cordoned-off area of patchy snow and winter stubble.

On Monday morning, her identity was all over the media. Twenty-two-year-old Bella Savchuk's body had been found by a footpath that crossed a wasteland at the back of apartment blocks near the Dnipro River.

The site was about two kilometres from Richard's apartment and the grocery shop, and only a few hundred metres from the building where Bella lived.

Police confirmed that — like Maryna Petrenko, the young woman murdered three weeks earlier — Bella's throat had been slashed. And although they wouldn't be drawn on whether it was the same killer, they confirmed that neither of the victims had been robbed or sexually assaulted.

In a state of numbness, Richard rode the metro to the city. On the news-stands and tucked under commuters' arms were images of Bella.

"Well, well," said Alexei, raising an eyebrow crookedly at him in the KSE reception area. "Number two in Dniprovskyi ..."

Richard knew it was an attempt to continue a darkly humorous vein they'd begun at the time of the first murder. But he shook his head at Alexei and reached a steadying hand to the wall.

"I ... knew her a little," he said. "From the grocery shop, you know? She was a really nice girl ..."

Bella in her leopard-print dress. Bella with her innocent flirty smile.

"You come back soon, okay?"

What a waste of a young life.

"Oh," said Alexei. "Richard, forgive me ..."

The mood at the KSE was sombre all morning. It wasn't until his advanced group in the afternoon that politics crept back into the classroom. Richard's habit was to let discussions run. He'd make notes and do individual feedback later. He saw no point in written exercises during contact time.

"... and I hear rumourings," said Galnya, "that Russia's Black Sea Fleet is supplying weapons to Yanukovych supporters."

"Rumours," said Sergiy.

"I keep telling to everybody. Kyiv is like a pressure saucepan lid cooker!"

Sergiy yawned hugely.

"There is no such things as a pressure saucepan lid cooker. Richard?"

Richard was looking out of the window, his thoughts drifting with the scudding clouds over the rooftops of Passazh. If Lola were here ... She'd phoned in earlier and excused herself, too upset to attend. If she were here, she'd cast politics aside and be livid over the murder.

Autumn & Winter, 1999 — 2000. London

Richard and Trixie were buoyed up with the buzz of being with one another. They went to see subtitled foreign-language films together then talked for hours in the pub afterwards, analysing merits and shortcomings. If they were out with friends, there were always intimate looks and touches.

At weekends, they bed-and-breakfasted in Stratford or Oxford or Winchester or Brighton. Trixie loved to wander through the old narrow streets, looking for second-hand bookshops and vintage clothing stores.

If she got them lost, neither of them cared.

Trixie was pretty lost anyway.

By November, she'd moved into Richard's ground-floor flat. She loved its minimalist style of wine-red carpets, white rugs, and the modest antiques his parents had given to him before emigrating to New Zealand.

But by the start of the new millennium, something was stirring beneath the happiness. It had been there all along, he realised.

The power of denial is a wonderful thing.

A growing malignancy dogged his days and poisoned his nights. He imagined it as a separate entity, clawing its way up from some putrid underbelly.

He'd be out with her in public and the heads would turn. The men's heads turned as if on castors. And Richard felt aggrieved and sickened by the cumulative effect of all those covetous gazes.

He began to study her, wondering if she were in collusion with her anonymous admirers. On the one hand, she was blameless in her beauty; on the other ... surely, she *knew*?

How can she not be aware of the effect she has on men? Naturally, she's enjoyed the attention. What girl wouldn't? But now she's with me. We're a couple. She can stop. She should stop. Men will still look ... but take away her conscious or unconscious part in the game ...

"I've been wondering," he said finally, trying but failing to keep the bitterness from his tone. "Wondering if you're aware of how men look at you?"

She came over to sit next to him on the sofa.

"Is that it? Is that what's been wrong with you?"

She kissed him tenderly on the lips.

"You can stop worrying then, Richie. You know I only want you."

So disarming and reassuring. Impossible to believe anything bad of her at that moment. Entirely possible to believe that the attentions were unsought.

They made love on the sofa. Then wrapped themselves in the Moroccan throw. And he fell asleep to the lullaby of Trixie's voice.

"I only want you ..."

Over and over.

But the predatory looks — like starved foxes eyeing a stray chicken. And her knowing little smiles and demure glances ...

"Only you, only you, only you ..."

eight

January & February, 2000. London

Richard tortured himself over Trixie as he paced the quiet corridors of the university. He'd left his English Lit undergrads watching an old BBC video of Harold Pinter's *The Lover*.

He thought about Pinter's play, a script he knew well. Was that what Trixie needed from him? A bit of fantasy?

"Would you like it if I pretended to be somebody else?" he asked her that night. "Like in a fantasy. I take you by surprise by arriving home at an unexpected hour, dressed differently, speaking differently. I pretend to be more suave or something?"

"No, Rich," she said. "What's this insecurity about?"

A few nights later, there was an administrator's leaving do in the pub. Richard arrived first and was talking with colleagues when Trixie walked in. He noticed the sudden drift of male attention, and watched in delight and horror as she approached wearing the slinkiest black cocktail dress. Stomachs were pulled in. Chests were puffed out. Thumbs were hooked into waistbands, fingers pointing cowboy-like towards genitals.

This sleazy display was tempered when it was clear that she was *with* Richard.

Then, close to the end of the night, *Moon* showed up.

The son of Swedish hippy parents, Moon Stillwater (formerly Larsson) was a professor of quantum mechanics, or — Richard mused — something equally beyond the ken of the sane masses.

And Moon really was a cause for concern.

Deny it she may, and did, but in *his* company, *Trixie's* behaviour changed.

"I thought your friends were mostly the psych and socio lot," he said.

"Yeah, well these are *new* friends, you know?"

Moon insinuated himself into the circle. He turned up around every corner, at every gathering.

Richard knew hatred, then — hatred for Moon's incandescent blue eyes, his perpetually flashing perfect teeth, his shaggy mane of blond hair, his snakeskin boots.

Beside him, Richard felt clumsy and stupid and tongue-tied. By contrast, Trixie shone brighter.

And was there an assumption — in the looks of strangers — that Trixie and Moon were an item? They would have looked right, for instance, in the pages of trashy magazines featuring galleries of celebrity couples coming out of nightclubs.

Moon was so beguiled by Trixie that he acted as if Richard didn't exist. He ponced on and on about the theoretical trajectories of invisible particles.

"I saw you tonight," said Richard. "Listening to him ... Enraptured. Starry-eyed. Understanding nothing."

"I *do* understand it," she said. "I want to know more."

Also, Moon was an accomplished blues guitarist, and at first even Richard went trotting along to the gigs, poodle-like, with Trixie and half the science faculty.

Within a few short weeks, fury underpinned Richard's every thought and deed. The intimacy they'd had was stymied. Verbal exchanges were reduced to the dead, functional stuff of shared habitation — like what time one of them might be late home because of a work meeting, or who would pick up the midweek bread and milk.

He would brood in his armchair pretending to watch a programme, or to read a book or newspaper. Her offers of tea, coffee, wine, beer, servings of food, were brushed aside; then moments later, he'd help himself to whatever it was she'd been offering.

One evening, they both flew into a rage. They argued half the night. Went off to work in the morning without speaking. Then ripped into each other again as soon as they got back. Their worst row ever. Door slamming. Shouting and screaming. The lot.

The neighbours banged on the walls.

By Thursday evening, they were too exhausted to argue any longer. Trixie spent an hour in the bedroom, getting ready.

"Drinks at the Riverside. Krista, Carl, Fazana, some others ... You're invited, if you're interested."

"No, thanks," he said. "I'd rather not have to watch you getting drooled over by Moon all night."

"See you when I see you then."

"Yeah. Just one thing. If you end up fucking him, don't bother coming back."

December, 2004. Kyiv

Annushka hung around after class, a pout on her bee-stung lips, her ice-green eyes trained on Richard.

From Siberia, he remembered.

"You know I like you, Richard."

"I ... have to go," he said.

"Yes, of course."

She smiled over the shoulder of her lime-green leather jacket as she crossed to the door.

"Er, Annushka, wait," he said. "Can you translate this for me, please?"

She came back and took the slip of paper from him.

"In English it would be ... *Closed ... for ... repairs.*"

"Until when?"

"Oh ... I don't know. It does not say. What is ...? It is a shop in Kyiv? A restaurant?"
"It's a café, a bar."
"But it's closed. Okay. No problem. I know a cool bar we could go to?"
Richard laughed and shook his head.
"You're stunning, Annushka. And I must be totally mad, but ... But."
"What is this *stunning*?"
"Beautiful. *Krasivi.*"
"Thank you. I ... really like to hear you speak Russian words. And for you I think there is ... somebody already?"

Back in Dniprovskyi, he trod the snowy, shadow-deep streets from the metro station. The grocery shop was open again and the two other girls saw him through the window. One gave him a broken wave.

He hesitated, nearly went in, then walked past even though he needed supplies. A sob and a queasy feeling swept through him. He leaned against the wall. He thought about Bella. And about Trixie's last walk along the river nearly five years ago.

Then he thought about Nadya ... Imagined her being shouted at by her aggressive boss, Pavlo. Or being sent out to hunt down beetroot and cabbages. Or huddling in her old raincoat waiting for a tram. He even thought about the throat-slash gesture she'd made at Café Oasis the first time he'd seen her, and he read into it some kind of distress plea. He'd found someone who looked like Trixie and was building a case for rescuing her.

Closed for repairs.

His hand found something in his coat pocket. It was the book he'd bought for Nadya, the dual English-Ukrainian collection of Emily Dickinson poetry. He took it out and leafed through, smiling thinly.

What am I really doing here? he thought.

What do I want? Who am I? Who is anybody? What is any of it really about?
He scanned the page the poetry book was open at ... *"I am out with lanterns, looking for myself."*

The last days leading up to the ballot saw the TV screening of a debate between the two presidential candidates. The pro-Russian, Yanukovych, alleged that Yushchenko was guilty of accepting financial backing from the West. Yushchenko — the Orange Revolution leader — denied the allegation. In turn, he drew attention to Yanukovych's criminal past.

In Independence Square, Yushchenko appeared again to speak to his supporters about the need for peace, unity and stabilisation.

"He says we are on the cusp of victory," translated Alexei. "He says that he, his team, Yulia Tymoshenko, the people, everybody — we have opened the eyes of the authorities, made them respect our rights."

On Friday, Richard realised that it was Christmas Eve at home and that it would be Boxing Day on Sunday, the day of the election. He hadn't sent a greetings card to anybody he knew.

In Kyiv, there was only a hint of Christmas in the air, created by the Catholic community. Alexei told him that Ukrainian festivities did not begin until New Year.

To monitor election fairness, more foreign observers poured into Ukraine, especially from Poland, stationing themselves in Kyiv, Lviv, Odessa, Kharkiv, Kherson, Donbas, Nikolayev and elsewhere. In an interview with the Italian daily newspaper *la Repubblica*, Yushchenko suggested that the imminent election was nothing less than an ideological struggle between Western democracy and Soviet authoritarianism.

***

From the street, he saw that the light was on in Café Oasis but the place was empty and the wall-mounted TV played to itself. It was late afternoon. He went down the well of steps to the yard.

Inside the door, Nadya's coat was on the coat-stand.

At the counter, Richard was about to call out when he heard muffled voices from behind the kitchen door. One voice was male and gruff, the other female and possibly distressed. He leaned forward over the counter. His heart thumped as the female voice sounded again — in a way that was not a scream but a small cry of alarm.

Or a cry of pleasure?

He scrambled under the counter flap and thrust open the kitchen door.

Pavlo had Nadya up against the wall by the cooking range. With one hand, he appeared to be grasping her hair and forcing her head back. With the other, he was trying to undo her trousers. Her shirt already hung open.

Then Pavlo's grip slackened and both his and Nadya's faces turned to Richard at the same time. Like a choreographed movement in some grotesque dance.

A second later, a powerful hand clamped onto Richard's neck. Pavlo's face jutted forward, and the clustered consonants of the language were ground out of his mouth like aggregate.

His eyes were coal-black and glittering.

At the end of his rant, he added "Dickhead" in English.

Richard flailed ineffectually as he was bundled to the back door. The door opened and he was sent staggering across the yard. He hit the opposite wall — just missing a rusty old iron bracket — and folded to the ground.

It was a soft landing onto some bulging grey rubbish bags. One of the bags burst under him.

The café's back door slammed and a bolt was shot.

He lay there, fighting for breath, the winter light harsh in his eyes.

To his right was the arched undercroft — wide enough for cars — leading out to the road. To his left, a small parking area with designated bays and a line of wheelie bins. A fierce wind cut through the yard. Bits of rubbish from the burst bag skittered over the cracked concrete.

Richard's ribs felt bruised. So did his throat. He could smell drains and rotting vegetables. Something slimy and spinach-green was coating his hand. He wiped it on the wall. It could have been food slops; it could have been vomit or diarrhoea.

As worried as he was about Nadya, it was another minute before he could stand. Clenching his teeth against a spasm of pain in his right ankle, he limped back across the yard and hammered on the solid grey door.

Nobody came.

He felt nauseous. The ground tilted and swayed. His heart galloped and there was a rushing in his ears. Everything grew fainter and paler, as if the world might lose substance altogether.

He moved towards the undercroft, steadying himself against the wall.

What have I been thinking all this time? I hardly know Nadya. What did I really witness in the kitchen? Can I trust my interpretation? Their faces turning together at my entrance ... Is it a perverse game? She lures unsuspecting foreigners and then they both get off on Pavlo's violence? Why not? Are they having sex in there now? Laughing at me?

Intrusive thoughts ... He hated himself for thinking these things.

Nadya ... What was she doing, or being made to do at this moment? He had to help her. She was in trouble.

With his body hurting in at least four places, he hobbled out to the street in the dusky light, and back around to the railings at the front of the café.

nine

Richard reached the front just as Nadya was coming up the steps. She had her coat on.

"Are you all right?" he said.

"Are *you*?"

One look at her was enough. He knew that none of his paranoid fantasies had any basis in reality.

Down through the window in the sunken yard, he saw that the café's interior was empty. Pavlo must still be in there somewhere, in the kitchen or the rooms above. Maybe he'd reappear at any moment. Come out to finish the job. Pummel Richard into the ground and drag Nadya back inside.

Richard's stomach lurched. He thought he was going to throw up but managed to hold it back.

"Let's go," he said. "We'll report him to the police."

"No. It was not how it looked. Not as bad as it looked."

He stared at her.

"You're confused. You have to get away from here."

"Everything will be all right," she said.

"No. I don't think so!"

From across the road, an elderly couple in heavy coats and fur hats looked over.

"Everything's fine," called Richard. "*Kharasho.*"

They exchanged dark mutterings before walking on.

"I know it may be difficult for you to understand," said Nadya, "but Pavlo could make a lot of trouble for me if he decided to."

"*What?* He was already making trouble for you!"

He put his arm around her shoulders and tried to get her moving. She resisted at first, then complied.

"Richard ..." she said as they started up the hill. "You are hurt. Your leg."

"Fuck the leg. What about you? If I hadn't turned up when I did, he would have forced you."

She lowered her eyes.

"What is it?" he said. "Is there something else?"

"No."

"Yes. Men can be intuitive as well."

"This word. Intu ... ?"

"Intuitive." He stopped walking and placed a hand on his stomach. "When you know something, and you feel it. Here."

"Yes. Intuition. I'm sorry. Pavlo ... has tried before."

"Even more reason to report him," he said.

"The police would do nothing. Believe me. Maybe in your country ... But in Ukraine, it's different."

He moved closer and took her in his arms. They were still within sight of the windows above the café and he was half hopeful and half apprehensive that Pavlo might be watching.

Nadya returned the embrace, then stepped away.

"I will take this evening off," she said.

"Good. You should leave completely."

"I can't," she said. "It's my job. I need the money."

Richard glanced over his shoulder, down the hill towards the café.

"I'll go back ..." he said uncertainly. "Talk to him."

"He does not speak English."

"Well ... maybe if ... I don't know."

"He said ..." She laughed. "Pavlo said that if he sees you there again he will suck your eyeballs out of your head and spit them down the toilet."

"*What?*"

"He talks a lot of rubbish, but he can also be dangerous. I am sorry, I should tell you more. He was the son of my father's friend, from many years ago. Then after my father left us, Pavlo started visiting. He helped my family. He still gives money to my mother. It is difficult. In the old days, I was *with* Pavlo. Not for long. One year or less."

"So now he thinks he can still —"

"Three times in the years that I have worked at Café Oasis ... he has tried, as you saw in the kitchen."

"And those three times ... Did he ever ... ?"

She shook her head.

"It must be nearly five o'clock," he said. "We could go to eat somewhere?"

She didn't respond, but she let him take her hand as they carried on up the hill towards the metro station.

Chandeliers and paintings, gaudy maroon-and-gold flock wallpaper, ranks of silent tables, an impeccable and painfully servile waiter — everything about the place made him regret his choice of restaurant.

"It's a bit quiet," he said.

"Yes," said Nadya. "Ukrainians don't go out like this much. Not like in your country. Of course, things are changing. Some people now have money and go out more. But traditionally, most people just go out for family celebrations."

In fact, the only other customers were a small family at a corner table.

Puccini played softly over an in-house system.

They both ordered *champignons julienne* for starters and chicken for main. On impulse, Richard ordered a bottle of Moet Chandon and a side dish of caviar. He did a quick calculation and realised with a mild shock that the food was cheap but the champagne alone was the equivalent of about ninety pounds.

He felt crass and dirty. For all he knew, the bill might be more than Nadya's weekly household income.

She drank a glass of the Moet and said it was "nice".

He laughed and said, "It's like a crypt in here. We should have gone to a bar instead."

"Yes," she said, smiling. "Perhaps. You have many friends in London that you go to bars with?"

"Not really. All the friends I grew up with or met at university, they all got married. Had kids. I still see them sometimes, but I'm the only one who didn't settle down. Just a few relationships that never worked."

She smiled.

"And you are nearly forty. Well, it is maybe unusual for me as a woman, at thirty-one, to not have married."

"Was there ever anybody special?"

"Special, well ... Not Pavlo. Somebody. But I don't want to talk about it today."

Richard nodded and said, "I wish you could just leave that job."

"Please stop saying that. Anyway, tomorrow ... Pavlo will be calmer."

Richard kept remembering the ease with which he'd been thrown out the back of Café Oasis. Pavlo's almost gleeful anger. His strength and height.

"By the way," he said. "I'm ... not afraid of Pavlo."

On Sunday, polls were predicting a win for Viktor Yushchenko even before voting closed. His supporters swamped Independence Square once again, and an impromptu rock concert sprang up that evening.

By Monday morning, it was clear that he had about 52% of the ballot compared with Yanukovych's 44%.

He showed up in the square, the Maidan, to thank everybody publicly and to declare victory.

"We have done it!" Alexei translated. "It is an end to the days of Kuchma, Yanukovych and Medvedchuk."

Amid cheers, Yushchenko was presented with a very long orange scarf.

"Ah," said Alexei. "The fifteen-metre scarf that was knitted especially for him in Poland. The woman giving it to him — Ruslana Lyzhychko — she is the winner of the Eurovision Song Contest. You knew that Ukraine won the Eurovision this year?"
Richard grinned.
He hadn't watched it and hadn't known.
"Hah!" said Alexei. "Victory! Victory for the non-violent Orange Revolution! Soon we will be members of the European Union and NATO."
By Wednesday, the majority of demonstrators had dispersed from Independence Square. But a core of supporters still lived in tents, and the stage and podium remained.

It was twilight when Richard arrived.
The ground was clear of snow and ice, but the wind carried a fine, cruel sleet.
Although four days ago in the restaurant, Nadya had arranged in advance to meet him outside the post office, he felt frustrated with her. How was he supposed to know if she was all right? He knew these thoughts were ridiculous, but he couldn't stop himself. Nadya could have phoned the KSE and left a message. She could have given him her email address. How was it possible that she didn't have an email address?
All around the square, teenagers chatted and larked. Some were hooked up to personal stereos. Some whizzed about on skateboards or rollerblades.
Outside the post office — which had a high, square-pillared entrance and a marble floor leading to a vast, dim interior — a group of five old men in greys, blacks and navy blues were having a heated discussion. Two wore peaked leather caps. All had moustaches. As with the snow-clearer from the apartment block, Richard felt

that he was glimpsing a fading Soviet world that wasn't quite ready to die.

Nadya was suddenly at his side. He leaned forward to kiss her but she turned out of reach and laughed.

"Hi," he said. "I thought we might go for a pizza. I found a place nearby. Pizza Perfect. It looks good."

"I am sorry, Richard," she said. "For me, it is a little early to eat. Can we walk?"

"Where to?"

"Nowhere. Just to walk."

"Yes. Is anything wrong? Pavlo —"

"Pavlo is nothing."

"Right," he said. "Pavlo is nothing. I wanted to ... I mean, here's my mobile number. Alexei gave me a mobile phone. I doubt if I'll use it much, but *you* could call me on it or leave messages or ... you know."

She took the slip of paper, glanced at it and put it in her coat pocket.

"I ... don't have."

"I know. No computer or mobile. I could maybe even ... If you'd let me ... Or you can call from your home phone, if ... or from Café Oasis?"

"I like you, Richard."

"I'm moving too fast?"

"Yes. Perhaps."

She linked her hand in his, which shut him up. As they left the square and began to walk along Khreshchatyk, they passed a line of three *babushki* sitting on wooden crates selling cigarettes.

"So many grandmothers on the streets," he said. "Don't they get a state pension or anything?"

"Only a small amount," she said. "Their lives are hard. Mostly they are the wives and sisters and mothers of dead soldiers. War widows."

"What about the rest of their families?"

"Sorry?"

"These women are old. They shouldn't be struggling to earn a bit of money on the streets like this."

Richard wasn't as shocked or naive as he sounded. He was looking for ways to get Nadya talking.

"It is perhaps difficult for you to understand," she said. "I know in your country the old are comfortable. Cared for. In Ukraine, it's different. A lot of old women here are completely alone, or they earn money to help look after other people in their families who can't work."

"Have you got a grandmother?"

"One grandmother died a long time ago," she said, "the other is in a special place for mad people."

"I see. I'm sorry. Shall we go to a bar?"

"You want to drink beer?"

Before he could stop her, she bought two bottles from a kiosk and passed one to him, the top already taken off.

"Thank you," he said. "And *za vashye zdarovye!*"

"Oh, more Russian," she said. "Cheers! It's shorter. Or, in Ukrainian, *budmo!* Also short."

"*Budmo!* I've seen how people drink on the street ... And it's all right?"

"Of course."

She smiled and took a slug from her bottle. Richard watched her in fascination. Another woman, another city, and it would be the behaviour of the gutter. Nadya even managed to make it look sophisticated.

Further down Khreshchatyk, when they'd finished their beers, she turned the empties in at a different kiosk, and that was acceptable too.

"Again," she said later, as the light grew dusky. "That look you were giving me. You do it often. What is it?"

"Oh, you remind me of ... somebody," he said, caught off-guard.

"An old girlfriend?"

"No. Yes ... Her name was Trixie. You look a lot like her. And ... you've got some similar mannerisms and idiosyncrasies."

"Oh, so many long words, Richard! Is that why you are interested in me? Because I remind you of another girl? So where is she now ... your *Trixie*? Maybe she wants to be with you? *You* obviously want to be with *her*."

"No ... She died. Nearly five years ago."

"Oh? What happened?"

"It doesn't matter."

"Yes, it does," she said. "You told me I remind you of her and you say that's not the reason you want to be with me. So you can tell me how she died."

"She drowned," he said, with an effort. "A drowning accident."

"*Drowned?*"

"Yes," he snapped. "You know. In water. In a river."

"Yes," she said. "I see."

"Is that enough then? Or do you want the forensic details, the scientific findings of the post mortem?"

He wasn't sure if she'd understood his words or his sarcasm. She looked regretful and hurt. But she had one more question.

"Were you with her?"

"*What?*"

"Were you with her when she drowned in the river?"

Richard felt sick. His voice was thick and strangled when he spoke.

"No. I wasn't with her."

ten

February, 2000. London

"So you weren't with her then?" said DS Dwyer, his eyes dull from sleeplessness or indifference.

The interview room was small and windowless and stank of cigarettes. The chair Richard was obliged to sit in had a moulded plastic seat, and sweat was spreading on the undersides of his thighs. The metal feet of the chair and the crude table were bolted to the floor.

"No. I wasn't with her. I told you already."

That morning, he'd been raised from his bed, told of Trixie's death and taken to the station to answer questions. Now, mid afternoon, he'd been brought back in for a second interview.

He felt oddly calm, but was aware of another person, another self — beyond reach somewhere abstract and timeless — sobbing inconsolably like a child.

The tapes were running as the detectives went over and over the same ground.

Letting Dwyer take the lead, DI Maugham sat back, adding one cigarette-end after another to the pile in the ashtray. She was grey of skin as well as hair, and was given to withering glances and mocking little smiles.

"*If*, as you maintain, she was indeed alone," said Dwyer. "Why do you —"

"I didn't say she was alone. I said *I* wasn't with her."

"Why do you suppose she'd choose that route? A quick squiz of the *A-Z* and anybody can see it's hardly a short cut. By going down to the river and then back up to Merrick Road and your flat, at least five minutes gets added to the journey. Why would a lone female take that route at night anyway?"

"Trixie liked walking along the river at night."

Dwyer made a snorting sound.

"Were going to bring your footwear in," he said. "Get the treads compared with the casts that forensics are preparing. Lucky for us, two days of rain had washed mud down the bank and slurried the footpath up nicely. Even luckier, the rain stopped sometime before or shortly after the incident, and held off long enough for us to find three or four clear sets of footprints at the spot we think Trixie may have entered the water."

"Good," said Richard. "That should help you catch the bastard."

"Hopefully. As I said, we're going to process your footwear first."

"Fine. Why don't you start with these?"

He reached down and started to undo the laces of his Caterpillar boots.

"I'd rather you didn't do that," said Dwyer.

DI Maugham raised a hand and Dwyer fell silent.

"Richard," said Maugham. "I've been sitting here all this while wondering how best we can help you with what's going on. I've been watching you, and I've been thinking here's a man who's in a lot of pain."

She spoke softly. Richard knew on some level that it was a strategy, but in spite of himself he warmed to DI Maugham.

"Let's go back a bit," she said. "Let's see if we can't sort this muddle out. Now, I wasn't at the crime scene myself and neither was DS Dwyer. DI Gooch was. All I know is that Trixie was found in the river by the dog-walker at seven thirty this morning. We haven't got the pathologist's report back yet, so we don't know if she was injured in any way. But I'm interested in what you said in our earlier talk with you this morning. You asked if she'd been attacked with a knife."

"Only because you said the dog-walker was receiving trauma counselling."

"Hm," said Maugham. "Lots of people receive trauma counselling for all sorts of reasons. The shock of finding a dead person can be enough in itself."

"Right," he said, shifting in his seat.

"But *you* mentioned a knife earlier. Not us. *You*. A knife is pretty specific. Do you own any knives?"

"Everybody owns knives."

"Do they?" she said.

"Kitchen knives. You know."

If there'd been a signal for Dwyer to jump in again, Richard missed it.

"At this very second," said Dwyer, "there's a team on its way to your house. They'll take the place apart. Room by room; drawer by drawer. Go through your stuff. And hers. Everything. Your dirty laundry and private letters. Photographs. Computer. Porn stash."

"There's no porn. We were enough for one another. We were happy."

"You weren't all *that* happy. The neighbours reckon you've been at each other's throats lately."

Richard stared at his fingernails.

"Just 'fess up," said Dwyer. "Save us the hassle."

"Listen, Richard," said Maugham gently. "Sometimes accidents happen. Things that aren't really anybody's fault. Things that we wouldn't *want* to happen. That we didn't *mean* to happen. But they happen all the same. Now, we know from Trixie's mother that she couldn't swim. Did you know that?"

"Of course I did."

"Unusual these days, don't you think? A non-swimmer adult? I'm a bit surprised she'd choose — of her own volition — to walk home along a river late at night if she couldn't swim. What do you think, Clive?"

"Yes, ma'am," said Dwyer. "A bit surprising all right."

"Richard," said Maugham. "I'm going to put a scenario to you ..."

She lit another cigarette.

"Some of it might be right and some of it wrong. I'd like you to listen carefully, then I'll invite you to discuss any discrepancies afterwards. Now, I know you've *said* you weren't with Trixie on the river. Let's pretend for a moment that you were. Trixie had a fair amount to drink at the Riverside pub. We know you weren't in the pub, but let's say you had a skinful at home and then took a walk and met her after she left the pub.

"You may even have suggested the river route yourself. It's dark on the footpath along that stretch. Just a bit of light coming down from the road. It's wet and muddy that night. Trixie slips and goes in. You know she can't swim. You try to help. It's difficult because you've had as much to drink as her, maybe more. You try your best. You *really* try, Richard.

"You get her to the side, but you can't get her onto the bank. You might get out yourself at that stage and call for an ambulance. You *might*. Except that you don't own a mobile. Trixie owns one, but that's lost in the river in her handbag. Is any of this sounding familiar?"

Richard shook his head. Maugham's illusion of safe harbour had dissolved fast. Not that Richard had believed in it, and he could now at least cultivate unwavering hatred for them both.

"Speak for the audio tape, please, Richard," she said. "Does any of what I've just put to you sound familiar?"

"None of it's familiar. None of it happened."

"Thank you," she said. "Now, we know from Trixie's friends that she wanted you to get a mobile, but you refused. Argued about it even. And I can tell you that we *have* recovered Trixie's handbag. With her mobile inside. So ... Mobile in handbag. Handbag in river. Girlfriend dead. Or as good as. What do you do next? You go home, that's what. Except for one small problem. Do you know what that problem is?"

He wasn't even going to dignify it with an answer. He wished he'd said yes to a duty solicitor. Was it all right to make the request now?

"Richard," said Maugham. "I asked you if you could tell me what the problem with the scenario is?"

He stared at the floor.

"For the tape," she said, "Mr Farr isn't responding. Do you know, Clive?"

Dwyer made an extended grunting sound.

"Yes, ma'am. Most people would find the nearest phone-box or stop someone with a mobile. And call an ambulance anyway. Dead or not."

"I would've thought so," said Maugham. "But Mr Farr isn't most people. And what I think really happened, Richard, is this: You're walking back along the river and you're having another argument. Except that this one is bigger and nastier than the ones your neighbour Ms Burlington says she's been hearing. This one's a real stinker. Concerning a certain Moon Stillwater ..."

Richard looked up.

"Yes, we know all about *him*," said Maugham. "So at some point along the river, without really thinking and without intending harm, you push Trixie — "

"No. I wasn't there. You're not listening."

"She falls in the river. You're so drunk anyway, and so *angry* that you keep on walking — "

"No."

"By the time you come to your senses. Get over yourself a bit. Remember through your booze-addled brain that the poor girl can't swim. By the time you go back, it's too late. Repeat of earlier scenario. Except that we've now got our reason for you not attempting to call anybody. Guilt. Fear. Blame avoidance. Film over. Fade to black."

Maugham stubbed her cigarette out. Lit another. Inhaled deeply. Blew a stream of smoke up to the ceiling.

Dwyer chuckled and rubbed his hands together.

"Very good, ma'am," he said. "Very good. Articulate, that was. If you don't mind me saying."

"Thank you, Clive. We can't all be university lecturers like our friend Mr Farr. But that doesn't mean some of us can't string a few phrases together in the right order now and then."

December, 2004. Kyiv

"I've been meaning to ask you," he said as they walked again, continuing along Khreshchatyk. "The first night I met you ... I got off the metro at the wrong stop. When I came into Café Oasis, you did this strange gesture — "

"Strange — ?"

"You swiped your finger across your throat. Like this."

"I don't understand," she said. "You are saying that I did this ... *gesture*?"

"Yes. When I entered. You looked at me and did that ... so I thought maybe it meant the bar was closing or ..."

She frowned.

"No," she said. "I don't think so."

"I remember it very clearly. Then ... the first murder happened that night — "

"*What?*"

"But not until later and ... but ... So you really don't remember?"

"No, I am sorry, Richard," she said. "I have never used a gesture like that, so I don't see why I would use it on that night."

"But ... you *did* do it."

"No," she said, agitated. "You want me to try harder to remember something that I don't remember?"

"That's not what I meant."

"You think I am lying?"

"No."

"So maybe you imagined it?"

Richard shook his head and said, "I ... suppose I must have done."

"Don't worry," she said. "Maybe I did do it. Who really knows?"

Then he remembered something else. He took the Emily Dickinson book from his coat pocket.

"I forgot about this the last time we met. You know, what with the Pavlo thing."

"It's for me?" she said.

"Yes."

"A gift?"

"Yes."

She leafed through it page by page, smiling.

Then she put it in her pocket, took his hand and led him into the recessed doorway of a closed shop. She looked in his face, her gaze direct but at the same time unfocussed. It made him think of how somebody who was partially sighted or almost blind might respond to movement and changes of light — the look of somebody who can't see you properly but wants to give the impression that they can.

He understood what she was waiting for, too — what she was offering — so he placed his hands on her waist and stood closer.

And it was a kiss that made his head spin and his blood fizz — a kiss that was long, deep, sweet and dark.

eleven

Two days later, on Friday, which was New Year's Eve, Christmas trees and lights were up everywhere. At dusk, early fireworks began to crump and flash in the skies above Maidan Nezalezhnosti. One extra-loud bang shook the air and set dogs barking and car alarms wailing.

As Alexei had explained, the country usually came to a standstill during the fortnight spanning Gregorian New Year on the 1st of January, Orthodox Christmas on the 7th and Julian New Year on the 14th.

"This year is a little different," he added, "with our Orange Revolution. You know how pro-European I am, Richard. The KSE will be business-as-usual except for the national and religious holidays. And you'll find a skeleton metro service still operating."

That evening in Independence Square — where stage, podium and sound systems were all still in place — massive crowds turned up in a mixture of New Year's Eve revelry and political fervour.

From beside Richard, Nadya chatted with Alexei and the KSE tutors and some of the students present.

Amid the drinking and laughter, the mood was ultra buoyant, and shortly before midnight, a group of dignitaries arrived on stage. Guest of honour was Mikheil Saakashvili, president of Georgia, on a surprise visit. Flanking him were Viktor Yushchenko, Yulia Tymoshenko and the mayor of Kyiv. Best wishes were delivered to the hundreds of thousands gathered.

***

January, 2005. Kyiv

New Year's Day fell on the Saturday, and it was overshadowed by two things. The first was that gas supplies from Turkmenistan were cut off, followed soon after by the cutting off of gas from Russia's Gazprom.

"The bastards did it," said Alexei, in a call to Richard's new mobile. "Happy New Year to you, too, Mr Niyazov and Mr Putin! They cut us off and then they dare to announce — *cynically,* Richard, *cynically* — that the move has no political connotations! Bah!"

The second overshadowing was the latest update on the murders of Bella Savchuk and Maryna Petrenko.

Police now believed that it was the same killer, and were dismayed to admit that a serial killer was at large. It was feared the killer could strike again soon.

Women, in Dniprovskyi especially, were warned not to go out alone in darkness.

Nadya had said she was busy with family commitments on New Year's Day, but would meet Richard on Sunday.

As he stood waiting outside the post office, he saw — in the quietest conditions since his arrival — that Independence Square was vast. Its flatness was relieved by monuments, shrub gardens and skylight outcrops for whatever lay beneath. Grandiose buildings lined parts of the perimeter. Some were hotels. Others were banks, restaurants, bars, a McDonald's.

He thought Nadya looked cold when she arrived and, in a moment of confused chivalry, he offered her his coat to wear on top of her own. She refused, but eyed the thick material with interest.

"This is a new coat for you, Richard?"

"Alexei gave it to me."

"He is like your father," she laughed. "He gives you a phone and now an expensive overcoat."

"Oh, he made fun of me with my double-lined fleece from London, told me it was a 'spring jacket'. Said he never wears this and I should have it."

"Alexei is very nice. In Passazh that time, he offered me a job teaching at the KSE."

"*Really?* Well, that's —"

"But I have never taught. For me, it is really quite a crazy idea."

A blast of static over speakers drowned the end of her sentence. Then rock music filled the air.

"A band?" he said.

"No, it's playing over the street speakers at weekends. Khreshchatyk and the Maidan are more like a normal weekend today. Closed to traffic, and with music playing, so that people can walk and enjoy."

Elsewhere in the square, hawkers were offering the chance to be photographed with an owl or a falcon or a monkey. *Babushki* sat at trestle-tables selling books, maps and patriotic paraphernalia.

Near by was a marquee with the logo *Obolon* all over the dark-green awnings, and Richard wondered if it were the name of a local beer. Through plastic windows, he saw people sitting drinking and others queuing at a bar. Outside were plastic tables with parasols, where a few weather-impervious customers sat.

"You would like to drink beer?" asked Nadya.

"Maybe later."

He leaned towards her for a kiss.

She kept it brief, then looked down and smiled and said, "You always want to know more about my life?"

"Yes."

"You think I am a big mystery. So, come on, this way, I would like to show you something ..."

She stopped outside a large, drab-looking department store along Khreshchatyk, and said, "This place is called

Tsum. It's a Russian shop. At one time, it was the only big shop in Kyiv."

"You want to go in?" he said.

"No. I prefer the shopping places beneath, you know? Beneath the Maidan and beneath Khreshchatyk. They are small but very modern and ... shiny. Like in Western Europe maybe."

Richard thought about the skylights he'd seen across Independence Square.

"Only to look," said Nadya. "I cannot buy anything. But I wanted to ask you what you call these models in the windows of Tsum? These ... pretend people. Are they dummies?"

"Yes. Dummies. Or mannequins."

"Mannequins. Thank you. I told you that we lived in Volgograd for some years. It was a difficult time. My father was an engineer but he could not find a job to have. He drank a lot and sometimes hit my mother. After I left school, I could not find a job myself. I tried very hard. Factories, shops, bars. When I was seventeen, I had my first job. I worked as a mannequin."

Richard laughed, then stopped as he saw that he'd offended her.

"You ... pretended to be a mannequin?"

"In some big shops in Volgograd — and all over Russia — they paid girls to be mannequins. To show what fashions they are selling. Still now, in Russia, I think this is a job that girls do."

"Just girls?"

"Mostly."

She smiled in a way that made him feel naive.

"I don't understand," he said. "Human mannequins? You stood in shop windows all day?"

"Not standing. Dancing. A special dance. Like a robot, I suppose."

"Like a mannequin that's come to life?"

"Yes, exactly. I got tired after all day. You can imagine. The pay was poor. Two and a half *roubles* only for each hour. And the things you had to wear! Short skirts, of course. Swimming costumes. Nightdresses. And men would stand outside, watching."

Richard looked from Nadya to the winter-coat-and-fur-hat-wearing mannequins in the windows of Tsum, then back to Nadya.

Tears pricked at his eyes. And at the same time, the intrusive thoughts surfaced ... *picture her behind display glass, dancing in a bikini.*

He shook himself.

"I'm sorry ..." he said. "Sorry you had to do that job."

He put his arms around her, but she stepped back.

"There are worse things," she said. "Much worse."

As they continued walking, she said, "You like the city of Kyiv then, Richard? You think it's beautiful?"

He tried to look past the concrete, granite and tarmac, the forbidding buildings — past the winter colours of lingering snow, ice and slush.

The boulevard was impressive. Conceived on a grand scale. Perhaps when the trees were in leaf and the sun shone from a blue sky ... ?

And then there was Nadya ...

"Yes, I think it's beautiful," he said.

At that moment, they passed a 3D advertisement in the form of an eight-foot tall model of a mobile phone, which rotated on the end of a pole. How could the administrators of such a tasteful city allow this hideous piece of *kitsch* a place on the streets?

Nadya saw him scowling at it, but she only shrugged.

"I thought we might go back to the apartment in Dniprovskyi," he said.

She laughed.

"Of course you are thinking that, Richard. And ... on another day, yes."

She stopped and looked at the boxing-machine. He'd seen the contraption in the vicinity before, but he'd never seen anybody having a go. It was a crude set-up draped with tarpaulins and a poster of Muhammad Ali. There was a padded round leather attachment at chest height — the punch zone — and a tinny speaker that crackled with a rousing crowd-cheer.

"Would you like to try?" said Nadya.

Richard laughed and shook his head.

"Of course not! Why *would* I?"

She resisted when he tried to walk on.

The attendant's face lit up and he gestured at the machine. Nadya squeezed Richard's hand.

"Not my kind of thing," he said.

"But if you want to try," she said.

By now, the attendant was shadow-boxing and doing some fancy footwork. From beneath his beetling brows, he fixed Richard with a dark gaze.

"Five *hryvnia* only," he said, punching the air.

He produced the boxing-glove and held it out. The rousing cheer crackled from the speaker again.

Nadya unfolded a note from her purse.

Richard glanced up and down the boulevard. Dusk was beginning to fall. The artificial light from streetlamps, cars, kiosks and shop windows refracted and splintered in the cold air.

Nadya handed the money over.

Richard stepped forward, fretting that something indefinable but valuable could be lost if he didn't have a go on the stupid machine.

He took the boxing-glove and thrust his hand inside. Not bothering to lace it up, he made a fist and threw a punch at the padded disc. The squeaking smack of leather on leather was followed by a dull clunk. There was a pause, then a short announcement in Ukrainian came over the speaker.

"Good score?" he asked, handing the glove back.

"Yes," said the man in a flat tone. "Good score."

Nadya smiled, though she looked disappointed.

Was a bell supposed to ring if you packed a powerful enough punch? Did lights flash? Did the cheering crowd go crazy?

"One more time?" said the man.

Richard was already striding away.

Nadya followed, laughing.

"It was like you were training for your next fight with Pavlo!" she said.

"*What?*"

His limp returned for a couple of steps and his throat went into spasm briefly, like a muscle memory of Pavlo's hand clamped about his neck.

"Oh, I am sorry," said Nadya. "Was this a bad joke?"

"No ... no. It's fine."

Soon, she led him into another doorway. Like teenagers. Which was fine by him. And the kisses were even longer, deeper, sweeter and darker...

twelve

Alexei had been right about the Dnipro freezing over. A few days after seeing Nadya, Richard got off the metro at Hidropark Station and walked across. It was satisfying to hear the soft crunch of his boots on the snow-dusted expanse of ice. He swung his arms and breathed the sharp air, watching it ghost up in front of his face.

The only other nutters on the frozen river were a gang of children trying to harness up and get a thoroughly pissed-off-looking wolfhound to pull them on a sledge.

The mood during the part-time holiday hours at the KSE was relaxed, and students and staff were happy.

On an afternoon of heavy snow, Nadya failed to show at the next meeting outside the post office. Richard waited an hour before giving up. He thought she might at least try to reach him on his mobile. She didn't.

In the evening — in spite of the Pavlo situation — he went to Café Oasis, but it was shuttered and dead.

The KSE was closed the next day, and he wandered about the city centre. There were ice patches on the footways and jagged sculptures of frozen slush in the gutters. He turned up the collar of Alexei's overcoat. A light, icy rain bombarded his face like blunt needles.

Plenty of people were out, fur *shapkas* and other hats pulled down over their ears.

At weekends and holidays, promenading in downtown Kyiv seemed a social activity for its own sake. And the soundtrack was rock music, blaring from speakers that were grey and industrial-looking, as if installed originally for public announcements, or for disseminating Soviet propaganda maybe.

He bought a beer from a kiosk and drank as he walked. It was funny to think that in London it would be unlawful and be seen as the behaviour of an alkie, a waster, a yob. Nobody looked that way here. The well-dressed women and men in one small gathering were sipping wine from glasses, and laughing over some joke as if in a park on a summer's day.

Heavy snow fell again that night.

At Café Oasis, he found the steps, doorway and window half buried by drifts. It looked abandoned. The next day, the sunken yard had disappeared altogether — topped with snow to the level of the pavement.

The place might never have existed.

In January, the media confirmed that it was an unusually cruel winter. More than fifty people died and hundreds were hospitalised with frostbite and hypothermia. The majority of these were homeless.

Temperatures dropped to -24C in the capital one night and as low as -40C in other parts of Ukraine. In shops, demand for heaters outstripped supply as people tried to supplement their antiquated, state-controlled systems.

Richard spent a lot of time holed up and stranded in Dniprovskyi. He stood at his tenth-floor window looking out over the snow-blitzed landscape. He slept fitfully, kept company by the gurgle and clank of the plumbing, and by the rattle of the fridge every time the condenser kicked on or off.

On arrival, he'd judged the Dniprovskyi apartment buildings a high-rise slum. Then he'd found that although in a state of decay and disrepair, there was cleanliness and respectability. So far he hadn't seen a single glue-sniffing adolescent in the stairwell. No drug dealers. No abandoned syringes. No pimps. No mafia. Nothing.

Unless it all goes on quietly behind the steel-plate doors? he speculated.

It was as if the worst London tower-block estate, in expectation of a royal visit, had been given a superficial makeover and had all the low-life airlifted away.

And yet Dniprovskyi was a place of murder.

He thought of the second-floor apartment, still in the burned-out condition it had been in six or seven weeks ago. And he thought of the murdered victims — the first found near Hotel Yalta on the other side of the metro tracks, the second, Bella, an employee at the grocery shop halfway between Darnitsya Metro Station and Richard's apartment. *Bella* ... found several kilometres further west, close to the river, not far from her home.

He didn't talk about her with the other girls in the grocery shop. They'd been subdued since the murder.

For a short time, there was a flurry in the media about another suspect — a tram-maintenance engineer from the Marinsky Park area — but, like the previous suspect, he was released without charge the same day.

Now the press were growing critical of the police for having no leads, no profile, no motive.

Time weighed heavily for Richard.

The isolation was turning him into a paranoid loon. He'd pass the bulldozer man in the stairwell and think, *Is it you?* Or exchange *dobray vecher*s with the old snow-clearer out the front and think, *You?*

There was a man from the ground floor, who — every day in all weathers — tinkered with the engine of a rusty yellow Moskvich. Its wheel-less axles stood on bricks. He was a wiry, tough-looking man in his thirties. He worked hard, treated his tools with respect and was always whistling. Richard thought, *How about you?*

In mid January, the snowy, deep-freeze conditions lifted during the last holiday-season weekend. Only then was Café Oasis "dug out" and reopened. He hadn't seen or heard from Nadya in twelve days.

Apprehension jagged through him as he turned off the footway and descended the steps.

Pavlo ... Pavlo ...

Richard had to show Nadya that he wasn't afraid.

It was a relief to find her looking after the place by herself. She seemed on edge, but refused to admit that anything was wrong.

Her eyes darted about, or she'd flinch at the tiniest noise from the kitchen or from upstairs.

"Please," she said quietly. "You really should go. But tomorrow, Sunday, I will come to Dniprovskyi. You can meet me at the metro station at three o'clock?"

They reached the tenth floor to see the spider-brooch woman and the bulldozer man kissing on the landing.

Post kiss, the woman looked coy, girlish and radiant. She wore a rose-pink dress and her big furry boots. When she spotted Richard and Nadya, her expression became flinty. The bulldozer man turned his cobble face, too, and Richard imagined them as carved and wooden, an eccentric couple shunted into view from the innards of an old-fashioned clock striking the hour.

After some awkward parting touches and words, the spider-brooch woman went into her apartment and the bulldozer man went into his.

Richard opened up his own apartment.

Once inside, Nadya walked around the main room, asking permission with her eyes before swinging open each door and looking in.

"This is very nice," she said.

Richard laughed, then felt sad.

If she saw this place — which was small and unimaginative and crudely furnished with mismatched items that were clean but looked as if they'd been salvaged from across four decades — if she saw this apartment as "very nice", what must the apartment she shared with her mother and sister be like?

She went to the window and gazed down into the twilit street. It had started snowing again. Despite the interior warmth, she still had her coat on.

Richard stood behind her and reached around to undo the belt and buttons, then he slipped the coat from her shoulders. She jiggled her arms helpfully. He tossed the coat on the sofa and put his hands on her waist. She was wearing the black trousers and black jumper he'd often seen her in. It was a limited wardrobe she rotated day after day, and it struck him that she may even be poorer than he'd imagined.

Poor — but clean, dignified and beautiful.

Ever so slightly, she leaned back against him. He noticed it as small changes in pressure and weight rather than as a movement.

He kissed her on the neck.

Nadya turned to face him, turned into his arms.

Then he kissed her deeply on the lips and pulled her close. She returned the kiss before extricating herself in a sinewy action that left him puzzling over how she'd managed it. She stood in the middle of the room. Flushed and a bit breathless. Hair dishevelled. Eyes wide and dark.

"Nadya, I wanted —"

"I know what you want," she said, raking strands of hair from her face.

She glanced towards the door, and he wondered if she were calculating her chances of escape should he decide to "attack" again.

He raised a hand in a calming gesture.

"I meant to ask," he said. "Have you thought any more about Alexei's offer?"

"Oh, I don't see how I could teach," she said, relaxing. "You studied for years and you know all the right names for the language rules."

"What if I helped you? Showed you? It's only the more advanced students who get hung up on grammar. If you worked with beginners, you could pick up the rest as you go along. And I could help you. I *would* help you."

She smiled and shook her head.

"Beginners are easy," he said. "It's hard work, and I know you're not afraid of that. But really, technically, it's easy. You can spend weeks and weeks just working on the basics. An example —"

"Richard, I don't ... I know it's easy for *you*."

"Present tense. That's how they begin. The *Simple Present*. Daily routines. Listen ... *I get up. I take a shower. I brush my teeth. I have breakfast. I go to work at Café Oasis. I hate my boss. I come home. I kiss my boyfriend.*"

She laughed.

"Seriously," he said. "You could do it. You ... Your understanding of English isn't just good. It's brilliant. I can't understand how you're this good and you're not using it. Your family wouldn't need money from Pavlo if ... You wouldn't need to be there. Yesterday ... when I came to the café. You were on edge."

She sat on the sofa, hands in her lap, and he went to sit next to her.

"Richard, there is something I have to tell you about myself. Something ... very terrible. Worse than Pavlo. I thought it would be the right thing to come here today and tell you, but I know that it's not. This is a good place. I don't want to spoil it by speaking of terrible things."

"You wouldn't. You can tell me anything."

"Thank you, but can you be patient ... a little longer?"

For another hour, he made her laugh by playing around with the simple present and trying to convince her that she could be a tutor. When she said it was time for her to leave, he called a taxi service. She accepted on the basis of the destination being undisclosed.

Richard insisted on paying.

"This is enough," she said, taking only a few of the notes he offered. "As a foreigner, you would pay more, but this is the correct fare for seven or eight kilometres."

"Seven or eight kilometres?" he said.

A worried look crossed her face, but then she relaxed, and he realised that she hadn't really told him anything. Seven or eight kilometres in any direction?

A horn sounded below and she went to the window.

"It's here," she said. "Tomorrow and Tuesday I work long hours and have some family things. Wednesday I have the day off but work in the evening."

"I've got Wednesday afternoon off," he said. "Would you like to meet me at Passazh near the KSE for lunch? One o'clock. My treat."

She skipped over and kissed him, then hurried from the apartment. He knew not to accompany her. He might overhear her telling the driver where to go!

Her heels clacked down the stairs.

Richard watched from the window as she appeared below and got in the taxi. She didn't look up, but he waved anyway. The taxi moved off, its tail-lights casting a red glimmer on the fresh snow.

thirteen

Amid the intoxicating smell of ground coffee, waiters in black bowties and black aprons sailed about. Music with a Latin beat played beneath the buzzing conversation of the suave-looking clientele. Every table was taken.

Richard was about to suggest going somewhere else when Alexei spotted them and stood up.

"Have this table," he called. "We're leaving."

They went over and Alexei gave Nadya a kiss on the cheek. As they chatted in Ukrainian, the shaven-headed KSE administrator Oleg Skarshevsky stood up beside Alexei and tucked a laptop under his arm.

"So," said Alexei. "Enjoy your lunch you two and enjoy your afternoon off, Richard. By the way, Danica leaves us at the February break in four weeks. So I can offer you a longer-term position. Until summer. Think about it. You may have other plans, of course. Off to teach English in Vladivostok or Nairobi or Ho Chi Minh City!"

He laughed at his own fluency and inventiveness and Nadya laughed along. Oleg narrowed his eyes and tapped a fingernail to his wristwatch.

"Ah, yes, the meeting," said Alexei.

"I'll take the job," said Richard.

"Just like that?" said Alexei. "Good. Oleg will amend your contract."

"Office tomorrow," said Oleg. "Nine. Don't be late."

Richard nodded.

He could never tell if Oleg was joking or serious. A man of few words and rare smiles, everything from him was so deadpan. But there was a flicker of the hooded eyelids as he appraised Nadya.

"Be careful," he told her flatly. "The killer."

"*What?*" said Nadya.

"Oleg!" said Alexei. "This is not an appropriate comment. Of course all women must be careful, but ... All right. No matter. Nadya, please forgive my nephew for his poor social skills."

Oleg raised his chin. His face remained a mask of clinical detachment.

Alexei kissed Nadya's cheek again and punched Richard lightly on the arm. Then with Oleg at his heels, he edged away, still showing off: "*Do pobachennya. Dasvidanya.* Goodbye. *Au revoir. Ciao.*"

Richard and Nadya sat down, yielding their coats to a passing waiter, then ordering coffee and sandwiches.

"Alexei is very nice," said Nadya. "After lunch, we have the rest of the day. What would you like to do?"

Back in the apartment, she released herself from his kiss and his embrace, and stood smiling.

"Poor Richard," she said. "I say no to everything. Give you nothing."

She kicked off her shoes and lay a hand feather-light on his shoulder.

"I expect you want to leap into bed with me?"

"Not leap," he said. "Get in slowly. With lots of kissing and tender touches on the way. And only doing things we both want to do."

A first, sweet shock of pleasure.

The falling away of any reserve over breathing and sighing. And the approach to something so good he could barely believe it. Until he lost the thread of things. Lost all sense of time and space and self. In what the French so accurately called *la petite mort*.

Then the cushioned sounds of voices and vehicles below, the light of afternoon sky at the window — the world of forms beginning to make gradual sense again.

And as they lay side by side with the sheet thrown off, they exchanged lazy, dreamy touches under the feathery movement of time.

In a while, Richard propped himself on one elbow and looked into her face. He'd thought that her eyes were completely black, but he'd been wrong. Her irises were the same colour as her hair — very dark but not quite black — and if he looked close enough, he could make out the fine concentric circles of her dilated pupils. She gazed steadily back at him.

"What is it?" she said.

"*You*. You're really something."

She looked away towards the window.

"It's been years," said Richard. "I've not felt this good, this happy, this *alive*, in years. What I'd like ... with you ... Us. I'll work at the KSE until the summer. You could as well. I'll help you. Alexei would help. Then ... in the summer ... both of us could go back to London."

He felt a sudden tension in her body.

"I am happy, too," she said. "But there are things I have to tell you. Not here. I don't want to spoil *here*. So we have to go somewhere else. A bar underneath the Maidan. Bar Zavtra. There, I will tell you everything."

Beneath the city centre were dank, dingy, pedestrian passages lined with sellers of flowers, cigarettes, drinks, CDs, optic-fibre ornaments, remote-controlled cars. The smells of damp stone and smoke drifted on the air.

Along some stretches, there were shops — tiny, narrow shops, flush to the wall, slotted side by side like bullets in the magazine of a gun.

In one such underpass, a door opened onto a softly lit bar with low ceiling beams, dark-stained wooden tables and bench-seats. Out through the back, terrace tables overlooked a two-tier shopping centre — an ultra-modern triumph of glass and steel and designer stores.

As Richard and Nadya sat on the terrace drinking cold beer and snacking on pistachios, he thought about the *babushki* and the down-at-heel vendors hoping to shift their wares back in the underpasses.

He waved a hand towards the elite shoppers milling below and said, "It's like we're in a buffer zone. Two retail worlds at opposite ends of the spectrum, with Bar Zavtra in the middle. It means *tomorrow*, doesn't it? *Zavtra* is tomorrow in Russian."

"And the same in Ukrainian," she said.

"And we're under Maidan Nezalezhnosti here? It's a bit of a mouthful, don't you think?"

"It fills your mouth?"

Richard laughed.

"Yes," he said. "I keep thinking of it as Maidan Nez. Do people call it that?"

"I don't know anybody who does. We mostly say the Maidan."

He took her hand across the table, and waited ...

"His name was Vernon," she said. "I was twenty-four, so — seven years ago. I worked as a waitress in a restaurant in Volgograd. Vernon was an English businessman, or so he told me. He was friendly and always left big tips. On his next visit to Russia, to Volgograd, he took me out a few times and bought me an expensive bracelet.

"The third visit, he offered me a job at his London company. An import-export business. He said I would earn a very good wage because of speaking Russian and English. I should go alone with him and then my mother and sister could join us after some months.

"To live in London ... It was our dream. It was why I had learned English. And anyway, Vernon was so kind to me. I thought I was in love with him.

"When I arrive in London, at a house in a place called Pimlico, I have to sit in a room and wait. Vernon says he has some quick business then he'll be back. I never do see him again. I know something is wrong. It feels like in a waiting room at the dentist.

"I go out to the hallway. A very big man stands by the door. As I take a step towards him, he looks at me with cold eyes and shakes his head. That's all he has to do. And I know I have to go back in the room. In a few more minutes, two men come. I don't have time to struggle. I'm held tight with a cloth over my mouth and a chemical smell and I'm soon asleep.

"I wake up in a basement. I don't know if it's the same house. There are other girls. Three from Russia, one from Moldova, another from Ukraine. And Greta from Lithuania, who I become close friends with. A big room with sofas. Other, small rooms with beds.

"A man called Wayne always brings our food down, locking the door behind him every time. He tries to be friendly but he is still like a jailer to us. For two months I am in that basement.

"The men come. The customers. Five, six, sometimes ten each night ...

"You cry, Richard?"

He wiped his face, took her hand again and kissed her fingertips.

"I told you it was terrible," she said. "But it's over soon now. Greta has a plan. She tries to get all the girls to help, but they are afraid. Some of them have been beaten before. Or there are threats to their families in their home countries.

"When Wayne is putting the lunch things on the table, Greta hits him on the head with a wooden chair and he is only half awake after that. I get the keys from his pocket and we both run up the stairs to unlock the door. One of the Russian girls follows. So many keys. We can't find the right one. Then Wayne is shouting into a mobile phone and staggering across to the stairs. His head is bleeding a lot. We find the right key, but as soon as we get into the hall of the house we don't know what to do. The big man is at the front door to the street. Two more men come down from upstairs.

"I run to the back of the house. I do not look behind. I only think about saving myself. And I am so very lucky, Richard. The kitchen door, the door into the garden, it is not locked. I still have the keys in my hand but I don't need them. I run outside. It's sunny. My eyes hurt from the sunshine. A man is operating a noisy mowing-machine near the bottom of the garden. I can smell the cut grass. He doesn't see me at first. Then he does. Because I am frozen, worrying about Greta.

"All I can think is, *Where is Greta?* But of course she would have been caught and be back in the basement by now. The noise stops. The lawnmower man comes towards me. Another man comes out from the back door of the kitchen ..."

fourteen

"I run to the side of the garden. There are trees and a high wall. And I don't know how I do it — I could never climb trees or anything when I was a child, not like my sister — but I remember the branches scratching my face and the top of the wall digging into my legs. I climb over. I climb over and jump and twist my ankle when I hit the ground on the other side. But I ignore the pain and run so far with my chest hurting as well. I run until I come to some shops. Then I see a station of the Underground.

"I go down the escalator and over the barriers without paying. Somebody shouts after me. I keep going. I get on a train and travel for many stations before I get off. I don't know what I will do next, but at the barriers some guards are waiting.

"I cry as I try to tell them what has happened. I don't think they believe me. The police are called. After talking with them for a long time, other people are involved. Social services. Customs. The next day, the police drive me all over Pimlico. They want me to show them the house where I have been. But it is impossible to find.

"I am transferred to a detention centre. I have no money or passport. It was kept by Vernon. Everybody at the centre thinks I am an economic illegal immigrant, but I say, 'No, I only want to go home'.

"So they send me home."

They sat in silence. Anything Richard thought of saying never reached his lips. He held her hands and looked into her face.

"So maybe you can understand now," she said, "why London, and even speaking English has been spoiled for me. And so asking me to go to London with you in the summer is ... stressful."

Back in the underpasses, he stopped to buy roses. Thirty-five *hryvnia* each was expensive, he knew, but he wasn't going to barter with an old *babushka*.
"Very nice for lady," said the woman.
The long-stemmed roses were fresh and velvety and a rich crimson. Nadya was waiting a little way off, smiling. There were only two roses left, so he bought both.
"Thank you," said Nadya when he presented them.
He leaned in close for a kiss, then noticed that she was gazing at the roses with a puzzled look.
"Is something wrong?"
"No," she said. "They are very beautiful. But I think in England you must have different customs I didn't know about yet. In Ukraine, people give flowers like this in odd numbers. One or three maybe. Never two. Two flowers, somebody would maybe bring to a dead person."
"Er ... I'm sorry. It's probably not different customs. It's probably me not knowing. I'm sorry."
"Don't worry," she said, shrugging. "One for today, one for tomorrow."

Fat snowflakes fell as they stood at the railing outside Café Oasis. Nadya was resting her head against his chest. She said something in Ukrainian. He didn't understand and she didn't translate, but her sweet voice resonated with something deep in inside him.
I am out with lanterns, he thought, *finding myself*.
Following the revelations about London, he couldn't believe that she would still work an evening shift, and had to remind himself that the brutal story was fresh for him but historic for her.
Richard saw down through the café window that the old woman Olga stood watching. She smiled toothlessly,

brought her hands into view and made a theatrical show of rubbing her left ring-finger.

He smiled back. Since Trixie's death, he'd doubted if he'd ever come close to happiness again, but at that moment it was beginning to seem possible. He imagined resettling in London with Nadya later in the year. They'd have a good home. Kids. A big dog of some kind. Kite flying. Beach holidays ...

Pavlo appeared at the window beside Olga. He had his arms folded, and his mouth was working itself slowly in a shit-eating grin.

Nadya was facing away from the window, her head on Richard's chest still. He drew her closer, with the intention that Pavlo should make no mistake about how the situation was to be read.

Pavlo's grin broadened as he carried on looking up through the dusty window in the sunken yard.

A worm's-eye view, Richard remembered.

For the rest of the week and into the weekend, they met often. Walks up and down Khreshchatyk. Swan lake at the National Opera House. St Volodymyr's Cathedral. Pechersk Lavra — the famous Caves Monastery — where the bodies of the saints had been preserved for centuries.

Deep underground they shuffled with other visitors in single file. The air was fragrant from the incense that burned everywhere, and from the beeswax candles they held to light the way. They passed through a network of tunnels and cells, where monks still spent their lives praying, meditating and writing. Even for a faithless person like Richard, it was humbling.

On Sunday, finally — after weeks-long procedural hold-ups and complaints from the Yanukovych camp — the media voices resounded with Viktor Yushchenko's inauguration as president of Ukraine. It took place in the Parliament Chamber and was attended by over sixty foreign delegates including Aleksander Kwaśniewski, Sergei Mironov, Colin Powell, Jaap de Hoop Scheffer, Javier Solano, and Jacek Saryusz-Wolski.

Later, Yushchenko appeared before an estimated crowd of half a million in Independence Square. He emphasised maintaining strategic ties with Russia while at the same time pursuing integration with the European Union. The next day, he named Yulia Tymoshenko as prime minister.

And amid the political fanfare, even though the body of another murdered woman was found on the Sunday of inauguration, news didn't filter into the mainstream until Monday.

Richard had a sense of *déjà vu* as he rode the morning metro into the city. Fingers were being jabbed at newspapers; voices were raised in anger and disgust. There weren't any pictures. Just big bold Cyrillic text screaming out from the pages.

Along Khreshchatyk, the last few die-hard Orange Revolution protesters were finally removing their tents in the wake of the presidential inauguration.

In fresh public unrest, though, an incensed crowd jostled outside a television shop. Richard approached. Something serious was happening and he doubted that it was to do with politics.

On the screens, a police spokesman was talking to the press. The image shifted to a copse of trees at a roadside, and pale grass mottled with snow — the area cordoned off with crime-scene tape.

A grave-looking newsreader came on, and Richard was already suspecting that the killer had struck again.

It was confirmed when he saw one of his advanced students, Galnya, in Passazh, also on her way to the KSE.

"They believe it happen yesterday, Richard," she said.

Richard's heart thumped.

"The same time," Galnya continued. "The time when Viktor Yushchenko is giving his speech in the Maidan."

"Who was the victim? What else are they saying?"

"Very little. Only that it was a Ukrainian woman. Her body is found this morning. Near trees at the side of Parkova Road. Eastern edge of Marinsky Park."

"Marinsky Park? But that's near Arsenalna Station."

He thought about how Café Oasis was downhill from the park.

"Yes, that is correct," said Galnya. "Alexei may know more ..."

A minute later, they were sitting in Alexei's office.

"I cannot reveal the woman's name," he said. "And you must understand that anything I say is in the *strictest confidence* ... But listen: my friends in the courts and in the police tell me that her throat was slashed the same as the other two, and they are wondering if there is a political angle to the murders."

"How?" said Galnya. "Why?"

"I may have already said too much," said Alexei. "But listen: the woman found near Marinsky Park has her hair in the style of Yulia Tymoshenko. Blonde, with a long plait fixed around her head."

Relief flooded Richard's veins. It wasn't Nadya.

"Oh," said Galnya, "but this style is so popular now with Yulia's fame, and the other girls did *not* have that style of hair."

"Just so," said Alexei. "Unless the killer was *warming up* with the earlier murders. Or it's a coincidence."

"I don't understand how any of this makes it political."

"No, Galnya," said Alexei, "and I really cannot say any more, but, well ... there is the possibility that the killer is planning to kill Yulia herself."

"What?"

"If you look at the murder locations ... Now that there are three, it can be seen that they are in a line. That line begins at Hotel Yalta near Darnistsya Metro Station ..." — he glanced at Richard — "... continues with number two on the east bank of the river, and then number three crosses the river to Marinsky Park. If you extend that line, it would lead to Independence Square."

"The security services poisoned Yushchenko," said Richard. "You think it's them again? That they'll —"

"No, not that," said Alexei. "How could it be? Pro-Russian agents would act directly; they wouldn't mess about killing other women first."

"The hairstyle thing is a coincidence," said Galnya.

"Yes, most likely," said Alexei. "However — and I will be in big trouble if I say any more — but listen: *in strictest confidence*, I hear that as a precaution there are moves to put extra bodyguards in place for Yulia."

fifteen

In the coming days, the media showed pictures of the murdered woman. Polina Boyko was a twenty-eight-year-old office worker. As Alexei had confided, she had a long plait of fair hair wound about the top of her head. It looked like a crown, and was in the style favoured by prime minister Yulia Tymoshenko.

Police spokespeople confirmed that Polina Boyko's throat had been slashed and confirmed that they had a very dangerous serial killer on their hands, but they played down any suggestion of political motives.

"Sergiy Dralo," said Sergiy, standing from his seat. "I thank you Mr Richard Farr our tutor for invitation you give. To tell you our story. A small bit. Just the modern bit. Mikhail Gorbachev, from him the *perestroika* and *glasnost* policies. Then, 1991, the USSR is falling into pieces. The Berlin Wall is broken down. The people are angry. We end with fifteen independent countries. We have — in alphabet order, as I write down here in my notebook — Armenia, Azerbaijan, Belarus, Estonia, Georgia, Kazakhstan, Kyrgyzstan, Latvia, Lithuania, Moldova, Russia, Tajikistan, Turkmenistan, Ukraine, Uzbekistan. Okay, finish. That is my turn."

"Well done, Sergiy," said Richard. "I'm noticing much better pronunciation from you, and better grammar."

"Oh, thank you."

Annushka stood up.

"I continue from Sergiy to what happens next. In the year of 1991, Mr Kravchuk is elected president of new independent Ukraine. But sadly his policies, they are, they were, like photocopies of old communist system.

We have privatisation. Some few people in Ukraine are suddenly very rich, so rich it is disgusting when others cannot eat. Business becomes controlled by oligarchs. It is like a mafia state."

"Thank you, Annushka."

Yvan Shevchenko stood up.

"That time it was bad. Inflation is bad. Ten thousand per cent, Mr Farr! I remember my early twenties, in 1993 or 1994. Ukraine, it has then a temporary currency notes. Coupons. Cut-out coupons. They wear out quickly. Many people, we use bread and cigarettes for currency instead. Most shops are closed or empty shelves. People buying goods in streets. People working their jobs and they do not get paid."

Galnya stood up.

"Yes, then Leonid Kuchma was elected in 1994. It was meant to be an alternative to communism with him. He was seen as a *progressive nationalist*. Somebody who could unite all people of Ukraine. So Ukrainian culture was made important. In 1996, Ukrainian language was now the official language of our nation. But a problem at that time, and still it is a problem now, is that the Russian-speaking Ukrainians, particularly in the east, they prefer the old ways of the Soviet Union."

Lola Tismenetsky stood with her laptop open.

"Yes, Galnya — and Kuchma was again elected in 1999. Some people say he was corrupt, abusing his power. Men and power, you see! The story never changes. There were ideas that he was incented ... excuse me, *involved*, I think, in the killing of some Ukrainian journalists at that time not so long ago. Democracy, I think, was in big trouble. Until we have our beautiful Orange Revolution."

"Very good. Thank you, Lola."

"But, really, Mr Farr, I think you are nice man and good teacher, but we cannot pretend that another woman has not had her throat cut open with a sharp knife. Her innocent blood on the grass and the snow. A young, sister Ukrainian woman. Ahh! *Why this is happening? Why must men always hurt and kill women to feel powerful?*"

Towards the weekend, Nadya agreed and planned to stay at the apartment on Saturday night. But then on Friday, things changed.

"I'm sorry," she said. "My aunt. She lives in a village at the Black Sea. She's not well. I must visit her with my mother and my sister. You understand?"

"Yes," he said, distracted.

"And you are disappointed," she said. "But there is something else. You had that look. Were you thinking about *her* again?"

"*Her?*"

"Your Trixie?"

"Er ... only for a moment."

"Yes, and I am sorry to say this, but I wonder if you have told me everything there is to know about ... Trixie. Of course, you don't have to tell me anything. But we have been talking about the importance of *trust*. And after all that I told you about London — "

"Trixie drowned."

Nadya stared at him, and he knew that *she knew* there was more.

"All right," he said. "Trixie did die from drowning. But it was murder ... and the killer was never caught."

Her eyes widened and she put a hand to her mouth.

"Oh ... oh ... I am sorry."

Richard can almost believe the promise of the early sunshine. Almost deny the scene of horror laid out at his back. It's a winter morning. The sky is blue and the

countryside glistens from last night's rain. Don't look behind, he tells himself. Why ruin such a nice day?
He could step into the meadow and enjoy the February sun. He could take off his boots and socks and feel the wet grass flatten beneath his feet.
Could walk away and keep on walking, as innocent as the sleeping oaks.
But he turns and looks.
He laughs at first, wondering why somebody would dump a perfectly good mannequin in the river. But it's not a mannequin. It's a dead, naked woman with her head shaved. Trixie. She hangs six inches below the surface. One eye is closed, the other partly open with only the white showing. There's a movement in her left nostril. Something small and black wriggles out, curls around and swims up the right nostril ...

Sweating and full of panic, he woke in darkness.
"Trixie!"
Trixie died nearly five years ago.
"Nadya!"
Nadya's at the Black Sea visiting her aunt.

February, 2000. London

Richard had been staring out of the window of the Merrick Road flat for he didn't know how many hours when the phone rang. He'd won a holiday. At least that was what the ebullient young man was saying.
"Yes, Mr Farr! From millions of phone numbers, yours was randomly selected by our computer. All I need you to do is answer a few short questions."
"That's great," he said flatly. "Where's the holiday to?"
"Costa del Sol!"

"A holiday would be good," said Richard. "I'm feeling a bit low today. My girlfriend was murdered last night. What do you think to that?"

"And I have to tell you, Mr Farr, it's a fantastic holiday! I'm excited for you myself! You're very lucky! I just need you to complete a short, simple survey about popular everyday products. As an added bonus, you'll be entered into our Grand Prize Draw, and could even win a brand new Toyota!"

"I was interviewed by the police earlier," said Richard. "I'm the prime suspect."

"So, Mr Farr, are you ready for the first question?"

The old man with the long grey beard had arrived on the open-plan park opposite. Today he was wearing a transparent raincoat over his tweed suit. As usual, he squatted on the grass to unzip his canvas bag.

"Here's the first question. When you do your laundry, would you say that you use fabric softener *always*, *sometimes* or *never*?"

From the bag, the pigeon-feeder produced handfuls of white sliced bread, which he shredded and scattered about the grass. Twenty or so pigeons landed or strutted into view and pecked at the bread.

"If you're not sure, I can put you down as *sometimes*."

In moments, the numbers had swollen to about fifty. The old man dived his nimble hands in and out of the bag as if speed were vital. He shredded the slices rapidly and threw the bread about in a way that suggested thankful relief from a burden.

"Mr Farr? Are you there? Mr Farr?"

The feeder shuffled off, trailing the empty bag from his fingers, head hung. It was as if the business with the pigeons drained him.

"I'll never know your story and you'll never know mine," Richard said aloud.

"Mr Farr? Mr Farr? Did you say *never*? I think you said *never*. Is that right? Okay, the second question ..." Richard lowered the handset back into its cradle.

One week after Trixie's death, Moon Stillwater rang the doorbell. Richard didn't ask him in. Just leaned in the doorway, glaring, his right fist clenched and trembling at his side. The light had gone out of Moon's eyes.

"I've never pretended to like you, Richard," he said. "I still don't."

Richard said nothing.

"Okay-dokey," said Moon. He sniffed and ran a hand through his shaggy blond hair. "Me and Trixie. I wanted to. I don't mind telling you I tried hitting on her. She wasn't having it. She was in love with *you*. Everybody knew that. I thought it was right that you should know we didn't do anything ..."

He sniffed again and looked down at his feet. Snakeskin boots.

"Is that it?" asked Richard.

"Well ... yeah ... I guess," said Moon.

Richard closed the door.

January, 2005. Kyiv

Around ten o'clock on Sunday night, he kept hearing a dull knocking. It took him a while to realise that it was somebody at the door of the apartment. That hadn't happened before. He wondered if it was the spider-brooch woman, the bulldozer man, the snow clearer, or maybe even Alexei.

When he saw that it was Nadya, he kissed her and was so happy that he all but dragged her inside.

"You are pleased to see me?" she laughed.

"Just a tiny bit."

She half raised her travelling bag.

"I thought that because we missed out on Saturday, I could stay with you tonight instead. If you wish?"

When they were sitting on the sofa, he said, "How's your aunt?"

"Oh, a little better, I think. A false alarm."

"Aunt Katerina," he said.

"Yes."

"Katerina ... ? What's her family name? I don't know your family name yet. Is it the same as your aunt's?"

"So many questions. My family name is not important for now."

Richard laughed. He laid a hand on her leg.

"Aunt Katerina's village ..." he said. "Where is it?"

"It's on the Black Sea, as I told you."

"The Black Sea has a very long coastline," he said. "What's the name of the village?"

"I ... What is this game you are playing, Richard? I don't understand."

He reminded himself of the horrors she'd experienced in Pimlico.

"It's not a game," he said. "But don't worry."

Wake from this dream:

He laughs and screams and crows at the night sky, his raised hands dripping blood. Blood all the way down to the elbows like devil's gauntlets.

A fantastic tide of stars sweeps the vaulted indigo. Cicadas chirrup. The warm breeze smells of wet copper. In the sand at his feet, he knows, lies a carcass. A fresh kill. His kill. Close by, hyenas circle. He'll kill them too if he must. The indigo night. The stars. His hands. The blood ... Whose blood? An antelope's? A person's?

Below the horizon of his vision only darkness.

He cannot see what he's killed and he cannot wake.

sixteen

January 2005. Kyiv

Feeling drugged and gluey-eyed, he woke. The contours of Nadya's warm body were curved into his. Her back was against his chest and her bottom in his lap.
Spoons.
He raised himself up and saw that she was awake, gazing towards the light at the gap in the curtains. The bedside clock showed 7.45 a.m.
Nadya turned onto her back.
"Did you sleep badly, Richard?"
"No, I ... slept fine," he said, though the nightmare he hadn't woken from flashed across his thoughts.
"You were making ... some noises in the night."
"Oh?" he said. "What sort of noises?"
"Strange noises." She laughed. "Before that we were lying how you say, like spoons. And you had your arm around my neck, my throat."
"I ... didn't hurt you, did I?"
"No. But it was like you were afraid I might run away. You were holding me tightly. Then you got up and went to the window. You stood between the curtains and placed your hand on the glass. That was when you made the noises ... I don't know, like a wild animal."
His heart sped up, but he laughed.
"Sleepwalking?" said Nadya.
"I ... wasn't sleepwalking," he said. "I remember going to the window."
She blinked three times rapidly — something he'd noticed her doing if she was being sceptical.
"You remember?" she said.

He hesitated.

"Yes. And the noises."

She blinked again. He'd entered into a lie and he didn't know how to backtrack. He couldn't backtrack. He didn't want her to be alarmed. To doubt his mental stability. Didn't want to do anything — *anything* — that might give her second thoughts about him. Gaining her trust this far had already been a mammoth task.

"Sometimes I wake in the night," he said. "Not often. I like to look out at the sleeping streets. And I don't know why, but when I'm doing that I make strange noises, sort of off-key singing or humming. I've even been told that it sounds like a wild animal. Isn't that what you said?"

No mater how implausible and ridiculous, he knew that he had to stand by it now or be exposed as a liar.

Nadya looked less than convinced.

"I came back to bed then, didn't I?" he guessed.

She nodded slowly.

"Have you *ever* sleepwalked?" she said.

"Once. When I was a child." He laughed. "My dad found me downstairs wearing my school football kit!"

She laughed, too, but he regretted what he'd said. Blanket denial would have been better than throwing in an historical truth.

He went to make tea, but discovered he was out of milk. He told her he'd go to the shop, and she asked if she could use the shower.

Overnight, there'd been a fresh dusting of snow. A few delicate flakes were still floating down. The Moskvich man already had his head under the bonnet, whistling as he tinkered. The old yellow car now had wheels and tyres, but half the transmission components were laid out on the ground.

Richard felt happy. Felt a sense of belonging in this crumbling district. He knew the apartment buildings were where labourers and factory workers lived, but also where a large proportion of the middle classes lived. Any number of those getting into tatty cars or waiting at the metro station might be doctors or teachers. And always the women were so immaculate in appearance, picking their way around the pot-holes in footways with such dignity that they might have been on their way to the opera rather than the office.

As he walked back with the milk, his thoughts were of Nadya. Maybe they'd set up home somewhere on the south coast of England? He'd always fancied Brighton. He'd find a job at another university. Nadya could work at an adult-education college. They'd be happy to boast Russian language classes on their curriculum (Ukrainian might be considered too obscure).

Getting a visa for Nadya could be tricky because of the circumstances of her last visit. He might have to marry her in Kyiv before she'd be allowed back.

At the apartment, he went straight to the bedroom. He could hear the shower running in the *en suite* and could smell apple-scented shampoo.

Nadya's weekend bag was on the floor and some of her things were on the bed — a magazine, her jumper and trousers, clean underwear, her open handbag.

It had never been in his nature to snoop, but his eyes devoured the visible contents of the handbag — make-up items, a hairbrush, tissues, a small bunch of keys.

As he moved closer, he made out the black vinyl cover and page-edges of a slim book, possibly an address book or diary ...

"Richard. I *thought* I heard you."

He spun around.

Nadya stood naked in the *en suite* doorway, beads of water glistening all over her. He went to her and she settled easily into his arms.

"Your clothes will get wet," she laughed.

"You think I care?" he said, pulling her closer.

It was fine. She hadn't suspected he was about to rifle her handbag for the diary. He kissed her, then said he'd make tea and breakfast.

"Richard. You have work this morning?"

"Not until the afternoon."

"You would like to go somewhere together? It's the last day of January today. When I was young, my father liked to go out and do things on the first day of each month, but my mother thought it was better to celebrate the last day of each month in some small way."

It was a day of sunshine. Clear skies stretched in every direction, filling their eyes with blue. The ground was white with snow, the air crisp. The edges of things were highly defined in the clean light.

"I come here sometimes to walk and think," said Nadya as they overtook a stout old couple meandering at snail's pace.

To Richard, Hidropark — an island in the middle of the Dnipro River — seemed a place of little interest. Accessed by a metro station directly off the river bridge, it was a grid of paths amid acres of scrubby grass and trees. There were bench seats everywhere and a few cafés and kiosks, many closed for low season.

Nadya led them along a path to the shore. The river was still semi-frozen with ice floes bobbing about. On the opposite bank, the wooded hillsides were punctured by the domes, belfries and green-tiled rooftops of Pechersk Lavra. Downriver, the Motherland Statue — Rodnya Mat — towered and shimmered in the sky, a shield raised in her left hand, a sword in her right.

"It's gigantic," said Richard.

"She was built in the days of Brezhnev," said Nadya. "Inside her, elevators and stairs go up to her right hand."

Richard dropped his gaze to the opposite shore.

"The woman who was killed?" he said. "The latest murder. Is Marinsky Park near Rodnya Mat?"

"No. The opposite way. To the north."

He turned and looked upriver to get his bearings. At the same time, a metro train trundled across the bridge towards the city. He scanned Hidropark again — the spindly trees, the grey tufts of grass poking up through the snow, the bleak loneliness of the place.

Nadya laughed at his expression.

"Hidropark is a beauty spot," she said. "Where we stand now, it is sand under the snow. In the summertime, people come to swim and sunbathe. Have picnics and play games. Eat ice-cream.

"I came here as a child with my family. My parents were happy at that time. My father made everything into an adventure. We had picnics here, and he told stories about kingdoms and princes, witches and spells. He made me and my sister characters in the stories. We were princesses. That was before he drank too much and before he ever hit my mother."

"What do you want from life?" said Richard.

"Oh ... What a question!"

"Most people hope to find happiness."

"Yes," she said. "I don't know. Maybe a family of my own one day."

"Do you believe in fate?"

"I'm not so sure. I used to have *faith*. Religious faith, you know. But since Vernon and London, everything ... I suppose everything has been broken."

"I don't believe in fate," he said. "Nothing is pre-determined. I don't accept the inevitability of something somewhere written and unchangeable. What I believe is that we can take our lives in any direction we choose. We live in a random universe. There's only action and its consequences."

Nadya stared at him.

"What do *you* want from life?" she said.

"I want *you*. Want you in my life. I'm sorry that your father hit your mother and that your family broke up. Sorry for all the hurt you've had. Especially Vernon and London. I wish I could fix it. I want to fix it. If you came back to London with me ... If we ..."

He took her hands in his, but she went rigid and lowered her eyes.

"*I'd* never hurt you, Nadya," he said. "You know that, don't you?"

seventeen

February, 2005. Kyiv

She stayed at his apartment again on Wednesday. Earlier that evening she showed him where to find good quality, cheap produce at the markets, and — putting his barely equipped, barely functional, barely *there* kitchen to uses he'd never imagined — she cooked a delicious *borscht*.

Although she hadn't arranged to see him again until Saturday, he crossed paths with her in Independence Square on Friday afternoon. She was with a woman who had a ruddy complexion and a broad forehead.

"Richard ..." said Nadya. "Er, you remember Alla?"

"Hello, Alla. Two months ago, back in early December, I think? One of the demonstrations. Then you both came to Passazh afterwards."

"Alla doesn't speak any English," said Nadya.

The other woman's blank stare gave nothing away. Nadya spoke with her in Ukrainian for a moment, then stroked a hand down Richard's arm.

"I am sorry, Richard. We must go."

And they went.

She glanced back and said, "Please don't follow."

Dusk had fallen when he stood at the railing above Café Oasis. The only customers were a group of men in leather caps smoking cigarettes and throwing back vodka. The old woman, Olga, tended the bar. At one point, Pavlo leaned against the counter speaking pleasantly with her.

Richard was about to walk away when a black Land Cruiser with tinted windows pulled up. He remembered seeing the same or a similar vehicle here before. He went up the hill a little way and waited, then saw the familiar occupants get out. The oldest man wore dark glasses and had long grey hair in a pony-tail, the younger two had gelled hair and wore leather jackets.

They were laughing as they filed down the steps. Richard moved closer and saw Pavlo welcome them inside with hugs and vodka.

Still no sign of Nadya.

Some twisted part of Richard's imagination conjured an image of her preparing herself for the men in an upstairs room. Painting her eyes dark and her lips red. Slipping on lingerie. Spraying herself with perfume. Selecting a tarty outfit from a wardrobe.

On Saturday evening, she was by his side as he tried his card in the fourth cash-machine to be out of service.

"Nadya," he said. "Are you sure the Marquise doesn't take card payments?"

"I don't think so," she said. "There is another machine in the next street."

They walked around the corner, narrowing their eyes against the wind and trying to avoid the slush and puddles. The machine was scratched and tatty and looked as if it might have been one of the first in Kyiv.

"It's working," said Nadya. "But only notes of ten *hryvnia* are available."

Worried that some new restriction on withdrawals might be in place or imminent — as during the recent political uncertainties — he keyed in two thousand to see what would happen. It was far more than he needed short term and he didn't expect the machine to deliver it anyway, but after some clicking and whirring, the notes began to drop into the chute.

As Nadya stood back and waited, Richard became conscious of a pot-hole at his feet, the broken step of a nearby doorway, a tear in Nadya's coat that she poked at absently with her finger.

Suddenly, a gust of wind tore the notes from the chute and they spiralled into the air. He ran to catch them. Nadya helped. The machine was still spewing out notes and the wind took them as well. Drivers and passers-by stopped to watch as Richard and Nadya chased the notes through the air and into the road. When the last one had been picked out of the gutter and dried on a sleeve, Nadya held out the stack she'd collected.

By the time they reached the Marquise de Chocolat, Richard was feeling obscurely dirty and crass — over money, over being from the West. It was a mood that was compounded by a lingering irritability at Nadya because of yesterday's scene with Alla.

"I didn't like it when you told me not to follow you," he said now.

"Oh," she said. "You mean yesterday. But Alla doesn't understand — "

"That's not the point. Don't you see? I thought ... thought we'd *got* something. Trust. You don't have to tell me anything about yourself until you're ready. But, really, I *wouldn't* have followed. You didn't have to say that."

"Oh! You are in a bad mood now? Should we cancel going to the Marquise?"

"No. That's not what I'm saying either. And I'm not in a bad mood."

"I think you are."

They walked on in silence.

At the Marquise de Chocolat, he opened the door onto music he recognised. The Grateful Dead.

They sat on one of the lip-form sofas and within a minute a waitress had taken their order for cappuccinos. In the low lighting, the reds of the furnishings and the brown of the unravelled-Flake decor creeped him out. He felt as if he were inside a belly or a womb.

Over by the window, Annushka — the blonde Siberian from his advanced class at the KSE — was sitting with a female friend. Richard quickly looked away before he was spotted.

"What is it?" said Nadya.

"Nothing."

Annushka had been flirty around him a few times and he'd begun to find her annoying. He wasn't sure why. Too vivacious maybe. Too alive.

In the periphery of his vision, he saw the two girls standing, ready to leave. He turned more fully towards Nadya, twisting himself at the waist and wedging his knees against the red plush edge of the sofa. It put him at an unnatural angle that made her frown.

"Richard!" said Annushka. "I *thought* it was you!"

"Oh. Yes. Hello, Annushka."

She stood over them, beaming, self-assured in her beauty. Richard felt Nadya shrink physically at his side.

"This is my cousin, Tina," said Annushka.

"Hello, Tina," he said.

Tina was buttoning up her full-length fur coat. In her own, more Slavic way, she was as striking as Annushka.

Richard glanced towards the door, hoping Annushka would take the hint. His armpits were sweaty and his forehead itched. When the awkwardness had stretched out for too long, he said, "This is my friend Nadya."

"*Nadya!*" said Annushka, offering a slender hand that was dripping with rings. "*Ukrayinets?*"

"Pleased to meet you," said Nadya, ignoring the hand.

Annushka looked puzzled.

Richard laughed to cover his discomfort.

The waitress appeared with the coffees, set them on the low table in front of the sofa and went.

"Good bumping into you," said Richard, glancing at the door again.

"Yes, really good! We will go now. See you."

When they'd gone, he picked up his coffee and sipped. He couldn't look at Nadya straightaway.

"One of my students," he muttered.

From behind the sofa, around the corner of the partition wall came the sound of high heels descending wooden stairs, and the sound of laughter.

"She is very pretty," said Nadya.

"Yes, I suppose."

"Have you fucked her?"

He laughed and shook his head.

"But you wanted to?" said Nadya.

He shook his head.

"But the way you acted with her," she said. "The way you —"

"I was embarrassed, that's all. She's been flirty around me. Hinted that she was interested. *I* made it clear I wasn't. Okay?"

He tried to take her hand but she moved it away.

"I promise nothing's happened with her," he said.

"Okay," she said, her voice flat, her eyes cold.

"There's something else?" he said.

"Well, you introduced me as a *friend*," said Nadya. "A friend! 'This is my friend Nadya,' you said."

"I ... didn't mean anything by that ... It was part of the awkwardness."

"Awkward? Why? If there's nothing between you ..."

Richard drank more coffee. He thought about the cash-machine episode of fifteen minutes earlier, the mad paper-chase in the street.

"I was feeling ... awkward about money too."

"Money?" she said. "Well ... I don't think money is a problem for Annushka. She is maybe the daughter or the niece of an oligarch. As for myself, I have enjoyed your *friendship*, and of course it would have been nice if it was more than a friendship —"

"Stop," he said. "All I'm saying is that I want to be with *you*. I don't care if you're poor and live in a rundown apartment block. I wouldn't care if — when times are tough — you and your family have to survive on snared rabbits and beetroot soup ..."

Although he doubted if what he'd said was true for Nadya, he knew it had to be true for some Ukrainians and Russians historically and even in modern times.

She was staring at him.

How could he expect her to understand the easy decadence of his culture? And how much harder must it be for people like Nadya to see pockets of it suddenly emerging in her own culture?

"I just want you to know that life could be different," he said. "For you. For both of us. I've got money in England. When I was ... when my university job ended, they gave me thousands. Not a fortune, but a lot. We could start a new life in London ... when you're ready. Your mother and sister could come. Like you always wanted ... You'd get a job easily. We could earn so much money between us! Have any life we wanted."

He knew that he had a big grin on his face. For a moment, he saw himself as if through somebody else's eyes — as if through Nadya's eyes — and his grinning face looked stupid and grubby and insincere.

He wondered how close what he'd just said would have been to Vernon's spiel of seven years ago.

Nadya looked sad.

"Could we talk about something else please, Richard?"

She stayed at the apartment with him over the weekend, and he dropped the subject of London. But — a week later — as he sat in the KSE office on Monday morning checking emails, his life was blown out of the water.

eighteen

"This is most irregular!" said Alexei. "Is it essential that you go to this funeral? The timing, Richard, the timing. Don't you see? We have the academic February break beginning at the end of the week. But you have now booked a flight for Wednesday night?"
"Not booked," he said. "*Available*. But I have to make the decision today."
"And you want my approval? How can I approve it? You will leave the KSE in a mess just days before the February break."
"I'm ... sorry."
"Anyway, I don't want to be insensitive, but you said it was the *sister* of a girl you *once* dated *years ago*?"
"It's more complicated than that."
"Bah!" said Alexei. "I cannot approve it, but I cannot stop you. So you have to decide for yourself. Please go now. Your students are waiting."

That evening, Nadya came to the apartment, and he told her about the trip during the walk from the metro station. As on earlier visits, she wouldn't take her coat off straightaway. She stood at the curtained entrance to the kitchen while he put the kettle on the gas ring.
Then she went to the living-room window and looked down into the street.
"I'll worry you about you," said Richard, standing behind her and putting his hands on her waist.
"I will miss you, too," she said.
He kissed her neck and smelt her musky perfume.
"It was the best flight I could get," he said. "The funeral's next Tuesday. I'll be back on the Friday."

"And Alexei will forgive you," she said.

"I wish I didn't have to go."

She turned into his arms and they kissed for a while. Then she took her coat off and they sat on the sofa.

"Nadya," he said. "Before this trip ... Are you going to let me have a phone number or something?"

"I have *yours*."

"I ... yeah, okay. You know, it's really easy to set up an email address if you don't have one. We could do it together at the KSE or the library. I've only been using email myself in recent years. I didn't trust it at first. Or computers. And I've only just got my first mobile phone. Courtesy of Alexei. Maybe now's a good time for you to learn the basics with computers and email? If you work at the KSE at any time, it might —"

"I won't be working at the KSE."

"No. Right."

There was an odd smell he couldn't identify, and he realised that it must be somebody burning rubbish out the back again.

"I am sorry," said Nadya. "I *want* to trust you."

"You *want* to trust me? What does *that* mean?"

"I ... don't know. You are having a difficult time. Your Trixie died, or was killed five years ago and now her sister dies from cancer. It is —"

"Please stop saying *your Trixie*. Okay? I don't like it. Yes, it's difficult. I don't even want to go to London, to the funeral. I knew her, but not well. It's ... complicated. Her parents ... The link I have to her family and our mutual friends ... after everything that happened."

"So you will see all your old friends and remember your *real* life in London and you may not come back."

Richard made a snorting sound.

"You've made it clear you don't trust me anyway!"

"Oh!" she said. "And you made it clear to Annushka that I am only your *friend*."

She stood up.

"Don't go," he said, standing too.

For a full minute, neither of them moved nor spoke. They stood frozen with broken gestures and mask-like faces, like creatures suspended in amber.

Until Nadya said, "Richard, what is that smell?"

He rushed across the room and tore the kitchen curtain aside. The kettle had boiled dry. Long ago. A sharp pong of hot metal and cinders filled the tiny space.

He grabbed a tea towel, soaked it with water and used it to snatch the kettle from the gas ring. He threw the kettle in the old porcelain sink.

Nadya joined him at the curtain as he stepped back, and they stood watching as the kettle hissed and smoked and clinked.

Trixie lies half in the reeds, half in the water.

Her face is turned towards the opposite bank, her long dark hair fanning out in the slow current. Richard smiles tenderly, admiring the familiar curve of her neck and shoulder ...

Furniture shapes were fuzzy in the swimming semi-dark, but he knew that he wasn't looking at *his* furniture. The door was in the wrong place, too, and the ceiling was lower than it should be.

Even as his eyes adapted, nothing was right.

He was naked and sweaty.

A blanket felt scratchy against his skin.

It was all right though. It was all right because *she* was here. In bed beside him. Asleep. He stroked her bare shoulder. He could hear her breathing.

She was warm. Safe. Alive.

But ... she'd cut her hair. Why had she cut her hair?

"Richard?"

She spoke ... but the voice was wrong.

She turned her face to him.

She *looked* strange. She *was* a stranger.
Who the fuck is she?
"Who are you?"
"Richard, what is it?"
Of course ... of course. I'm in Kyiv.
The girl next to me is Nadya. Not Trixie. It's good that Nadya is here. I care about her.
I cared about Trixie once. Then she was killed by someone who was never caught. It's bad that Trixie is dead, good that Nadya is alive.
"Go back to sleep," he said. "Bad dream. It's all right."
He went to the bathroom.
The nightmare was cloying still, dragging at his heels like the swirling waters of a storm drain.
As ever, the details had been wrong. There were no reeds or meadows along that stretch of the river. It was an urban environment.
He turned on the tap and dashed cold water into his face. He pressed his forehead to the mirror.
Breathe. Keep breathing ...

The days passed too soon.
On Tuesday evening, they joined forces in the kitchen and cooked another *borscht*. Elbow to elbow in the tiny space, Nadya bullied him, snapping if he didn't chop things right. He pretended to be cowed by her manner, and thoroughly enjoyed himself.
Later, he suggested going to a bar, but she wanted to stay in. It was good to see her more relaxed in the apartment. She half sat, half lay on the sofa watching a dubbed Hollywood movie.
"Good film," he asked.
"Yes. Good film."
Richard thought it looked utter crap, but had to admit it was lent a comic element by the voice casting of Hugh

Grant's character with somebody who sounded like a Ukrainian Al Pacino.

He wondered if they'd be in a flat together in London one day. As he tried to talk to her again about contact details and about a trip to London in the summer, her expression clouded and she turned to him and said:

"This feels like pressure. Like before. Making me feel that if I don't decide quickly, it could be too late."

"Like before? Vernon, you mean?"

"No. You're not like him. But I don't want pressure. I haven't said that I would *not* come, ever, have I?"

That was good enough for him. He took her hand and kissed her fingertips.

Wednesday evening. Six o'clock. The taxi ticked over at the kerbside, waiting to take him to Borispol Airport. Nadya was in his arms. Behind her was the yawning entrance to the metro system.

"So I will see you in ten days," she said.

"Yes. On the Friday of next week."

It was cold but fine. Diagonally across the Square, the giant digital screen flickered with coloured tropical fish and sea anemones.

"You've got Daz and Preeti's phone number safe?" he said. "Haven't you?"

"Yes."

He held her tighter. Thought about the difficulty of being apart. And here were the intrusive thoughts, to torture him with images of her destruction ...

Nadya lost in a world of heavy machines and manifold dangers. Being stalked by the killer. Washing up dead on the banks of the Dnipro River.

She stood back from his embrace, head slightly bowed, dark hair brushing her cheek. Anything he thought of saying would only be repetitions of his own fears and needs, clothed in paper-thin disguises.

Nadya held his gaze for a moment, smiled, and turned away. He watched her walk down the steps until she was out of sight. Until she'd been swallowed up by the metro system.

"I love you," he said.

nineteen

February, 2005. London

Rain lashed at the bedroom window.
 The clock on his mobile phone showed 7:50 a.m. He hadn't altered it yet, so London time was 5:50 a.m.
 Memories of the journey were a blur — airline food, delays at Warsaw, the shocking opulence of Gatwick Airport after so long in Eastern Europe.
 He went to the window. Apart from streetlights and the odd porch light, the *cul de sac* was in darkness. As new as the houses were, they looked soulless and depressing. In an instant, he cast his eyes over millions of pounds' worth of property and cars.
 Marjoram Fields. South London.
 Who are all these people? Civil servants? Office managers? Teachers? Their Kyiv counterparts live on breadline salaries in cramped, rundown apartment buildings with lifts that never work.
 He dozed for a while, then woke again when he heard noises downstairs.
 In the kitchen, the kids were spooning breakfast mush into their faces. Preeti was making coffee.
 "Terry's grown," said Richard.
 "Thierry," said Preeti. "Yeah, he has. Er, last night ... Sorry I'd had too much to drink by the time Daz got you back here."
 The kitchen was all daffodil-yellow walls and pristine white cupboards.
 "No problems repatriating Helen's body in the end, then?" said Richard.

"No. Pierre wanted her buried in Paris, but he gave in to pressure from her parents, you know?"

"That sounds like Pierre."

"I still can't believe how quick it was. I've heard that sort of thing before. With pancreatic. So close to the anniversary, too, you know ... Trixie."

Richard stared at the ceramic floor.

"You working today, Preeti?"

"Not till the afternoon. I'm part-time now. It's all a bit bollocks at the minute. We've got Ofsted in."

Richard was pretty sure that Daz and Preeti's biggest challenge in life was the length of check-out queues when buying their Pinot Grigio, mozzarella, *foie gras*, extra virgin olive oil and conveniently packaged 125g of oyster mushrooms. Or being pissed off that there was nothing to watch on the scores of channels provided by their satellite dish.

"Daz left early, Rich," said Preeti. "But he said you're meeting for lunch? You know, I wasn't surprised to hear about the Russian girl. I told Fazana last December that I thought you might meet somebody there. Do you think she's the one?"

"Nadya's Ukrainian." He smiled. "And, yeah ... She's the one."

Preeti beamed smiles and gave him a hug.

"This tastes like shit," said Daz. "Oi, waitress! Yeah, you. Take this back to the kitchen and tell them to try again. I wanted *granary* bread not wholemeal, and the lettuce is all floppy. Thanks."

"You're embarrassing," said Richard. "What happened to basic respect?"

"Embarrassing? Last I checked, *you* got the boot from the uni for being too drunk to teach, then spent the next few years sleeping on your sofa surrounded by pizza boxes and empty cans. *Anyway*, your round."

Richard laughed and went to the bar.

"So," said Daz, when they had fresh pints of lager, "where are you staying after the agreed *couple of nights* at our place?"

"Oh, I didn't — "

"I'm only winding you up, mate. So what's the deal with this Kiev woman? You can't be serious about bringing her back, can you?"

"Why not? It's the most important relationship I've had in years. Even if it's not the simplest ... Her boss treats her like crap and ..." He laughed. "I've even kind of had a fight with him!"

"You're fighting over her? Brilliant. What deep doggy doo-doo are you getting yourself into over there? You need some perspective. Stay in London for longer. A month or so. Then call her and see how you both feel."

"I can't."

"Can't what?"

"Call her. I haven't got a number."

"Email then. Whatever."

Richard shook his head.

"You can't contact her at all?" said Daz.

"No. Or not easily. Just maybe the landline at the bar where she works."

A slow smile crept over Daz's face.

"Not a hooker, is she? I ... No. Okay. Sorry."

"She's got trust issues," said Richard. "Life's been cruel. She's damaged."

"Like you."

"Like me."

There'd been nothing in the UK news about the Kyiv serial killer. He used Daz and Preeti's home computer to search Ukrainian news websites but found no updates beyond what he already knew.

The days ticked by to Tuesday's funeral.

He was disappointed, but not surprised, that Nadya didn't try to call his mobile or Daz and Preeti's landline.

Both Trixie's parents blanked Richard when he tried to speak to them in the pub after Helen's service and committal. It was even worse with Pierre:

"I didn't want you here," he said. "This whole chain of events began with you, Richard. You drove Trixie crazy with your jealousy. Then Helen's cancer was a result of grief over her sister. It's all you. Everyone thinks this."

"*Everyone?*"

"Yes."

Thankfully, Moon had never met Helen, so he wasn't there. Another old acquaintance Richard wanted to avoid was Krista. But she weaved over from the bar, spilling her wine, and cornering him by the buffet table.

"Richie, darling," she slurred, eyes out of focus. "What's this I hear about you and the drop-dead-gorgeous, mail-order Russian bride?"

Richard stared at her and said nothing.

"Not questioning your right to be happy," Krista went on. "Think about how you look to other people though. You're forty in a couple of months. This is such a midlife-crisis type of thing to do. Some blokes get themselves a sports car. Others get a mail-order bride — "

"She's not a mail-order bride."

"So you'll bring her back here? Next thing you know, three-quarters of her extended family'll be over expecting you to find them accommodation and jobs. How old is she, about eighteen or twenty?"

"Thirty-one."

"Respectable enough. Still, you really should ... Where are you going?"

When he got back to Daz and Preeti's place, it was past midnight. He tried to be quiet but stumbled over the shoe rack in the hall. Preeti was still up, watching some rom-com by herself. There were two wine bottles on the coffee table — one empty, the other half empty.

"I didn't see you leave, Rich. What happened?"

"I went to an old stomping ground. Marrakech."

"By yourself?" she said. "They still do that designer beer you like?"

"Yeah. Had too many, I think."

"Join the club. Uhh, I put a glass of Chardonnay down somewhere ..."

Not able to locate it, she lifted the bottle from the coffee table and took a long drink. She offered it to Richard and he had a swig too.

"I know you don't believe in fate," said Preeti. "But you and your lady in Kiev ... You have to wonder, don't you? That story you told me about getting off the train at the wrong stop and meeting her."

She had tears in her eyes.

"I'm glad I did," he said.

"Yeah," she said, sniffling. "You and Nadya. It's just so romantic. I really hope it works out."

Thursday night at nine o'clock — eight hours before the return flight — he came downstairs in a new midnight-blue Paul Smith suit and an open-necked white shirt.

"You're going out?" said Daz.

"One drink. At the ... Riverside."

"I'll come with you. You'll need a lift anyway."

"I'll get the tube."

The Riverside? said Preeti. "You're not serious, are you? Tonight? *Tonight of all nights?*"

"He knows what night it is," said Daz.

"Oh ..." said Preeti. "You want to be there by yourself? With your thoughts and memories? Before you begin the next chapter of your life?"

"Something like that," said Richard.

"You'll freeze," said Daz.

"I'll be fine."

"Take my Gore-Tex. It's by the door."

The Riverside had leaded windows and *olde worlde* relics on the walls. He found a table to himself and did only plan to stay for one drink.

And maybe it was the memories flooding back — like the last words he'd spoken to Trixie about not bothering to come home if she fucked Moon. Or maybe it was the group of young people at the corner table — among them a smiley girl with long dark hair.

He'd had four beers by last orders.

The girl with long dark hair stood and wrapped her coat about her. Kissed her friends goodbye.

And left ... alone.

Richard watched as the door swung shut behind her.

Counted to five.

Then followed.

If there'd been a taxi waiting, or a boyfriend, or a dad in a car, he'd have headed back to Marjoram Fields.

She was on the other side of the road taking the steps down to the river.

It was a cold night, but he was warm inside Daz's Gore-Tex. He crossed over and hurried down the steps. Instinctively, he looked to the right along the river path, the direction to the old Merrick Road flat. Nothing. To the left, he made out the lone figure of the girl.

Residual light from street-lamps and passing cars filtered down, but the surface of the river looked black and viscous. It had the appearance of obsidian. The air had a vegetal smell.

When he'd closed the gap to twenty metres, the girl turned and looked back. Richard stopped and pretended to be interested in something across the river. There was no opposite footpath along this stretch, just the blind walls of some industrial buildings.

He realised that the girl had started walking again.

The river was three metres below the level of the road, but felt deeper. Traffic noise was muffled and distant. There were intermittent glimpses of the moon between shifting clouds. Odd ripples and sploshes in the water. The click of her heels and the scrape of Richard's boots.
Why would she choose such a route at night? She could be attacked. Anything could happen.
Just before she reached the twin-arched bridge, she checked behind her again. Richard stopped walking.
Go on, he thought, *take the steps up to the street.*
She even looked between the certain safety of the steps and the dark space below the bridge arch. With hands on hips, she leaned forward to peer beneath. As she did this, her head was lost in deep shadow and, from Richard's perspective, she looked headless.
Then she moved forward and disappeared altogether.
At the bridge, he saw the reason for her hesitation. It was something he knew about but had forgotten. Depending on the water level, passing under this bridge could be tricky. The footpath sloped down into the river and the arch was low. His feet were close to the edge. He had to stoop and half crouch, and he doubted if it would have been any easier for the girl.
Keeping a hand on the overarching masonry, he moved through what was just about long enough to qualify as a tunnel. He had the illusion that the darkened space was in motion. It was alive with shadows and reflections and faint unidentifiable echoes.
Out the other side, he saw that the girl was a long way ahead. He increased his pace.

twenty

The girl looked back. Walked on.
Looked back. Walked on.
Why did she come down here? She could end up dead. Drowned. Her blind eyes staring up at the moon.
Across the river, the bank had widened. It bordered the razor-wire fence of an industrial compound.
On the river's nearside, the girl had reached what used to be a waterfront Italian restaurant, which had closed the previous autumn. The doors and windows were shuttered and a single abandoned chair lay on its side behind the low railing.
Here, too, was an exit from the river.
But the girl continued walking.
Richard saw a faint light at the side of her head, and it took him a moment to realise that it was a mobile phone. The lilt of her voice drifted downriver in fragments. He couldn't make out the words, but took comfort from knowing she was able to contact friends.
He passed the grimy rear elevation of the shuttered restaurant with its curved concrete roof-slabs and its defunct security lamps.
Concerned that he'd already alarmed her, he kept his distance to thirty or forty metres.
Minutes later, blue lights were strobing across the river. There were voices and radio static.
One moment, he and the girl were alone on the footpath; the next, people were everywhere.
Strong torchlight cut through the semi-darkness. Three figures took shape ahead. One remained with the girl, the others came towards Richard.
He turned and ran.

But in that direction — silhouetted by strobing blue light — more figures appeared on the footpath from the sides of the closed-down restaurant.

For a crazy moment, he considered diving in and swimming to the opposite bank. Trying to go to ground somewhere in the industrial graveyard beyond.

But he stopped and waited. Did not resist as rough hands took hold. Rifled his pockets and removed things. Twisted his arms behind his back. Led him away.

The interview room was different from the one he'd sat in five years ago. The table was black and rubberised. In the wall, there was a recessed mirrored panel that looked like a one-way observation window.

"Let's get this thing straight," said Detective Inspector Bradshaw, a thin man with snow-white hair. "Shortly before midnight, you're following a girl along the river. Said girl calls us. We lift you and find a knife in your pocket with all sorts of attachments, one of which happens to be a five-inch blade —"

"It's not my knife. The coat's not mine either. It's my friend's. He goes camping and hiking in Derbyshire."

"As you've said, Mr Farr. We also found a campsite receipt, a pen-light, some old wrappers from those high-energy snack bars the outdoor types are fond of — all of which would seem to support your claim. And we *will* be checking that story out against the name and number you gave us. To continue. When we asked you why you ran, you told us you're worried about getting delayed, about missing a flight you've got booked for five o'clock this morning..." — he checked his watch — "... in four hours' time."

"Right," said Richard.

"Can you really not see the problem? Man with knife follows girl late at night on river path. Said man leaving the country in a matter of hours."

"This can all be cleared up. Don't I get the right to a phone call?"

"Technically," said DI Bradshaw. "But it'd be easier for me to decide that you're too rat-arsed to be questioned properly. Not coherent enough to make a phone call. I could let you sleep the booze off and leave you for the dayshift to process."

"I'm coherent," said Richard. "We're talking, aren't we? If you'd just get hold of DI Maugham, she'd —"

"It's Detective *Chief* Inspector now. And you've been told, DCI Maugham's off-shift. I've left her a message. And I've seen that her name's all over the file we have on you. Moving on."

"Er, shouldn't you be recording this or something?"

"I don't know, sir. Should we?"

Bolts of panic kept shooting through Richard.

The idea of him getting charged with anything was ridiculous, but he had to make it to Gatwick.

"Think of it as an exploratory chat," said Bradshaw. "It's not as if a crime has been committed, is it?"

"No."

"Right. Let's talk about the girl you were stalking on the river then."

"I wasn't stalking her."

"Would you care to say exactly what you *were* doing? She thinks the man on the river was the same man she saw in the pub. Sitting by himself."

"All right," said Richard. "This is what happened. I ... noticed that she left the pub on her own. I ... followed her ... to see that she was safe ... and ... she went down to the river and ... I was watching over her. I'd like to say sorry to her if she was uncomfortable. I didn't know how else I was supposed to keep her safe ... I ..."

He stopped and looked at the floor. If he were Bradshaw, he wouldn't believe such a story either.

"Safe?" said Bradshaw. "You wanted to keep her safe?"

"Yes."
"Do you drink at the Riverside regularly?"
"No."
"Been watching that particular girl for a while?"
"No."
"Is it the first time you've followed her?"
"Yes."
"Is it the first time you've followed *any* woman?"
Richard hesitated a moment too long.
"Yes," he said.
DI Bradshaw drummed his fingers on the table.
"Mr Farr, we're going to keep you overnight. I'll leave an urgent message for DCI Maugham on her voicemail. If you're lucky, she might pick it up and come in tonight. More likely, it'll be the morning though. You can see the position I'm in, can't you? Sorry about the flight."

Before he left the room, he spoke briefly with the uniform at the door.

The uniform stepped over and said, "Belt and laces, please, sir."

Richard paced the cell in a state of suppressed rage and occasionally hammered on the door. Uniforms answered his calls but only to tell him nobody would be available until morning. Once it got to four o'clock, he calmed down, accepting the impossibility of making the flight.

He slept on the narrow bed and was woken around eight by a uniform.

Back at the interview room, he noticed three things: the uniform stayed outside; the mirrored panel in the wall had been covered by a curtain; the only person present was DCI Maugham. In front of her on the desk she had a fat manilla folder and two packs of cigarettes.

"Have a seat, Richard," she said. "I was thinking about you yesterday. Before any of this happened."

"Seriously?" he said, sitting down. "Why?"

She lit a cigarette and smiled across at him. Her grey hair was shorter than he'd seen it in previous meetings.

"Not as if we're strangers," she said, patting the folder.

"No. I suppose not."

"I thought about you because it was the anniversary yesterday. The fifth anniversary. February the 24th. And because my daughter's the same age as Trixie was then."

Richard nodded.

"You know how thorough we were over Trixie, don't you?" said Maugham. "More thorough than usual. Partly because of your persistence. But the inquest verdict was correct. Death by misadventure. I've explained it so many times. You know we identified the owners of the four sets of prints on the muddy footpath. You know that people came forward. That we corroborated iron-clad alibis. That it's incontrovertible that she was on the river alone. That your claim she liked walking there at night, even as a non-swimmer, was backed up by friends and family. That there were no marks on her, no signs of a struggle. It was a tragic accident. Not foul play."

Richard hung his head.

"And yet you still think she was murdered, don't you?" she said.

He shrugged.

"Don't pull any more stunts like last night, Richard," she said. "I'm sorry you missed your flight, and I'm sorry I didn't get DI Bradshaw's message until eight o'clock this morning. Your friend Darren is in reception."

She stubbed out her cigarette, picked up her things and stood.

"That's it?" said Richard. "The girl from last night ..."

DCI Maugham set down the folder but remained on her feet.

"I've spoken with her. She's fine. You saw her leave the pub alone, didn't you? You saw her go down to the

river. You worried about her being in danger. You followed at a distance to make sure she was safe."
"You believe that?"
"Absolutely. But you can't do anything like it again."
"No."
Maugham walked around the table and placed a hand on his shoulder.
"I hear you've been teaching English in Ukraine? And that you've met a woman out there? That sounds like a life. You want my advice? Leave the ghosts of the past behind you. Once and for all. Now. In this room. Go out there and live."

The rain was torrential by the time they reached the carriageway. It rumbled on the Vectra's roof and bounced off the tarmac.
"A night in the cells, then?" said Daz as he accelerated to seventy. "Another badge of honour, mate."
"Yeah. I know. Did they tell you much?"
"No, mate. Just that they'd kept you at the station overnight and asked if I could confirm it was my coat and knife. So what happened?"
"Oh, I was at the Riverside till closing. Got hammered. Went staggering off for the last tube or a night-owl bus and got picked up for drunk and disorderly. Don't remember too much else."
"You should have phoned last night."
"Yeah. I ... wasn't even capable of speaking."
"Right. Respect. Missed the flight though. What now? Snap out of fantasy land and look for a job in London?"
"Book another flight," said Richard. "Top priority."
They arrived at Marjoram Fields and he frowned.
He couldn't understand how his friends could bear to live in this new-build, dolls'-house, ghost-town.
A sickly-sweet smell drifted on the air. Its source was the "brook", a foam-fringed, toxic-looking stream at low

ebb in a concrete channel that cut crudely across the development.

"Is it the first time you've followed *any* woman?" DI Bradshaw had said.
And Richard had hesitated a moment too long.
He'd hesitated because there *had* been one other time. Around six months after Trixie's death, on sleepless hot August nights, he developed a habit of wandering the deserted streets. On one such foray, he spotted a girl, at 4.00 a.m., dressed in club gear, weaving her way through the dark forest of the slumbering market.
Skeletal frames. Bare stalls.
The flap of awnings in the warm air.
He followed — watching over her, as she made a long drunken struggle to a Victorian terraced house with multiple doorbells outside. And he waited as she dropped her key over and over, before getting it in the lock and letting herself in.
Then he'd turned for home.

twenty-one

His airline carrier said he'd breached the terms of the ticket. Its value was forfeit. Worse, they couldn't offer another flight for three weeks. He visited other high-street travel agents that morning and the best deal was a staggered journey with three stops and stupidly long waits, flying out Monday, not arriving until Wednesday.

"I've been to New Zealand quicker than that," he told the young man.

At Marrakech, he had curry and rice washed down with too much lager. He did at least have the landline number for Café Oasis on a slip of paper, but then he found that his mobile's battery was flat.

Back at Daz and Preeti's place, he put a ten-pound note under the landline phone, then connected with the international operator.

The patch-through resulted in a scratchy line, but he recognised the odd mix of good-natured sternness in Olga's tones.

"Hello," said Richard. "I'd like to speak to Nadya. Is she there?"

Olga spoke in Ukrainian.

"Olga. It's Richard, Nadya's boyfriend."

There was a pause, some muffled conversation, then a male voice.

"*Dobry den.*"

Pavlo. It had to be Pavlo.

"*Dobry den,*" said Richard. "Do you speak English?"

"Some little," he said in a heavy accent.

"I would like to speak to Nadya."

"Nadya?"

"Yes. Is she there?"

Silence.

"Hello? Er, Pavlo ... ? It's Richard. Listen, I know that we've ... Anyway, if Nadya's not there, can you give her a message? Before I left, we arranged to meet outside the post office today ..."

The line went dead.

Pavlo hung up. He must have hung up.

Richard slammed the handset down into its cradle, then remembered it was somebody else's property and checked that it wasn't damaged.

He used Daz and Preeti's home computer to search for flights. It was a rubbish computer with a slow connection and the afternoon passed with no progress. Except that he found a Ukrainian news website reporting that the Marinsky Park tram-maintenance worker had been questioned again but released.

On Saturday, he rang the travel agent who'd offered the staggered journey that left on Monday and arrived on Wednesday.

It was no longer available ...

For the rest of the weekend, he did searches on Preeti's computer and achieved nothing. On Monday morning, he slipped another ten-pound note under the phone and made a call to the KSE.

"This is very inconvenient," said Alexei after he'd been fed Richard's lie about the airport bus breaking down. "Are you saying that you won't be here today at all? The first day of the new term? I don't understand."

"I'm working on it. Whatever happens, I'll be there ... tomorrow ... or Wednesday at the latest."

He thought he heard Alexei do some kind of breathing exercise, but he couldn't be sure.

"Oleg Skarshevsky has been trying to reach you on the mobile," he said.

"Sorry. The battery was flat."

Silence.

"I think I left the charger in Kyiv, in the apartment ... and my friends' mobiles have a different connector. I'm buying a new charger today ..."

More breathing exercises, then:

"Keep me informed, please, Richard."

Another day of dipping in and out of travel agents. Not even a business-class seat was available.

March, 2005. London

The next day, Tuesday, he realised he could have been *en route* by now if he'd taken the staggered flight without hesitating. Now, back at the same agent, the same young man laughed as he cobbled together a similar journey.

"Same deal, buddy," he said. "Leave *next* Monday, get there next Wednesday. *Groundhog Day*, innit?"

"Seriously?" said Richard. "That's the best you've got?"

He paid a reservation deposit, even though the flight was a week away. What choice did he have? What if nothing else came up? Something else *would* come up.

Over lunch in Marrakech again, he called Alexei, and Alexei's mobile went to voice mail. He phoned the KSE.

"Ah, Richard," said Alexei. "You must be ringing with good news. Are you at Borispol?"

"*Nn*-no."

"Heathrow? Gatwick?"

"I'm having problems securing a flight."

Silence.

"So, I was wondering," said Richard. "If ... I don't know, if maybe you could pull some strings at your end?"

"*Pull strings?* Richard, I run a language school, not a travel agent."

"Yes. I'm on a number of cancellation lists, so I'm sure that ... I mean, I could even be flying out tonight."

"Good," said Alexei. "That's good news."

"I wanted to ask ... Do you remember Nadya?"
"Yes, of course."
"Has she by any chance dropped into the KSE? Or phoned? Left any messages?"
"Not that I know of. No."
When he got back to Marjoram Fields, Daz and Preeti and the kids had just finished eating in front of the TV.
"Plenty of casserole left," said Preeti.
"Thanks," he said.
He was about to go to the kitchen when Preeti added: "Your girlfriend rang. Nadya. Half an hour ago."
"Nadya rang? *She rang here?*"
"Yes," said Preeti. "You told us you'd given her the number, so —"
"What did she say? What did she say?"
"Oh, Daz took the call —"
"The line was a bit crap," said Daz, avoiding Richard's gaze. He put his empty plate on the arm of his armchair and sat back. "She was only on for a minute. Asked for you and I said you were out."
"And? And?"
"That was kind of it really."
"*Kind of it?* Did she leave a message or a phone number? Is she calling back? Where was she was calling *from*? Did it sound like a bar? Music or voices in the background? Or traffic? What did she say *exactly*?"
"Uh, well —"
"Half an hour ago?" said Richard. "Half an hour?"
He looked frantically about, spotted the landline handset on the coffee table and fell on it like a bird of prey. Punched in 1471. Listened to the automated voice giving the last number to call.
"A local number!" he said.
"I had a work call ten minutes ago," said Preeti.
"Shit!"
Thierry began to cry. Saffron giggled.

"Er, Rich," said Preeti. "I know it's ... but can you calm down a bit, please?"

"I *am* calm! Daz?"

"Like I said, mate, she asked for you and I said you were out. She mentioned something about asking for you at the Casey as well?"

"The KSE?"

"Yeah. And someone named ... Lego?"

"Oleg?"

"That's it," said Daz. "Oleg told her he didn't think you were going back to teach there, or back to Kiev."

"*What?* How can he say that? It's bullshit."

"I dunno, mate. I — "

"Where's all this coming from anyway? You said a second ago that Nadya hardly said anything?"

"Yeah, I'm just remembering now ..."

Richard paced the room.

"You told her I was going back?" he said.

"Er ... she asked about that and ..." Daz's eyes danced about as if the answer might be floating in the air. "I said you *were* as far as I knew."

"*As far as you knew?* Why did she even ask? She *knows* I'm going back! Why didn't she call my mobile? *As far as you knew?* Why did you say that?"

Preeti led the children out of the room.

"Dunno," said Daz. "I didn't think you ... When we talked before, you said you might stay on in London. See how you feel? Didn't you?"

"No. They were *your words*, Daz. *You* said something like that. Not me."

"Did I? Right. Sorry, mate."

"This is bullshit!"

Richard went out of the patio doors, into the twilit garden. Crows cawed and squabbled in the treetops at the bottom. It was about six o'clock, making it four in Kyiv. He took out his mobile — now charged up from a new charger — and rang the KSE office. There was no answer so he rang Alexei's mobile number.

Alexei wasn't aware of Nadya being anywhere near the KSE or of any conversations she may have had with Oleg.

"But I trust you are now on your way back, Richard?"

"I'm ... working on it. Still got the reservation for the rubbish flight next Monday, but obviously that's no good. I'll get something sooner ..."

Alexei made a clucking sound.

"It is already Wednesday tomorrow," he said.

"I know," said Richard. "Alexei, could I ask a favour? I've been trying to reach Nadya at Café Oasis. Pavlo, the manager ... we've had our differences. He hardly speaks any English. Could you phone and try to speak to Nadya? Or leave a message for her that I'll be back ASAP?"

Alexei was doing his breathing exercises again.

"I'll see what I can do," he said, and rang off.

Over the next few days, Richard phoned all the travel agents who'd been looking out for cancellations and last-minute deals. He avoided leaving Daz and Preeti's house in case Nadya should call again. But there were no calls from her, and nothing from Alexei either.

A voice in his ear. He strains to make out what she's saying. It's her. Nadya. Her voice is faint, then loud. Faint, then loud.

He replies, but she doesn't hear. She keeps repeating the same phrase over and over, and he can't make out what she's saying.

The line goes dead.

He's standing on an empty metro platform. Or not quite empty. He glimpses somebody in a dark suit passing between the marbled columns and the archway, towards the escalators. A man with very short hair, or possibly a shaved head.

It's night. There's a smell of sewerage.
Most of the wall and ceiling lights are out. One flickers. He looks at the phone in his hand. It's an old-fashioned Bakelite receiver with a curly flex. His eyes follow the flex to where it dangles in mid air, frayed wires connected to nothing.
Further along the platform, he sees the body of a woman. She's wearing a crumpled old mackintosh.
He goes to her, squats down and turns her over.
Her face is lost in deep shadow.
He tries to lift her by the shoulders and a red slash across her throat gapes open wider as her head lolls back ...

twenty-two

The door burst open and Daz entered in his boxer shorts.
"*What's going on?*" he said. "All the noise. Sounded like you were fighting off feral dogs or something."
Richard sat up from the tangled, sweat-soaked sheets and gazed wildly about the small room.
"I'm all right," he panted.
Preeti and both the children appeared, sleepy-eyed, on the landing.
"What's *wrong* with you?" said Daz, in anger now.
"Nothing," said Richard. "Go back to bed."
"Don't tell me to go back to bed in my own home!"
"Sorry. I've been a crap guest. Sorry for everything."

Friday afternoon. He'd accepted — saw no choice but to accept that he'd be flying out on Monday and arriving on Wednesday. He abandoned the high-street travel agents and the online searches. Gravitated towards Marrakech with its pounding music — Radiohead, Muse, Arcade Fire, Eels — and the frost-coated glasses topped with delicious Czech lager.
In the early evening, he went out to the beer garden at the back and called Café Oasis.
A gruff Pavlo responded with: "Nadya? Nobody name Nadya is work here. Wrong number."
Richard immediately phoned Alexei.
"Yes, hello, Richard. Thank you for calling. What is happening? I expect you have landed at Borispol?"
"I ... no."
Silence.
"I'll definitely be there next Wednesday."
Silence. Then:

"I should tell you," said Alexei, "that another tutor is starting at the KSE on Monday. Omaha. He is from Washington DC."

"You're giving him my job?"

"Not exactly. I have work for you if you come back."

"Definitely I'll be back," said Richard. "And ... I was hoping ... Have you had a chance to call Café Oasis and speak with Nadya?"

"This number you gave me. I spoke to a man. Pavlo. He was quite rude. He says he has nobody working there called Nadya. Not now. Not ever."

"That's impossible. He's lying."

"Richard. Are you drunk? You are slurring a little ... Were you aware of that?"

Marrakech. Weirdly lit by Moroccan lamps. Cigarette smoke hanging against the ceiling like a cumulus. The roll-down big screen showing *The Nightmare Before Christmas* with the sound muted. Instead, Frank Zappa playing over in-house speakers. Another glass of Budvar and moments of accidental synchronicity between the video and Zappa.

Late night. Tripping out of Marrakech. Thoughts of Nadya ... His imagination working on him like an instrument of torture.

Drift around this corner and into a thoroughfare. A blur of bar fronts, music, screams, laughter, handy-looking doormen. And the shining faces of youngsters in brand labels, toying with their camera phones, shouting to each over great distances, largeing it up.

He stumbled into somebody and was pushed aside.

The next street. Past the little Art Deco theatre and cinema. Memories of foreign-language films with Trixie. Directors' names popping into this head. Almodovar. Truffaut. Von Trier. The thrust stage with its 120-seater auditorium. Experimental dance and drama. They'd once seen the punk poet John Cooper Clarke perform there.

At the end of the street, the dual carriageway. Too busy and too dangerous to cross. But he knew a way. Down these steps ...

Magazine Walk. A pedestrian underpass with graffiti on the tiled walls. Old beer cans and fag packets. Whiff of urine. Bare concrete ceiling with strip lights, mostly out of action. A tunnel of shadows to the other side.

A great place to get mugged.

Three days to the flight. Don't screw up now.

His hand trailing against the wall that dripped with condensation. His footsteps echoing weirdly. Memories of Kyiv. Then he realised why. He'd read somewhere once that this part of the district — Magazine Walk and the nearby buildings — had been designed by a Russian architect.

He was not a big fan of sci-fi or theoretical physics — and not only because the latter was Moon Stillwater's field of expertise. But he pressed his hands and face to those cold, damp tiles. And gave himself up to a drunken fantasy. Imagined a wormhole opening up and delivering him to a similar passage beneath Maidan Nezalezhnosti.

March, 2005. Kyiv

The final descent. Dropping smoothly through blue skies. The clunk and whirr of the undercarriage.

Clusters of apartment blocks cradled among the hills. Traffic threading arterial roads. Sunlight silvering the Dnipro River.

He'd been on and off planes and hanging around in departure lounges for forty-two hours. He was tired beyond belief.

Following a half-hour wait in the customs queue, he was about to step forward when an officer raised his hand, smiled and shook his head.

Behind the officer, a steel roller-shutter came down. Richard looked to the left and the right, and the same thing was happening at the other gates. There was a crackly announcement over a speaker. With sighs and grumbles, everybody about-turned and wandered away. He waited for an English translation that never came, then trailed after the others.

Across the airport concourse, at a different set of customs gates, the fronts of the old queues had now become the backs of the new queues. He protested, but was frowned into submission by people more tolerant and more bafflingly protective of this Kafkaesque code of etiquette.

Once through, he took a taxi straight to the apartment block in Dniproskyi.

The Moskvich man was outside — a wiry figure in a boiler suit — standing by the open driver's door pumping the accelerator, revving the engine. He was smiling. The engine note sounded sweet.

Inside the building, the scratched and dented lift-doors bore the usual sign, so Richard humped his bag towards the stairs.

On the tenth floor, he couldn't understand why his key wouldn't turn in the lock. He put his shoulder to the steel-plate outer door and bounced against it while trying to turn the key again. No go.

The door of the apartment on his right opened and the bulldozer man appeared on the threshold in his vest and braces.

"Problem with the key," said Richard. "Have to phone my boss."

The bulldozer man's gaze was impassive. He sniffed and rubbed a large hairy hand around his neck.

Richard took out his mobile, hit a name on the contact list and waited.

"Alexei Koval. Kyiv School of English."

"Hi, Alexei. It's Richard. I'm at my apartment but for some reason I can't get in."

"The locks have been changed," said Alexei. "Standard policy when a tenant leaves without returning the keys."

"What? That's not ... I'm fired?"

"I didn't say that. But your ten-day trip turned into a twenty-day trip. You have been infuriatingly AWOL. And I can't co-ordinate every little thing. Oleg did what he thought was best."

"Oleg?"

"Of course Oleg. He is the KSE's administrator."

"Yes. I'm sorry. I realise I let you down ... Can I ask if Nadya's been into the office? Or phoned? Left any messages?"

Alexei sighed before answering.

"Not that I am aware."

"Okay. Uh, do I need to come to the office to get another key, then?"

Alexei sighed again.

"The new tutor, Omaha, is in the apartment now. And he is taking all of your previous groups. Which will continue. We had no choice. Any possessions you left behind were collected and are being stored here."

"Uh ... so I *have* been fired?"

"It's Thursday tomorrow," said Alexei. "I suggest you come to the KSE on Monday and we'll talk about getting you started part-time with some new groups again. Which days, hours. Another apartment possibly."

"Thank you, Alexei. So ... can you suggest any hotels?"

"Yes. Try the New Bratislava on Khreshchatyk."

As the call ended, he realised that the bulldozer man was still watching from his doorway.

"Looks as if this is *dasvidanya*, friend," said Richard.

"*Dasvidanya*," said the bulldozer man.
They shook hands. Richard half expected his hand to be crushed, but the grip was firm and warm.

Richard almost got off the metro at Arsenalna, even though he'd been told that Nadya didn't work at Café Oasis any more, or — according to Alexei's conversation on the phone with Pavlo — had *never* worked there.
Richard would, of course, be going there to look for her. But he was unwashed, unshaven and dog-tired. Probably looked like a vagrant. He'd check in to the hotel and have a shower first.
The train clattered in to Khreshchatyk.
Up the escalators. Through the sprawling passages and chambers. Hand over some *hryvnia* to a stick-thin blind woman singing an aria. Out to a breezy afternoon with the sun's rays angling across the Maidan.
"Richard! So very good to see you!"
It was Annushka.
"Hi," he said. "How are you?"
"Oh, I'm really well. I recently was promoted at work."
"Congratulations."
"I did not know if I would see you again, Richard. It is wonderful! And our new tutor, Omaha, is very nice! But ... you will be back at the KSE now?"
"Yes."
"Good. I have a work meeting to go to." She gave him a business card. "But please call me if you like to meet for a drink."
When they'd said goodbye, he followed Khreshchatyk away from Independence Square — as Alexei had told him — and soon found the marble entrance and revolving doors of the New Bratislava Hotel.
Brown leather armchairs lined the walls of the huge foyer and the marble floor stretched to a brass-trimmed

reception desk. Maroon-jacketed porters stood about like statues.

After a fifteen-minute check-in, he took the lift to the sixth floor and let himself into Room 626 with a key on a big wooden fob. There was a double bed. A television on a wall bracket. The essential *en suite* bathroom.

He'd soon had a shower, and was towelling himself dry back in the main room when a movement in the wardrobe mirror caught his eye.

It was his own reflection, but even as he began to relax, an uneasiness remained.

It had to be the mirror, a trick of light, lack of sleep.

He moved closer. He recognised the face as his own. At the same time, he was convinced that it was the face of a total stranger. The skin was too pink to be real. Glowing, almost. Like a plastic rose internally lit.

"*O rose, thou art sick!*"

He couldn't be sure if the voice had originated inside or outside his head. It wasn't, he assumed, Mr Blake making contact from beyond the grave. Feeling giddy and on edge, he hurried to the window and opened it.

A panic attack. Nothing more.

He looked out over Khreshchatyk.

The world was there. Life continued.

twenty-three

He only intended lying down for a short while.

When he woke, hours later, the sky was dark at the window. Following the earlier episode, and the sleep, he felt refreshed but fragile.

Instead of wearing his new cotton suit, he put on jeans, a tee-shirt and a black roll-neck jumper, thinking — in a moment of superstitious weakness — that the thicker clothes might offer protection from some obscure threat or force he was unable to name.

Nearing Café Oasis, he heard music and keening voices.

Through the window, he saw three men on stools. One played an accordion, the other two played *bandura*s — large, many-stringed, tear-shaped instruments.

Tables were set in a line down each side, spread with an array of dishes. About a hundred people were crammed in the small space.

At the bar, Olga was grinning toothlessly, her usual blue-and-white flower-print dress exchanged for a shiny lilac number. A girl carried trays to tables. She had pretty, pixie-like features and dark hair cropped short.

As Richard stood at the railing, a large man in a suit and tie staggered through the open door below into the yard. A woman with dyed red hair came out behind him, said something and led him back inside.

Richard went down the steps and caught the edge of the door before it closed. The music warbled at him. There was a burst of conversation, laughter, singing. And a smell of something sweet and vinegary.

Because of how crowded it was, and how the extra tables had been arranged, the aisle through the middle was narrow. He squeezed towards the counter, while on both sides people swayed to the music in an animated, clumsy way, as if on a boat.

The waitress was back at the bar for fresh drinks.

"Do you speak English?" asked Richard.

"Yes," she said. "A little. How I can help you?"

"I'm trying to find Nadya. She works here. Or ... she *did* work here?"

"I don't know," said the girl. "This is private party. Only the manager and his family, his good friends ..."

She stopped as she was distracted by something over Richard's shoulder.

"The English!" came a slurred voice. "Welcome!"

He turned and saw Pavlo. *Welcome?*

Pavlo's slumped posture took a few inches off his height, but his broad face still hovered high. His eyes were out of focus, his cheeks flushed. He had spittle at the corner of his mouth and a stain down his shirt.

While clapping a heavy hand on Richard's shoulder, Pavlo spoke to Olga. A moment later, a glass of vodka appeared in front of Richard.

He drank it in one swallow.

Pavlo grinned lopsidedly and signalled for Olga to set up another. He spoke to Richard in Ukrainian. Richard shrugged and looked at the waitress.

"He say you can stay," she said.

There was a rough tug on Richard's arm. He grabbed the fresh vodka and allowed himself to be led to a table.

All Pavlo's friends were drunk. One spoke reasonable English and introduced himself as Pavlo's brother, Roman. Richard wasn't certain, but he thought Roman might be one of the men he'd seen visiting the café in a black Land Cruiser previously. Across the table, he spotted the older man from the Land Cruiser, the one with grey hair in a pony-tail. Between singing tunelessly to whatever the musicians were playing, Pavlo kept grabbing Richard's arm and speaking to him.

"He say you must sing," said Roman.

Richard laughed and shook his head.

"What are they singing about?" he said.

"Women. They sing about women and vodka."

Pavlo swayed as he sang louder and louder. From all over the little café, there was much table-slapping and foot-stamping.

Amid the chaos, a beetroot dish tipped off the table and landed upside-down in Richard's lap. He felt the quick, cold spread of it on his thigh and groin. All he could do was scoop the worst back into the dish with his hand. Pale-blue jeans. Purple stain. What a mess.

Pavlo laughed and grabbed his arm again. Richard pulled away and stood up. The girl was at the bar with a tray of empties. He went to her.

"What's your name?"

"Tamara," she said. "I'll get a cloth. Your trousers."

"No. Listen, Tamara. My name's Richard. I can't stay any longer tonight. It's too difficult. Pavlo is drunk. Do you understand?"

"Yes. Great party! You are good friends with Pavlo?"

Another vodka was slid across the counter. From behind the bar, Olga gave Richard a wink. He smiled back and swallowed the vodka.

"There's a woman called Nadya," he said, addressing Tamara. "She was working here recently?"

"Sorry. I don't know."

"Her name's Nadya. She's older than you. Thirty-one. I don't have a photograph ... She didn't like ... Her hair's longer than yours. Cut in a bob. Like this." He used his fingers to demonstrate.

Tamara was shaking her head.

"You're new," he said. "How long — ?"

"Yes, quite new. I work here only one week."

Richard turned to Olga.

"*You* know Nadya, Olga. Me and Nadya."

"Ah," said Olga, nodding. She spoke in Ukrainian.

"What does she say?" asked Richard.

"She say you have been here some times before," said Tamara. "She remembers you."

"I know that," he said. "But ..."

Pavlo was hanging off his arm again.

Richard tried to ignore him.

"Tamara. Tell Olga I'm looking for Nadya. Can she tell me where Nadya is? Or her phone number? Can you ..."

His voice was drowned by explosive laughter from the entire room.

"That's very funny," said Tamara, her eyes sparkling. "The music man. He tells some very funny jokes. He say that when he was in the army —"

"Tamara. Please. Listen to me. Tell Olga I'm asking about Nadya."

She did as he asked.

"What did she say?" demanded Richard.

"She say you have been here before. She remem —"

"I know that! She said that already!"

Is Olga simple? he thought angrily. *Or just drunk like everybody else?*

He was close to breaking-point.

Then he felt Pavlo's fingers digging into his arm again.

The accordion man pumped out a fresh tune. The twanging *bandura*s joined in and everybody stamped their feet. Beer was spilled over Richard as somebody barged against him.

Pavlo grunted something in Richard's ear. Tobacco and booze were strong on his breath.

The fingers in Richard's arm dug deeper.

He turned and said, "Can you piss off and die?" He wrenched his arm free and tried to talk to the girl again.

A stream of Ukrainian flew past his ear.

Tamara flinched and gave Richard an urgent look.
"Pavlo say you must go now," she said.
Richard placed his hands on the counter.
"Tell him I don't want any trouble. Ask him where I can find Nadya. Three weeks ago —"
"He say you must sing or go."
"What?"
"Sing or go," she said.
Pavlo gripped Richard's arm.
"Sing or go!" he growled.
Richard laughed and tried to push him away.
Pavlo slapped him a stinging blow across the back of the head. Then hustled him down the aisle between the tables. Richard didn't bother to resist. As drunk as Pavlo was, his physical strength was alarming.
In a moment, Richard was dispatched out to the front yard. He climbed the steps without looking back.
He had little choice but to return the next day, in the hope of Olga being sober enough to help.
What else can I do? he thought. *Go back in and sing?*

The next morning, he was out on Khreshchatyk by nine o'clock. He wore his new suit with his fleece jacket over the top — the winter coat Alexei had given him was presumably stored at the KSE with his other things.
Along the boulevard, the usual wares were being sold from trestle-tables or boxes. Drinks. Cigarettes. Maps. Books. The latest fad-products were tee-shirts printed with the smiling faces of the new political leaders and champions of the Orange Revolution: Viktor Yushchenko and Yulia Tymoshenko.
Richard withdrew a pile of cash from the nearest machine, then went down to the pedestrian underpasses.
He came up at the base of the hill on the diagonally opposite corner of Independence Square. As he passed the huge digital screen, it was showing sunflowers from

every angle and magnification. Swooping aerial shots over fields stretching to the horizon. Extreme close-ups of heads and petals.

He'd worked out on the last trip that, from here, the road uphill led towards Arsenalna Metro Station with Café Oasis about halfway between.

He felt good today. Healthy. Felt that he could run up the hill. But he walked. Quickly.

At Café Oasis, Tamara was by herself.

"I was here last night," said Richard.

The girl folded her arms across her chest and looked him over.

"Ah, yes," she said. "Pavlo's friend. You leave early."

Richard laughed.

"He threw me out."

"Yes. You want coffee? Beer?"

He glanced around. There'd been a big clean up overnight or early this morning. Tables and chairs were back in their original positions. The only customers were a man and woman sitting by the window.

"Pavlo is have a day off today," said Tamara.

"I came to ask about Nadya," he said.

"Ah. You tell to me last night. Is she before work here? I am here since one week. So. I don't know. Pavlo, me, Olga. Nobody other work here."

"Is Olga here now?" said Richard. "In the kitchen?"

"Olga come in night."

"Tonight? This evening?"

"Yes. She come eight o'clock."

That evening, with Tamara translating, Olga said that Nadya *had* left the café. Two weeks ago. Without notice. Simply failed to turn up one day. Apparently, she'd since phoned Pavlo to say she wasn't coming back.

But we've only got Pavlo's word that Nadya phoned him and said that, thought Richard.

Tamara translated that Olga didn't know how to contact Nadya. Any information about employees would be kept upstairs, confidentially, in Pavlo's office.

"If Nadya drops in," said Richard. "If you see her ..."

He gave Olga and Tamara a page of hotel stationery, on which he'd already written his name, room number and mobile number. It was always possible that Nadya had lost the contact numbers.

Friday afternoon, he called by again. Tamara said Pavlo had been in briefly, and — in response to her and Olga's questions — told them to "tell the English he's wasting his time". Nadya had worked on a cash basis. Had never given personal contact information. Not even her full name. Pavlo had suggested, too, that her real first name may not even be Nadya.

Knowing Nadya, some of that sounded plausible. But then, Nadya had also told Richard that Pavlo knew her family, and sometimes gave them money. So ... Lies from Pavlo? Had he assaulted her again? Assaulted her so badly that she was afraid to come anywhere near?

On the way back down the hill, he phoned and left messages on Daz and Preeti's landline and mobile numbers — with the instruction that if Nadya was to ring they should give her his hotel details and make sure she had his mobile number.

For most of Saturday and Sunday, along with all the other promenaders, he wandered up and down traffic-free, rock-music-drenched Khreshchatyk. Swigging beer and fully expecting to come face to face with Nadya at any moment.

Straight after the hotel's buffet breakfast on Monday, he walked over to Passazh and the KSE.

He'd assumed he'd be meeting with Alexei, but Oleg fetched Richard from reception and said, "Follow me, please, and I will tell you what is going to happen."

twenty-four

Oleg's office was as scrupulously clean and clinical as his shaven head. The walls were hung with a series of frameless abstracts. Each had a yellow background overlaid with an arrangement of black rods. The black rods were orbited by polyhedrons and purplish splotches that resembled brain matter.

"A new contract will be drawn up this week," he said, as cheerless as ever. "We have another apartment for you, but it won't be ready for a while."

He pushed his swivel chair back, put his feet right up on the corner of his desk and regarded Richard with a reptilian smile.

"The apartment is located in a rough area. Regretfully, it is not the best of our accommodations."

Richard nodded, unsurprised.

"I hear that Nadya came in while I was away?" he said.

"Nadya?" said Oleg.

"You know who I mean. You met her in Passazh once. She came here while I was in London, asking about me. You told her I wouldn't be back."

Oleg snorted.

"That is incorrect. I told her you had failed to be here for your students. You let everybody down. I *may* have said I *doubted* if we'd see you again."

"Why would you say that? Did she leave a message for me? Some way of contacting her?"

"No. Nothing. Anyway, this *Nadya* is bad news for you. I think I may have seen her at a men's club. Yes, I think so. Taking her clothes off."

Richard's face muscles twitched.

The air in the office felt charged. The walls with their strange paintings undulated and closed in.

"You're wrong," he said. "She wouldn't do anything like that ... I know she wouldn't ... Where? When?"

Oleg steepled his hands.

"Maybe two years ago. Somewhere. I don't know. I go to many clubs. I think it was her. Talking her clothes off. She had very nice tits."

Richard's chair shot backwards and clattered to the floor as he leaped up and leaned across the desk.

Oleg barely flinched.

"Calm down, Richard," he said. "Hey, maybe I was mistaken. Like you say. Maybe it wasn't her ..."

Alexei shook hands with Richard and invited him to sit.

"Thanks for seeing me, Alexei."

"You look tired or ill, Richard. You haven't brought bird flu back with you, I hope? And the New Bratislava? It's comfortable?"

"Yes. Thank you."

"I expect you want to know more about the outreach project? Maybe Oleg already ...? No? We are to provide courses for a successful software company. It will not begin yet, but I have you in mind for the introductory sessions, and later to maybe head up the whole programme if you ... if I —"

"If I win back your trust?" suggested Richard.

"Yes."

"You said *outreach*? Is it still in Kyiv?"

"Yes," said Alexei. "Outreach only as in reaching out from the KSE. Their own offices are less than half a kilometre from here. Don't worry, you're not being sent to Siberia for punishment. Not just yet."

They both laughed.

"Alexei," said Richard, "could I ask a favour of you?"

Alexei had been toying with a glass paperweight. Now he set it down on his desk and gave Richard a wary look.

"What favour?"

"I'd like you to come to Café Oasis with me. Talk to the manager, Pavlo, in person. The one you phoned when I was in London. He claims he knows nothing about Nadya, but he's lying. He's known Nadya's family for years. Gives them money sometimes ..."

Alexei was shaking his head and smiling sadly.

"Seriously, Richard. What kind of relationship do you believe you were having with her? If you don't even have the means of contacting her?"

"She's ... got trust issues."

"Trust? You know nothing about her except for what she told you and what she allowed you to see. Forget her and move on to greener pastures."

"Pavlo's been aggressive ... violent. With Nadya. With me. That time you asked me about my bad leg and the bruises around my throat. I lied."

Alexei spread his hands.

"I'm sorry," he said, "but if Nadya cared about seeing you again, she wouldn't be so difficult to find."

"But she doesn't even know I'm back. Because of Oleg's ... careless comments, she probably thinks I'm *not* coming back."

He was tempted to tell Alexei everything — about Nadya's past involvement with Pavlo, the assault in the kitchen at the café, Vernon and London — but that was a line he didn't want to cross.

"Will you help me?" he said.

"No. I can't do what you ask, Richard. I am sorry. I have my reputation to think of, both social and professional. I can't go questioning some violent bar-manager about a waitress. You understand?"

***

For the rest of the day, he visited all the places he'd been to with her. The Marquise de Chocolat, Bar Zavtra, Pizza Perfect, Hidropark.

He even went to Dniprovskyi and was lucky enough to find the new tutor, Omaha, just arriving home, fresh from a day at the KSE. Omaha was friendly and helpful. He took Richard's mobile number and promised to do all he could if Nadya should show up there.

By sunset, Richard was exhausted. Back in his hotel room, he flicked the TV on and threw himself on the bed. It was six o'clock and a news programme had just begun.

Through drooping eyelids, he saw a scene near the west bank of the Dnipro River. In the middle distance was the metro bridge. In the foreground, a police launch churned about in the water. From another launch, a short way off, frogmen were going over the side.

These scant clues and images were all it took.

Richard ran from the hotel and out to Khreshchatyk and to the metro steps, with the aim of getting the first train to Dnipro Station.

Police, paparazzi and crime-scene ghouls crowded the waterfront. He couldn't get close. Emergency vehicles were parked diagonally everywhere, and officers were guiding people away.

Richard slunk back, wishing he hadn't seen what he'd seen — the dripping bundle in the twilight. Being winched out of the water by a boat-mounted derrick. A bundle that was bloated and discoloured. Hideous. Recognisably human, but only just. Quickly shrouded from the eyes of ghouls and voyeurs and to protect the fragile sensibilities of the general public.

But Richard was already doubling over, vomiting.

***

It's not her. Not her.

Such was his mantra in the coming days as the *Kyiv Post*, and the rest of the media, stated that the recovered body was a woman of about thirty. She'd had her throat slashed and was likely the fourth victim of the serial killer. It was not known who she was, when she'd been killed or how long she'd been in the river.

For long nights, Richard hardly slept. On Thursday morning, he bought a carton of peach juice from an early-bird kiosk and sat drinking it in the Maidan.

Except for the city cleaners in their sleeveless orange jackets, it was almost deserted. Though many people would be on their way to work, the Maidan and Khreshchatyk were always quiet at this time of day due to the high volume of commuters using public transport, primarily the metro.

At ten, his dazed wandering delivered him to Café Oasis, and it took him a moment to understand what he was seeing.

Parked by the footway was a silver BMW.

Richard's heart beat faster as he saw — among some paperwork on the rear passenger seat — a letterhead bearing the KSE logo.

At the sound of voices from the yard below, he backed off and squashed himself into a shallow doorway.

Seconds later, Pavlo and Alexei appeared at the top of the steps. They stood by Alexei's car, speaking in low tones. Then they shook hands. Pavlo went back into the café and Alexei got in his car and did a three-point turn.

The wildest conjectures flew through Richard's head.

While the BMW was still manoeuvring, he ran into the road and rapped on the passenger window. Looking startled, Alexei brought the car to a halt. Richard wrenched open the door and jumped in.

"What a surprise ..." said Alexei. "Can I offer you a lift somewhere?"

"*A lift?*" said Richard, breathing heavily. "What the fuck's going on? What are you doing here? How do you know Pavlo?"

"Please do not speak to me in this manner."

"Just answer the questions."

A truck rumbled up behind, horn blaring. The BMW was blocking the road. Alexei pulled over to the kerb calmly and switched off the engine.

"Now, Richard. I'll gladly answer your questions if you can stop behaving as if I've done something suspicious."

"I'm waiting."

Alexei pursed his lips.

"I'll explain," he said. "Afterwards, I would like you to get out of my car. Nothing has been *going on*. I have never met Pavlo until today. As for why I am here: I had a change of heart. I came to ask about Nadya for you."

"What about her? What did he say?"

"Only what you already know. That she left and there is no information on her. She was employed casually. Paid in cash. No questions asked."

"He's lying. And you ... *We* were supposed to come here together. Why did you come by yourself?"

"I thought it would go better if I was alone," he said, looking down the hill and tapping his fingers on the steering wheel. "You are right about Pavlo not liking you. Even the mention of your name and he was agitated. If you'd been there, it would have gone badly."

"But you haven't found anything out. It *did* go badly. Pavlo's lying. I thought you would have —"

"I understand that you are feeling upset," said Alexei. "Despite my misgivings, I try to help you. Instead of gratitude, you show nothing but suspicion and contempt. And you look terrible. Perhaps you should see a doctor?"

Richard opened the passenger door.

"I suppose I've blown the job?" he said.

"You have blown something," said Alexei. "Maybe a gasket in your brain?"

Richard got out, slammed the door and began walking down the hill.

A moment later, the BMW cruised past.

twenty-five

The whole of Friday saw him travelling the length and breadth of the metro system. Getting off at random stops to look around. A day in the ancient carriages. Clunking on and on. And — adorning the walls of some of the oldest stations on the Red Line — glimpsed art relics of socialist realism.

Media reports hinted that the body from the Dnipro was so badly decomposed that identification was going to be challenging.

It's not her. It can't be her.

In the evening, he combed through restaurants and bars close to the centre. Street by street. Nadya was a survivor. She'd have another job by now.

He knew it was an imperfect method, ducking into places to look the staff over. She could easily be in the back, or on a different shift. But until he came up with a better plan, he had to keep searching.

She hadn't called or left a message with Daz and Preeti. Nor with the KSE. Fortunately, incoming calls at the KSE now went through a receptionist, so he was able to keep checking there without the need to go through Oleg or Alexei. And according to Omaha, the new tutor staying in the Dniprovskyi apartment, Nadya hadn't been looking for Richard there either.

Like a worm, Oleg's spiteful comment about seeing her in a "men's club" bored into his thoughts, but he kept pushing it aside.

Bar Zavtra was busy. It was Friday night, after all. The terrace tables and the tables in the main room were full, but he found an empty stool up at the bar. Food sizzled on hotplates in the open-plan kitchen. He ordered and ate a tasty goulash dish and washed it down with cloudy wheat-beer.

In a corner by the main door, a mixing desk was hooked up to a battered old computer. Nobody attended the equipment. He supposed that the trippy, ambient music bouncing around the place was being downloaded and the mixing desk was on an auto setting.

From the next bar-stool, a man with a scar under his eye offered cigarettes and tried to make conversation. Richard wasn't in the mood to be social. His gaze swung to the door every time somebody entered.

Each track of the hypnotic music ran on and on through various mixes, then blended seamlessly into the next track.

At midnight, the man beside him said, "*Boovay*" — an informal *goodbye* — and left.

The stool was quickly taken by somebody else, a man who Richard noticed from the periphery of his vision was a good head shorter than the average adult.

"Fuck your Statue of Liberty," said the new arrival. "and fuck your apple pie."

Richard nearly choked on his beer.

Even before he looked, he knew who it was from the mocking, croaky voice.

On the neighbouring stool sat Nikolai Gaidak. The former suspect who'd been questioned and released without charge. The man who — around the time of the first murder — had kissed Richard's hand and spat in his face on a metro platform.

"Fuck the European Union," he said. "Fuck the West."

Richard ignored him and had a leisurely swallow of beer. Gaidak's drink arrived. A brandy by the smell of it. A double. Gaidak thanked the girl behind the bar and took a delicate sip. Richard finished his beer and looked towards the exit. The bar girl lifted his empty glass and jiggled it about in the air. He gave her a nod.

"Fuck NATO," said Gaidak.

A moment later, he slipped down from the bar stool and started taking off his overcoat. Richard risked a glance. Gaidak stood no more than four foot ten. Richard began to relax as he considered that he could probably knock the man flying with one good slap.

Wait, though ... What was the game now?

Between exaggerated grunts and groans, Gaidak was speaking to the customers at the nearest table. He appeared to be struggling with his coat. *Appeared* was the right word, because Richard thought that any idiot could see that it was faked.

But two people got up.

Richard watched in disbelief as a swankily-dressed couple helped Gaidak. And beneath the overcoat he wore, not the hotel doorman's purple livery of the last encounter, but a plaid shirt and jeans.

Gaidak gave the couple a theatrical bow, folded his coat neatly into a cushion and set it on his bar stool. When he'd climbed back up — sitting a few inches higher — he chuckled to himself, then drank his brandy.

Richard's beer arrived. He thanked the girl and had a long drink with affected indifference in case Gaidak was watching him.

"Fuck the Orange Revolution," said Gaidak.

Richard remembered he was wearing the orange scarf Alexei had given him in the Maidan. He glanced at Gaidak. The man's eyes were shining with amusement. His thin lips were curled in a sneer over rotten teeth.

The music from the download-and-mixing-desk set-up had segued into something frenziedly hypnotic, with clashing cymbals and strangled sax.

"Fuck your mother," said Gaidak.

Richard's heart jumped against his ribcage.

With the force of his gaze alone, he dared Gaidak to repeat what he'd said. Just when he thought Gaidak was going to back down, his lips parted in a horrible smile.

"I said ... Fuck. Your. Mother."

Richard threw a punch at Gaidak's face.

Gaidak was lightning fast and surprisingly strong.

He stopped the blow inches from its target, his little hand whipping out and encircling Richard's wrist like a manacle.

There was a scrape of stool legs.

In the next instant, Richard was unseated with no understanding of how that had happened either. He had to spread his footing to regain balance.

Gaidak moved in. Close quarters. All but hugging Richard. A knee was driven into Richard's groin. He folded over. At the same moment, Gaidak retreated to the open floor and threw up his arms.

"No, please!" he yelled in his croaky voice. "Please, sir, don't hurt me!"

The couple who'd helped Gaidak with his coat stood up. The woman said, "No making trouble in Bar Zavtra."

A man came out from behind the bar.

"You go home now," he said.

Clenching his teeth with the pain, Richard leaned against the counter. He met the hostile glares and raised a calming hand. He did up his coat.

Gaidak was back on his stool.

"I mind *my own* business," he said to the onlookers.

They nodded. He reached a theatrically trembling jazz-hand towards his empty brandy glass. In a moment, the bar girl had set down another.

On the house, probably, thought Richard.

"*My own* business," said Gaidak.

As Richard shambled away, Gaidak winked at him.

***

The pedestrian underpasses beneath Independence Square were in near darkness. The air was dank and stale. Smoke drifted from a little wood-fire a group of figures huddled around.

Richard strode along, Gaidak's face and the electronic rhythms of the bar music filling his head.

He shook himself. He was confused and a bit drunk. Couldn't even find any steps to the outside world now.

One weary-looking man, squatting by the underpass wall, was still hoping to sell toy robots. Five or six were beeping and trundling about the concrete on their caterpillar tracks. Cuboid heads swivelled. Red eyes flashed. And Richard ... intrusive dark thoughts ... pictured himself kicking the robots across the ground.

A brief sob in his throat. He stopped and thrust a hundred-*hryvnia* note at the man and told him to go home for the night, assuming he had a home.

Back on surface level, he got into the first taxi he saw. He didn't know why. It was only a two-minute walk to the New Bratislava. When he was slow to speak, the driver made suggestions.

"Hotel? Nightclub? Dancing? Casino? Girls?"

"Yes," said Richard, thinking of Oleg's taunts again.

"Girls?"

"Yes."

The taxi swung out along Khreshchatyk.

After a minute, the driver turned into a network of alleys, then stopped at an entrance guarded by a mountainous doorman. On the wall, a vertical pink neon sign said in English: Extreme Pink.

Richard paid the driver.

He was waved into the club by the doorman. After paying at the window of a booth, he climbed narrow, creaking stairs. At the top, a padded door opened onto a pink-floodlit environment of glass columns and studded white leather. The bar was a blinding sparkle of mirrors, bottles, glasses, and spirit optics.

Topless girls in pink thongs swanned about with drinks on trays. The music was high-octane jazz that put him in mind of Courtney Pine.

Elsewhere, men sat watching the floorshow — a dirty-eyed girl in a silver outfit contorting herself on a heart-shaped stage.

Richard had just reached the bar when a blonde approached him. She wore tiny shorts and a sparkly top.

"You want buy me drink?" she said.

"Okay. What — ?"

"Double vodka," came the reply.

Richard ordered the same for himself. When the drinks arrived, the girl led him to a private room.

There was a single bed, a wooden chair, a dressing-table. The jazz music played low through an unseen speaker. Beneath a whiff of *pot pourri* were trace smells of cigarette smoke, sweat and lubricant.

"Okay," said the girl, a hard look entering her eyes. "Hand job, one hundred fifty. Blow job, two fifty. Fuck, four hundred."

Swaying her hips to the music, she eased her shorts down a little. Then she whipped her top off and her large pneumatic breasts bounced free.

"I want to fuck you," said Richard, and handed over the money.

She checked the notes, posted them through a slot in a metal box that was fixed to the wall, then produced a packet of condoms.

"Wait ..." said Richard. "Has a girl called Nadya ever worked here?"

"Maybe," she said. "Is a common name. So ... *I* can be Nadya for you."

Richard shook his head.

"I've ... changed my mind," he said. He glanced at the metal box on the wall. "I suppose a refund's out of the question?"

That weekend, he continued the search. By day, he rode the metro, getting off at random stops and checking bars, cafés, restaurants. By night, he visited as many clubs as he could, looking for and asking about Nadya.

Kept at it until tiredness took its toll. Until the boundaries between the search and simple voyeurism became blurred. Until he felt guilty that he'd listened to Oleg's taunts and that he'd doubted his instincts about Nadya. Until, at five o'clock on Monday morning, he threw himself onto the hotel-room bed.

It was gone midday when he woke. He had a headache and the sensation that the backs of his eyes had been packed with sand.

He found the remote and switched on the TV.

A grave-faced man with white hair spoke to-camera from the steps of a building. He had medals on his uniform. Then the screen cut to images of the murdered girls. A recap.

There must have been a development ...

The roll-call of names ... and ... *her* name.

A meat cleaver in the back of his head.

His heart-rate doubled in a instant.

His vision went dark around the edges.

Cleared. Went dark.

Clear, dark. Clear, dark.

Pulsating.

A cut to the officer on the steps again.

The name Richard had heard? It could have been a mistake. Could just as easily have been Natalya. Or Danya. Could have been almost anything.

Couldn't it?

But his skin grew prickly and hot. He felt nauseous. A sound like escaping gas filled his ears. He tried to focus on the Ukrainian words from the TV. Tried to listen out for any names.

His head felt like a bag of blood that beat and beat, close to bursting. The darkness at the periphery of his vision increased with each pulse. Until he had the impression of looking down a cone, a funnel.

Then ... a voice from far away.

twenty-six

He nearly lost consciousness, but not quite.

The process reversed itself. His vision cleared.

But he was struggling to remember who he was and where he was. He recognised that he was sitting on an unmade bed. What bed? Whose bed? The tangled sheets were a shade of green he'd expect to find in an operating theatre ... Had he been in an accident?

The voice repeated something again, and again.

He looked up and saw that the door was partly open.

"Excuse, sir," said the woman. "Room cleaning."

The New Bratislava Hotel ... Kyiv ...

He gave her a nod and she brought her equipment in. He knew he was expected to leave the room. A news programme was finishing on the TV and he was holding a remote control. *Yes ... The news ...*

"Excuse, sir."

"Yes, I'm sorry," said Richard.

He grabbed his jacket and flew from the room. In his hurry, he collided with the cleaning trolley and got the wet end of a mop in his face.

In the corridor were another room-cleaner, another equipment trolley, and a trolley piled with more of the operating-theatre-green sheets and towels.

He hurried on.

The lift.

The hotel reception foyer.

Revolving doors.

Khreshchatyk. Sunshine.

A nearby kiosk.

News-stands. Cyrillic headlines and columns of text. A four-paned window picture of the murdered women —

the fourth, a greyed-out silhouette with a question mark in the middle.

Alexei strode to the table in his suit and tie, bringing with him a waft of spicy cologne.

Richard had been wearing the same clothes for two days and hadn't shaved or showered.

A little too eager to shake hands, he knocked his glass over. The tabletop swam with vodka. As a waiter swooped to clean up, Alexei pulled out a chair and sat down. He didn't shunt the chair back to the table though, just stayed where he was, briefcase on his knees.

After the waiter had gone, Alexei kept looking around at other customers, or out of the window. *Probably wishing he could be far away*, thought Richard, *among the sane and the rational.*

"So," said Alexei. "We agreed on ten minutes."

Richard filled two shot glasses and slid one across the table. Alexei set his briefcase beside his chair, rapped his glass on the table and knocked back the vodka. Richard did the same.

"I'm sorry again about the —"

"You apologised during your phone call," said Alexei. "Now you are in Passazh. A few doors from the KSE. No doubt uncertain about where you and I stand in any kind of friendship we may have had."

"Yes."

"I am also uncertain about this. But I sense that there is something else?"

Richard unfolded a newspaper on the table.

"Ah ..." said Alexei. "*Vedomosti*. I see that you are still learning the Russian language?"

"No. I usually buy the English-language paper, the *Kyiv Post*. But that's only a weekly publication. For now, I just grabbed any one of the dailies. Is the *Vedomosti* a rubbish paper?"

Alexei smiled enigmatically.

"I read it myself on occasion. In fact, it carried a good article a while back by Yulia Tymoshenko. She wrote that Russia has not lost anything with the Orange Revolution because we are still strategic partners. That the only losers were a handful of 'political technologists' — and of course the oligarchs who would have preferred their Yanukovych as president, in the hope of continuing the criminal privatisation of Ukraine's wealth."

Richard nodded, paused politely, then said, "Has something happened in the murder investigation? Some development?"

Alexei scanned the front page of *Vedomosti*.

"There has been anger at the police for not cracking the case. Continued difficulty with the identity of the new body. And difficulty determining when the woman was killed ... length of time in the water, you see. But the current media attention is summing up what we already know. Maryna Petrenko, killed on the 28th of November, the night of your arrival. Bella Savchuk, killed on the 16th of December. Polina Boyko, with the Tymoshenko-style hair, killed on the 23rd of January, the day of President Viktor Yushchenko's inauguration. Then the unidentified woman — killed we don't yet know when — recovered from the Dnipro River on the 14th of March."

"That's it?" said Richard.

"I think the new focus is because the media have settled on a name now. It *was* simply the Dniprovskyi Killer. But following the third murder, and in the time of your absence, the killer has become known as the Chort."

"Chort?"

"Slavic mythology. A *chort* is a demon. The media needs labels for society's monsters. Like your Black Panther. Or the Yorkshire Ripper."

"Anything else? What do your contacts say?"

Alexei laughed.

"Contacts?" he said.

"In the police and in the courts."

Alexei laughed again, then looked serious. He glanced around the busy, noisy café, and leaned across the table.

"I will be in big trouble if you repeat this, Richard. You understand?"

"Yes."

"Very well. *In the strictest confidence* ... identification is a challenge. Dental records have turned up nothing. Either the woman never had dental work done, never visited a dentist in Ukraine, and/or she lived off-grid."

Richard frowned.

"A name was mentioned on a TV new programme. It sounded like Nadya."

Alexei shook his head.

"There's a new investigating officer on the case: Danya Valentyn. Danya. I think you misheard. But you are worried that the victim might be Nadya? Why?"

"She's missing."

"She left her job. She does not contact you. You cannot contact her. That does not make her a missing person. You have to stop all of this, Richard. Can you not see? It will take you in one direction only."

Alexei pointed at the floor and made a downward spiralling motion with his index finger.

The moment Annushka pulled up outside Café Oasis — in her spanking white Porsche — Richard emerged from his doorway.

"Richard!" she gushed. "I am happy that you called me. I don't mind helping."

She offered her cheek and he gave it a peck.

"I can tell you, however," she said, "that I now have a boyfriend."

"Congratulations," he said. "This wasn't meant as a date anyway."

"No, no. Of course. My boyfriend is Omaha! The new English teacher. He is a very handsome and charming man from Washington, USA."

"Right," said Richard. "Great. Omaha. I met him. He seems like a great guy."

Annushka peered at the little café in its sunken yard, grimacing as she took in its time-worn features and obscurity.

"I ... want to help you," she said with a brilliant smile.

"Shall we then?" he said, moving to the steps.

He hadn't explained why she was here other than to translate and to clear up a "small misunderstanding".

A middle-aged couple shared a carafe of wine at one table; two old men coughed over beers and a dice game in the corner. The place fell silent when the new arrivals entered. Richard sensed Annushka's discomfort at being here, even though *he* was more the alien than her.

Olga was at the counter.

Richard approached her and she smiled a welcome. Following intros and pleasantries, he said, "Ask her if she's heard from Nadya."

Annushka spoke with Olga then relayed to Richard.

"No," she told him. "Nadya has not been here. And the new girl, Tamara, she has not seen her either. Nothing."

Richard unfolded the *Vedomosti* on the counter, showing Olga the four-paned window picture of the murdered girls. He pointed at the fourth pane, the head-and-shoulders silhouette with the question mark.

"Ask her if she thinks it could be Nadya," he said.

Annushka's mouth fell open and her green eyes went into dilation.

"Oh ... Richard," she said, her bottom lip wobbling. "I ... You think ... Oh dear."

"Just ask her. Please."

She turned to the old woman and tried to speak, but all that came out was a quavering little cry.

Richard stabbed at the newspaper with his finger.

"*Nadya*, Olga? Is it Nadya?"

Olga drew in a breath. Her hands flew to her mouth.

"I'm *not* saying it *is* Nadya," said Richard. "I'm asking you if ..."

There were rapid footfalls on the stairs.

The stairs door burst open and Pavlo came along behind the counter. He assessed the gathering. He quizzed Olga, but Olga was too upset to answer.

"Annushka," said Richard, "ask Pavlo if ..."

Pavlo's gaze was dull and languid. His lips were stretched back over his teeth. It was impossible to say whether he was smiling or scowling.

The shit-eating grin.

"You go out of here," he said.

When Richard didn't move, Pavlo lifted the counter flap. Olga wailed something at him. He hesitated, then grumbled a few words, nodded and went to the front door and held it open.

"You go now," he said.

"Yes, go now," said Olga.

Annushka touched Richard's arm.

She looked terrified.

He took her by the hand and led her out.

Pavlo shut the door behind them.

Annushka mounted the steps like a gazelle. Richard joined her beside her Porsche. She looked pale and the make-up on her left eye had run.

"I'm sorry about that," he said. "But thank you for trying to help."

Annushka was already starting the engine.

"I will see you, Richard. I'm sorry as well."

The new man sat for a minute, scanning hand-written notes and smiling through the pungent smoke of a long, thin, liquorice-paper cigarette. Outside the glass door, a uniform had been posted.

"You come one hour before?" said the new man. "You speak with the front desk and say you have urgent questions? You speak with my colleague. He makes this notes but he is not understand so well?"

"That's right," said Richard.

"Okay, Mr Farr. I am senior detective. Maksym Olearchyk. My English is not either very good, but is half okay, I think."

"Your English is fine."

It was the day after the episode with Annushka.

Richard had showered, shaved, put on a clean white shirt and his midnight-blue Paul Smith suit. He'd polished his shoes, scrubbed his fingernails and had his hair trimmed.

They were in a side room with two desks and an ancient-looking computer. Dusty files were stacked all over the floor. Through the glass door and the open slats of the partition windows, he saw personnel walking about or speaking on phones.

Maksym Olearchyk set down his notes.

"You give to my colleague a name and address of a café, a bar. We have now been phoning the bar and speaking with the manager, Pavlo. We are satisfied. We do not see that we can do more. We speak with the *babushka* of Pavlo as well. Olga. She is not knowing any girl name Nadya. A girl name Tamara is work there. Before Tamara, only Pavlo and Olga."

"*What?*" said Richard. "Olga said that? *No.* Olga ... ? *I was talking about Nadya with Olga yesterday.* Now she ... ? She's lying. They're both lying! Pavlo's telling her what to say. You have to investigate."

Maksym looked disappointed.

"This girl you talk of ... Nadya. She is ... was your *divchyna*? Your girlfriend?"

"Yes."

"Maybe you are confused? Maybe it was a different bar she works at?"

"No."

Maksym lit another of his liquorice-paper cigarettes.

"You as well are asking to my colleague about the Chort, the killer? What is your interest in this case?"

Richard sighed.

"I wondered ..." he said. "I've been worrying about the latest victim. The body from the river. Nadya didn't tell me much about herself. I don't know her family name. Where she lives. Email. Phone. Nothing."

"Yes. I understand. And so you cannot really know that she is missing, as you tell to my colleague? Unless, of course, you *do* know that she is missing because you are ... um, responsible?"

"What?" said Richard. "No. No no no no."

He got to his feet. Maksym watched him with interest, but made no move to stand up himself. Without looking behind, he raised a signalling hand. A second later, the uniform outside the door came in, closed the door, then leaned back against it and folded his arms.

"Mr Farr," said Maksym. "I have more questions."

twenty-seven

"You stay now in New Bratislava Hotel?" said Maksym, referring to his notes. "Before, you stay in the apartment in Dniprovskyi, near Darnitsya Metro Station? How long time you are in Kyiv?"

"Since the end of November last year," said Richard. "I've been teaching English at the Kyiv School of English, on Passazh."

"Okay. You have your passport, please?"

Richard took his passport from his inside pocket.

"I'm legal," he said. "Multiple-entry work visa."

"Your Borispol Airport stamp shows that you arrive on the 28th of November," said Maksym. "The same night Maryna Petrenko was murdered?"

"Yes. It was all over the news the next day ... "

The first night ... the night he met Nadya ...

How she was sent out into the snow. How, when she returned, he stood before her and prised her hand from her coat pocket. Found an aubergine. He remembered her docile reaction, her vulnerability. How she'd gazed at him with her beautiful dark eyes ...

"Mr Farr?"

"Sorry?"

"I am asking what you do that night?" said Maksym. "Late at night in Dniprovskyi, what do you do?"

Lost in the snow. Teeth chattering. The bulldozer man. A girl with red hair in a fur coat, pirouetting. The old-guard snow clearer.

Then, standing at the apartment window — feeling a hundred floors up instead of ten.

"The hours between midnight until two o'clock," said Maksym. "What did you do?"

"I was in bed asleep," said Richard.
"You are sure? And you were alone?"
"Yes."
Sweat erupted on Richard's forehead.
He felt shaky, panicky.
"You are sick?" asked Maksym.
Richard shook his head and shrugged his jacket off.
"Too warm."
"Okay," said Maksym. "And the night of December the 16th. What do you do then?"
"I ... don't remember."
"It was a Thursday. The night when Bella Savchuk was killed. The girl from the grocery shop ... Near your old apartment."
"Bella ... Yes, I saw her in the shop that evening."
"Tell me all about that night, Mr Farr."

An hour later, Maksym was concluding a recap of Richard's responses: "And on the 23rd of January, the day of President Yushchenko's inauguration, you tell to me you are at his speech in the Maidan. With colleagues and friends from the Kyiv School of English, and with your girlfriend. Then you are at the apartment from evening until morning. Alone."
"Yes. No. By then, Nadya was staying at the apartment sometimes. I think she stayed that night."
"You think? Or you know?"
Richard fought back a creeping sense of vertigo.
"I know," he said.
"You stay in Kyiv until the 16th of February," said Maksym, consulting Richard's passport again. "You go back to London but return in Kyiv again on the 9th of March. It is now near to ending of March. Springtime. How longer will you stay this time?"
"As long as it takes to find Nadya. Or find out what happened to her."

A woman in plain clothes brought in a sheaf of paperwork that looked like fresh print-outs. She left again without a word. Maksym read through the papers in his own good time.

"Okay, Mr Farr. You have a Russian grandfather."

Richard laughed.

"Yes," he said. "He died in the 1980s. And ... so what?"

"You were here during our recent Orange Revolution. You are a supporter? Or not?"

"What? Yes. A supporter. What are you —"

"Oleg Skarshevsy, the administrator at the school you work, he tells to us that you do not work there, not any more. That you are ... not reliable."

"Oleg? But he doesn't like me ... You should speak to Alexei Koval."

"At university in London, your master degree you make a thesis on Russian literature, and you —"

"*What is this?* Did you find that on the Internet?"

"Mr Farr, my colleague searches much information about you in the past hour. Tell me, have you read Dostoyevsky's *Crime and Punishment*?"

"Yes. *What —?*"

"It is a clever story of the criminal mind. It tells of how Raskolnikov ... how, he, after his murders at his lodgings ... he talks to the police, tries to help them with the case. Why would he go near the police when he is guilty? But Dostoyevsky has understood a criminal mind. Raskolnikov is ..."

Richard laughed.

Maksym tossed the pages aside, sat back in his chair and smiled.

"You should not leave Kyiv, Mr Farr. We may have more questions."

"Fine. I have nothing to hide."

"Okay. Is there anything another we can help you?"

Richard thought about the scene by the river ten days or so ago. Thought about the frogmen, the police launch, the bloated and waterlogged body dangling from the winch. Barely recognisable as human ...

But ... would I know? he thought. *Would I see or sense something?*

"The other reason I came here ..." he said.

"Yes?"

"Can it be arranged for me to see the body of the Chort's latest victim?"

April 2005. Kyiv

Khreshchatyk looked different. It was the chestnut trees. Bare only last week, they were now in young leaf. The air smelled cleaner, fresher, and people looked different too. Gone were the overcoats and swaddling furs. Hats were fewer. Hemlines had risen.

The latest copy of the *Kyiv Post* offered no updates, only that police feared the identity of the woman from the river may never be established, and that they still couldn't say when she'd been killed.

Richard's request to the police a few days earlier — to see the body — had been denied.

A lot of leopard print and zebra print was being worn, and leather of all colours, though white, red, pink, and lime-green were popular. Designer sunglasses, handbags and mobile phones were indispensable. Some women looked as if they'd stepped off the pages of Vogue.

He knew from the KSE receptionist that Nadya hadn't phoned or visited. He knew that she hadn't called Daz and Preeti in London either. And that there'd been no messages or attempts to call his mobile.

The Kyiv chic liked their skirts short and their boots high. Western European stereotypes rarely applied. Pick any of these women at random and the chances were that she'd be elegant and sophisticated, probably have a business degree and play classical piano.

What if it was Nadya they'd pulled out of the Dnipro? What if it really was her?

The one call she made to London may have been her last ... She could have been sensing danger. Been afraid. The Chort may already have been stalking her. Grooming her. Studying her routines and waiting for his moment.

The *nouveau riche* men favoured darker colours. Wore suits. Or fitted leather jackets and open-necked shirts. Expensive watches and sunglasses. Some had gelled hair and aspired towards a Latino style. Others wore *iffy*, pastel-shaded jumpers with V-necks and zigzag or diamond patterns. Judging by shop-window displays, such jumpers were the height of fashion.

Richard cringed, but wondered if Nadya would like to see him in one.

During another whistle-stop tour of the central cafés and bars, the sight of candles jogged a memory.

St Volodymyr's Cathedral.

He quickened his pace along Khreshchatyk.

In minutes, he was at the Shevchenko junction, where one of Kyiv's last remaining statues of Lenin stood.

Behind Lenin, a wide central reservation with a footpath and an avenue of trees led uphill.

Either side of the avenue, Shevchenko was busy with cars, taxis and trolley buses.

St Volodymyr's was another ten minutes by foot.

It was a bright yellow building set in plain grounds. Its windows were tall and arched. There were gold crosses atop domes that were blue with gold stars.

He remembered a day, back in January, when Nadya had brought him here ...

January, 2005

"It looks familiar," he said.

"Yes," she said. "You may have seen it in books or on post cards. Or, it is also on our one-*hryvnia* note."

She slipped a note from her purse and pointed out the picture. Then she smiled, put her hand in his and led the way to the entrance, stopping to cover her hair with a headscarf.

Inside, a stall was selling icons and other devotional trinkets. He waited while she bought something.

The place was all browns, golds, high-domed ceilings and huge paintings depicting the spiritual history. Dull-gold chandeliers bristled with electric candles. Real candles burned everywhere on plinths, and the air was slightly acrid.

Nadya led the way to an image of Jesus.

Richard stood by as she crossed herself and spent a moment in silence with her eyes closed.

"Do you still believe?" he said.

"No, I don't think so," she said. "Not since the two months in Vernon's basement in London. It is not often I come here now. I hope for an answer, I suppose, but maybe the world is simply too fucked up and nobody is going to save us. Ever. I thought to show you this place one time. That is all."

He was slightly shocked to hear her swear and speak that way in the cathedral, but — after what had happened to her — if *she* didn't have the right, who did?

"I think death is the end," he said. "I've never been religious. I've gone to funerals and weddings at churches, but I don't sing the hymns or make false gestures. It would be hypocritical."

Moments later, he learned that — for Nadya — apparently he was prepared to go against his own code.

She'd bought two "birthday cake" candles at the stall. Now she lit one using a book of matches. She set her candle on the devotional plinth where dozens of others burned. Then she looked into Richard's face uncertainly as she offered him the second candle.

He took it, lit it, and set it next to hers.

The two flames burned steadily, side by side, then flickered in a draft.

One went out. Hers, not his.

She laughed and relit the candle.

They moved on. He saw people snapping away with cameras, and several mobile phones had gone off. Nadya didn't seem to notice this, but Richard — even with his non-religious feelings — thought it was bit disrespectful. So he was doubly surprised when a black-robed priest confronted him. He couldn't understand the angrily whispered words. Nadya took a step away, her hands over her mouth as if to smother laughter.

The priest went to slap Richard's face.

He dodged away. *What the ... ?*

Still raving in subdued tones, the priest clutched Richard's wrists and began tugging. And only then did he realise that the objection must be over having his hands in his pockets. He took them out, and the priest strode off with a conciliatory grumble.

Nadya was waving from the doorway.

He followed her outside and she broke into laughter. He'd never seen her so spontaneous, her emotions so unguarded.

"Richard, that was so very funny!" she said, pulling herself close to him.

He laughed along with her, held her tight, and pressed his face into her hair that smelled faintly of apples.

twenty-eight

April, 2005

He understood — as he traipsed back down the hill, past the statue of Lenin, back onto Khreshchatyk to join the promenading peacocks and peahens with their newly *bourgeois* lives, and the long-suffering majority who had nothing — he understood that the reason he kept searching and believing was because he knew he wouldn't be able to take it if she were dead.

What would be left? Revenge? The impossibly slim hope of finding the Chort before the police did?

He thought about Trixie then.

There was something heavy she'd said once, years ago, something that had made the skin on the back of his neck prickle ...

November, 1999. London

"There's nothing," said Trixie, "nothing we can imagine or dream or make up, nothing too terrible or sick or evil that hasn't happened at some time, or that won't happen one day. Done to humans, by humans."

"Yeah," said Richard. "That's ... Look ... we're really stoned. I don't — "

"If we suddenly had, I don't know, psychic access to every bad thing happening around the planet at this moment ... If we saw it all now, our minds wouldn't be able to cope. We'd go insane in, like, three seconds."

April, 2005. Kyiv

Even as he reached the Maidan again, his mind was conjuring up horrors — real or imagined or remembered from movies or news footage, he couldn't tell.

Trixie. A bog-standard accidental drowning.

No lacerations, bruising or signs of struggle. No evidence of foul play. Not broken and twisted as he sometimes saw her in nightmares. But it didn't make sense that she'd slipped in and drowned. Her life snuffed out in such a meaningless, empty way.

And to consider suicide meant having to consider that his own behaviour — his jealousy and anger of the final weeks — was contributory.

He went to Bar Zavtra and chatted with an English-speaking waitress, Ruslana. Once again, he asked about and described Nadya. Nobody remembered her. Nobody knew anything. He bought a beer and sat on the terrace overlooking the underground shopping centre.

And he continued sitting there long after his glass was empty. He felt that his limbs had turned to concrete. Felt immobilised by a woolly kind of rage and grief.

His life had been simpler at one time.

Or had it?

Tutoring his undergrads in Beckett, Joyce, Austen, Brontë, Allende. Shakespeare's tragedies.

The star-crossed lovers ...

"Never was a story of more woe ..."

Richard's morbid fascination, in fiction, with doomed love. Trixie with her Nick Cave songs – his passion, his imagery, his tortured characters.

But with Nadya, it was Emily Dickinson. New hope ...

"Out with lanterns ..."

Because she couldn't be dead. The tragedy of Trixie, and then Nadya five years later? Nobody could be that unlucky. Could they? Not that he believed in any such thing as luck. But ... but ...

Maksym Olearchyk had asked how much longer he'd be in Kyiv, and Richard had said as long as it took to find Nadya. No ... He could do better than that. Could give her all the time she needed.

He'd live here for her. He'd live here.

If he got the chance now, that's what he'd tell her.

If time could be turned back, he would have skipped going to Helen's funeral.

Would have. If.

At night's end, he was in a bar several kilometres from the centre. The metro had stopped running and he couldn't find a taxi. He began flagging down cars. Any cars. It was accepted behaviour if you needed a ride. Another black-market supplement for those on low incomes. Ordinary people shifting shape to become impromptu taxi-drivers.

The one who pulled over seemed as drunk as Richard, but got him safely back to the hotel for fifty *hryvnia*.

He threw himself on the bed fully clothed.

Trixie was right. You'd go mad thinking about the horrors of the world too much. Somewhere, in any city, or in many cities, a killer would always be doing his thing. Would — an hour or a minute from now — attack some young innocent in a darkened alley stinking of piss. Bundle her violated body into the back of a beat-up old van. Drive out to the woods. Bury her in a shallow grave. Then skulk back to what ever depraved hovel he called home. Or maybe he was an upstanding citizen. A doctor. A teacher. A successful businessman. Like Alexei or Oleg. Clever and wily enough to leave no traces.

Dumping the stolen van and picking up his own car from where he'd stashed it. Driving home to a beautiful wife and cute children. With a smile on his handsome face. Bearing flowers and treats. He wouldn't be caught this time or the next. Maybe never.

Alexei? What am I thinking?

The next night. Two in the morning.

Deathly silence and darkness.

Not a drop of alcohol had passed his lips that day. He needed his wits to be razor-sharp.

The scene was what he'd hoped for, but was unsettling in reality. The street was so quiet that his own careful movements and presence felt clumsy, loud, criminal. The only light came from a quarter moon and a swathe of stars. Every window in every building was in darkness.

In the sunken yard, it was even darker, even quieter.

He'd chosen the front entrance because he knew — from the time Pavlo had thrown him out the back of the kitchen — that the back door was solid and featureless, with its edges flush to the brickwork.

Back or front, the risks of getting caught were high. A neighbour might hear and call the police.

He took a breath and raised the crowbar in his gloved hands. It was easy to slot the flat end in a gap.

One thing he knew: from the moment he forced the door, he had to stick with the plan.

A pause, then he exerted his weight on the crowbar and there was a shriek of splintering wood in the dead street. The lock gave easily.

He pulled open the door, stepped into the blackness and moved forward with a hand outstretched. Winced as he jarred a table and its legs scraped the floor.

His eyes were adapting. Weak moonlight through the window helped to render the rough shapes of the interior. He pushed forward to the counter. Found the flap, lifted it and moved along behind. Went through the stairs door and crept up the stairs in the dark. Onto a landing where street windows let moonlight in.

Doors off the landing opened onto a bathroom and cluttered storerooms. The door at the end was locked. Pavlo's office. It had to be. Richard hefted the crowbar and the door sprang open.

It was pitch black inside and smelled of dust. He found a wall switch and flicked it on. Under the low-watt bulb, he saw that there were closed blinds at the window, a couple of swivel chairs, a small desk with an antiquated PC, an unlocked filing cabinet.

He turned the PC on, unshouldered his bag and rifled the filing cabinet. He piled the contents on the floor — lever-arch files and loose paperwork.

Every document was in Cyrillic. He considered his bag's capacity and the pile of documents and files. Too many to fit; too much to carry.

The PC's desktop screen had loaded and was showing a password box. Not that he'd understand the contents if he had access.

His choices were limited and shrinking.

He had to do something meaningful and do it fast.

No sirens yet. No noises from downstairs.

Going through the files, he tried to make sense of the way the information was formatted. Some pages were simple lists. Others contained figures and looked like accounts or invoices.

He took sections of paperwork from each file — some chosen because they had phone numbers, names and possibly addresses, some chosen at random. He knew what Nadya's name looked like in Cyrillic but couldn't see it anywhere. When he'd crammed the stuff into his bag, he turned the PC off, turned the light off and hurried downstairs.

Back through the café. Out to the yard.

Stillness. Silence. Starlight across the sky.

He climbed the steps and looked both ways. No lights in windows. Nobody about. Keeping to the shadows, he walked back to the hotel but didn't see a single person or a single moving vehicle.

The next morning, he rang Annushka as early as he dared and talked her into coming to the hotel room. She examined all the documents, laying each sheet aside and shaking her head. Finally, she confirmed that there was nothing about Nadya or any staff members.

Later that morning, at the post office, he bundled the documents into big envelopes and sent everything back to the café anonymously.

April, 2005. Kyiv

Richard was riding the improbably long escalators again. From deep down behind, he could still hear accordion music and the husky voice of the old busker in the strains of a Slavic folksong.

It wasn't necessary to understand Ukrainian to know that the song was about tragedy and loss.

He watched the descending commuters falling away to his left. A man with a forest of beard. A teenaged couple kissing, eyes closed. A statuesque woman with overdone make-up, smothered in mink, a Siamese cat placid in the crook of an arm and a lapdog nestled in the other. Two uniformed police officers, the ear-flaps of their hats in the fair-weather, *up* position, their gazes lingering on Richard a moment too long for comfort.

And suddenly there — *there.*

He recognised the set of her shoulders and her threadbare mackintosh the colour of mushrooms. Her dark bobbed hair and perfect face in profile. Her slender hand on the grab-rail.

For five seconds, he didn't move or breathe. Simply watched as she was carried further and further down, the dry ruminating groan of the escalators increasing her distance from him.

"Nadya!" he called. "Nadya!"

Some people looked back, but not her.

He began to clamber on the no-man's-land separating the escalators. It was a dangerous, crazy stunt, and he only abandoned it because he realised how close he was to the top. He pushed by the last few people and swung around and onto the downward escalator.

Nadya had joined the "fast lane". She was overtaking the stationery riders. Passing the police officers. Passing the woman in mink, who was so broad that Nadya had to twist sideways to squeeze through.

Richard's heart hammered. His breathing grew fast and sweat broke out on his forehead.

Where space allowed, he leaped two steps at a time. Where space did not allow, he barged and elbowed, ignoring the angry glares and remarks, the scandalised shriek from the woman in mink with her exotic pets.

What's with all the fur anyway?

Doesn't she know it's April?

Down, down, down.

Arsenalna.

Deepest underground station in the world.

Near the bottom, he glanced back at the sound of a fresh disturbance. The uniforms — forging their own aggressive way down.

He jumped the last three steps, stumbled and nearly fell as he hit solid, unmoving ground. He looked frantically about. Over the heads and hats. Between the packed bodies.

Where is she?

The old busker pumped his accordion and sang. Commuters streamed around Richard, all making for the arched entrances leading to the platforms.

Eastbound. Westbound.

A hand gripped his arm. Tightly. An unhappy face with compelling eyes loomed close. Cigarette breath and words Richard did not understand. It was the younger of the uniforms, ahead of his partner.

He pushed Richard against the wall.

From the westbound platform, Richard heard the familiar clatter and hum of an arriving metro train.

He tried to barge the officer aside. No good. He head-butted the officer. It was pure instinct. He had no idea he'd do such a thing until it was all over. The officer staggered away, blood slicking the lower half of his face.

There was a nearby shout. The partner.

Richard ran for the westbound archway, battling though the crowd. He burst onto the platform and glimpsed Nadya getting on the crammed train. There wasn't time to reach her carriage. The doors were closing and more passengers were trying to wedge themselves in. He fought his way to the nearest door. Got a firm grip on the rubber-trimmed edge and hauled himself aboard. The doors rattled and hissed and finally shut.

The train lurched into motion.

Among the dozens left behind on the platform, he saw the uniforms. The one he hadn't head-butted was speaking into a radio.

twenty-nine

He estimated that Nadya was three carriages forward. He had to reach her as quickly as possible. Before he lost her again. Before she got off. He squeezed his way along the crowded aisle as aggressively as he dared.

One carriage. Two. He pulled himself through the gangway connection into the third, and there she was, gripping one of the overhead straps.

Richard paused. The first doubts creeping in.

Something was not quite right.

"Nadya," he called, pressing closer.

She still didn't respond, though he was almost beside her. He reached out and touched her shoulder. Said her name again.

The woman turned and gazed into his face. Smiled querulously.

Not her ... Not her at all.

Where on the escalator she'd borne an uncanny resemblance in profile, now — except for the same height and build, the same dark bobbed hair and pale mackintosh — she was nothing like Nadya. Her eyes were different — smaller and lighter in colour, a cast in the left. Her nose was broader. Her lips thinner.

The woman smiled at Richard, pointed to her ear, then dashed off some sign language.

"Sorry," he muttered, backing away.

People were staring at him. No wonder. He'd pushed past them moments ago. Some talked in amused or curious tones. Others looked angry.

A shudder. Cold sweat. Nausea. Gut-churning nausea.

Sounds grew sharper. He had the sense of something vast and dark and hollow opening up inside him.

From near by, a big man in sports gear hissed at him. Richard shrank back along the carriage, avoiding the stares. He caught a whiff of perfume from one person, body odour from another, booze from another.

A young man deliberately barged him.

Richard kept moving.

Irrational thoughts whirled around his head.

He wondered if he was mistaken about the woman. *Maybe she is really Nadya? Wearing a mask and pretending to be deaf?*

An old man spoke to him authoritatively.

Richard continued retreating.

He'd drawn attention to himself by barging through the carriage. And some of these people may have witnessed the head-butting incident.

Before he passed into the adjoining carriage, he glanced back. Many gazes were still directed his way, including the mackintosh woman's.

No. Definitely not Nadya.

The train was slowing down.

Braking.

Trundling in to Khreshchatyk Station.

His sense of urgency heightened. He had to focus.

What to do? Stay on until the end of the line? Get off as soon as it stops?

Assaulting a police officer. How seriously would it be treated? The partner had been on a radio. An alert would have gone out. The longer he delayed getting off, the higher the chances of being caught? The police could be waiting on the platform at the next stop. Or the next. Or covering all exits of every station all the way down the line. He just didn't know.

Apprehend on sight — a tall, brown-haired, north-west-European man in a dark suit and white shirt.

The interior lamps dimmed then grew bright again. Tiled walls slid by outside. The train halted. The doors opened and passengers poured out. No waiting police. Not visibly anyway. Time to move.

All the way up to ground level, his heart fluttered and thrashed like a bird in its death-throes. He kept his head down. Stayed in the thick of the crowd. Was ready to run at any sign of extra security.

Once at the top of the escalators, he slowed his pace on the approach to the barriers. Commuters flowed around and ahead of him. He searched his pockets and brought out a handful of coins and two of the little blue plastic metro tokens. He felt vulnerable, exposed. But then saw his chance. A black beanie hat on the floor.

The mother with the buggy hadn't noticed. The child hung over the side, looking back, waving his arms.

Sorry, buddy. I need it more than you.

Richard stooped and picked it up. He waited as the woman and buggy were obscured from view by the continuing march of commuters.

The hat was too small, but he managed to stretch it right down over his ears and eyebrows. His head looked like a bowling ball.

He walked. Mingled. Queued. Fed a token into the slot and went through the barrier. Walked again. Normal pace. Eyes to the floor. Expecting a hand on his shoulder at any second. Not even glancing to where he knew the usual transport officials would be stationed.

Keep going. Keep going ...

Outside, in the bright daylight, he kept his face down. Kept among the crowds. Spotted the woman with the buggy up ahead and hurried alongside her. Told her the hat had been dropped and gave it back. Checked both ways at the New Bratislava, then went inside.

Perhaps only out of morbid habit, he made a pass by Café Oasis late that Saturday night. On his way up the hill, he saw Pavlo's friends getting into their black Land

Cruiser. It was the old guy with the grey pony-tail and his suave-looking minders. Richard waited for them to drive off before going closer.

Down through the lit window, he saw that the place was empty. Chairs were stacked on tables. If he squatted at the top of the steps, he could see the new girl, Tamara, behind the counter. Pressed up against her back, was Pavlo. Nuzzling her. It looked as if he were kissing her neck or whispering in her ear.

She kept turning her head aside, but he would only smile and nuzzle her again. Any smiles that flickered across *her* face were forced.

His big hands were clasping her upper arms, but he'd keep trying to transfer them to her breasts. Each time he did this, she'd struggle to free herself, but he was too strong. He laughed at her efforts.

Finally, he gave up. With a face like a slapped arse, he stumped off to the kitchen. Tamara straightened her clothes and carried on wiping the counter.

Richard's heart pounded as he remembered the assault he'd witnessed on Nadya in December. At a guess, Tamara was seventeen or eighteen. She'd only been at the café for a few weeks and already Pavlo ...

Pavlo.

As Richard started back down the hill, a strange feeling settled over him. A sense of dawning. He felt that pieces of information and ideas were shifting around in his head. Sliding into place with one another. Adding up to something both obvious and appalling.

His guts and throat went into sudden spasm. The violence of it caused his head to shoot forward, his body to fold at the waist. The only sounds in the empty street were his retching and the splatter of his vomit.

The giant advertising screen and the kiosks were eyes of light onto an almost empty square. A long-haired young man in a combat jacket covered with badges was ranting loudly and smashing beer bottles.

There were plenty of these left about. He'd pick each one up, trickle any dregs into his mouth, then with a grunt shatter them against the ground. At the end of another Khreshchatyk Saturday, other late stragglers and revellers gave the bottle-smasher a wide berth.

A rocket whooshed up into the night then exploded in a cluster of orange stars, and Richard wondered if it had any political significance.

Nadya had to be dead. He should never have left her and gone back to London. She was the body they'd recovered from the Dnipro. How could it be any other way?

He'd failed to read the signs.

In the time between Trixie's death and Richard's exit from the university, he'd begun working on an essay. Part of that essay came back to him now ...

If a person is vigilant and analytical enough, bad experiences and even some tragedies can be averted. Of course, many events are random and beyond control. But bring together two dysfunctional people and there is often a degree of collusion.

People say things like, "Why does this always happen to me?" But they stop short of deconstructing their own collusion in the chain of events.

There are patterns and cycles in life — and patterns and cycles will always repeat.

Good luck or bad luck, or fate, are all fantasies.

Watch your life unfold, year by year. Record the important events — especially the dynamics of relationships and the dynamics of their breakdown — and see if there is not a pattern.

What some view as unavoidable destiny, others understand as the trance-like journey along a well-worn path from love to loss.

We all have proclivities towards potential romantic partners. Some of us seek out bullies. Others seek out victims. Or neurotics, egomaniacs, freeloaders. We all say we want happy, healthy relationships. But such a thing is rare. What's more common, is to say we want happy and healthy, while at the same time being unaware of dark hidden mechanisms clunking away inside us, leading us towards something other.

What's stranger, and also common, is when we see the mechanism for what it is but still allow ourselves to be carried along by its power, in full knowledge (and maybe with a smile).

Dark paths are thrilling and seductive.

And as Richard stood at the window of his hotel room, he added new lines ...

My own proclivity is towards tragic women.

Tragic, beautiful women marked for death.

My psychological make-up will lead me to them. In turn, they'll be drawn to me as surely as one day they'll be drawn to their killer, and their killer to them.

thirty

Richard showered, shaved and put on his suit. He had a plan to salvage something good. Skipping the hotel's buffet breakfast, he was out on the streets by nine. It was Sunday. More fine weather. Blue skies. Sunshine.

Khreshchatyk was busy with sauntering families. Something that sounded like Eastern European grunge warbled through the air. Children's donkey rides were available. Bands were setting up in the middle of the road. A small crowd had gathered to watch a young woman juggle flaming torches.

Further on, the boxing-machine man caught Richard's eye and began punching the air and skipping on the spot. The crowd-cheer crackled through the tinny speaker.

"Five *hryvnia*," he said with each blow. "Muhammad Ali. Roll up!"

Richard gave him twenty *hryvnia* and walked on.

A *babushka* crossed his path pulling a handcart. It was wooden, squeaky-wheeled and had a long shallow tray loaded with a pick-axe, a shovel, bags of cement and broken flagstones.

In the Maidan, all the glass debris from last night's bottle-smasher had been cleaned up.

Two girls skipped by, chanting, "Yulia! Yulia!" The most effusive of them wore one of the Tymoshenko tee-shirts that were being sold outside the post office.

"You're in danger. You have to leave here."

Until those words, Tamara had ignored him, polishing glasses and feigning indifference. Now she paused.

"Pavlo come back soon," she said. "Two minutes."

He wondered if she were bluffing.

"I saw you through the window last night," he said. "It was late. Closing time ..."

Tamara frowned.

"Spying on me?" she said. "Like — how you say — like a peeping tomcat?"

"No. Listen. I saw him. Pavlo. Hassling you. You know what I mean."

"Pavlo is my boss," she said uncertainly.

"He was Nadya's boss too. But I had to stop him from forcing himself on her once. Like with you last night ..."

A flicker of doubt entered Tamara's face. Then her mouth was a hard, thin line. She glanced at her watch and out of the window.

"Pavlo say if you come here, I tell him."

"Tamara, listen. Pavlo is dangerous. He's ... already hurt some women. You need to be careful. You're pretty and ... Don't worry, I'm not ..."

Tamara stared at him.

"When I saw you last night," he said. "Pavlo was trying to ... *do* things. He had his hands on you. On your ..."

Richard placed his hands on his own chest, then pointed to her chest. She gave him a look of disgust and backed away behind the counter.

"No, don't be alarmed," he said. "I'm not going to touch you. Or hurt you. It's Pavlo you need to be worried about. He's a bad person."

Tamara's eyes strayed to the window again.

The grey Mercedes had arrived. It was slowing down and swinging into the entrance that led behind.

"Pavlo," said Tamara with a tight little smile.

"You've seen the news?" Richard said quickly. "The women who've been murdered ..."

There were noises in the kitchen. The sound of the back door opening and closing. Footsteps.

"Come with me now. We'll leave by the front."

Pavlo came through from the kitchen.

Without another word or look, Tamara went into the kitchen and closed the door.

Richard stepped away and raised his hands.

"It's all right," he said. "I'm leaving."

Pavlo swung open the counter flap and came forward. He looked almost pleased to see Richard.

The next thing Richard knew, he was on the floor.

He hadn't seen the blow coming. Or felt it. He felt it now. He touched his fingers to his mouth and they came away bloody.

As he was getting up, a vicious kick caught him in the ribs. A sharp pain lanced through his side. He crumpled to the floor, and lay there, trying to gather his wits.

Pavlo's face was a long way up.

Impossible to say what his next move might be.

He's insane ... Capable of anything.

Half crawling, Richard made for the door. But he felt the grip of powerful hands — one seizing the collar of his jacket, the other the waistband of his trousers. He was pulled up, turned roughly about, and propelled to the opposite side of the room.

He collided with two chairs and the edge of a table.

Pain seared across the top of his head. His vision blurred. His face smacked into the cold linoleum.

He lay there.

Dazed and incapable of coherent thought.

Then he began to piece together the information being received by his senses. Pavlo standing by the door, holding it open, his lips moving in speech.

"You go now," he said.

Richard nodded.

Using a chair for support, he stood and took a step forward. His legs gave way and he buckled to the floor.

"Sorry about that," he said, struggling up again.

He knew that his voice sounded weak and frenetic.

Sounded as if he were begging for mercy.

Then he thought, *As if? No. I'm doing exactly that.*
He took one careful step at a time.
Important not to fall again.
He anticipated another attack.
Didn't think Pavlo would let him go.

But he made it safely over the threshold and out to the front yard. In confused relief, he even turned to thank Pavlo — as he might courteously thank anybody holding a door open for him — but the door was already closing in his face.

He felt very old as he clung to the iron banister and hobbled up to the street.

A short way down the hill, he stopped in a familiar doorway. He was shaking and hurt all over. It even hurt to breathe. His trousers were torn across one knee and the breast pocket of his jacket was hanging off. The front of his shirt was bloody. His tongue was swollen and a tooth was loose. During a brief coughing fit, he brought up a gob of blood. He waited, took careful breaths, and tried to focus on being calm.

Get back to the hotel, was all he could think. *Get back, get cleaned up and decide if I need medical attention.*

He'd barely set off again when a passing car screeched to halt. A police car. Two uniforms jumped out and rushed over. Richard's first thought was that Pavlo had called them, but that would be ridiculous.

Maybe they were one of a number units on the look out for him? In connection with the break-in, or the incident in the metro system.

He braced himself, but it seemed that the officers had only stopped out of concern for his wellbeing.

"You fight?" said the tallest.

"Attacked," said Richard. "There ... Café Oasis ..."

He lurched uphill towards the café, staggered and nearly fell. The other officer laughed and caught Richard under the armpits. The taller officer came alongside.

"Okay," he said. "What happen?"

Richard thought about the question. If he could get Pavlo arrested for assault, get the opportunity to tell them what he knew in a full statement ... If he played it right, perhaps he could even request to speak with the senior investigating officer in the murder inquiry?

He said he'd been the victim of an unprovoked attack. He was a respectable teacher working at the Kyiv School of English. All he'd done was asked for a coffee and the manager had responded with violence.

The tallest officer nodded.

"Okay. We go see."

At the top of the steps, the officer said something to his partner, then descended. Stupid with shock and confusion, Richard began to follow. The other officer laughed and held him back.

Pavlo appeared in the yard below and met the officer head-on, offering a hand to shake. After about three minutes, the officer came back up to the street. Pavlo slouched in the doorway with his thumbs hooked in his trouser pockets, looking smug and unassailable.

"What's happening?" said Richard.

The officer spread his hands.

"He say you are a crazy person. Always you come here to find Nadya. But there is no Nadya here. He is very patient with you. He say you come here today and make shouting shouting shouting. You hit him first. He hit you. Fair fight. After when you run away you fall and hit your face on the ground."

"Nadya used to work here," said Richard. "Ask him what he did to her."

The officer called a question down to Pavlo, and Pavlo replied at length in a bored, apathetic tone.

"He say many girls work here," said the officer. "They come, they go. Now it is Tamara. Next week, next month different. If any Nadya work here before, he does not know where she is or if her real name was Nadya."

"He's lying. He's got something to hide."

"I am not understanding."

"I think he might have killed her."

The officer looked sceptical and didn't bother to question Pavlo further. But Pavlo offered up some words anyway and the officer translated.

"He say you always come here and make trouble. Now his *babushka* is sick. You make shouting with her and now she is sick. He is a good man. Business man, family man. He is not understand why you make trouble."

"His *babushka*?" said Richard. "I didn't threaten Olga. She's been lying to me as well anyway. She ... He ..."

Pavlo still slouched in the doorway, looking up from the yard. He appeared to be enjoying himself.

Richard snapped. He made a move towards the steps. It took both officers to restrain him. He kept shouting and struggling to get free, until the tallest officer slapped him round the face.

Then he was bundled into the back of the police car.

The tallest officer sat beside Richard; the other started the engine and the car moved uphill. Richard reached for the door handle, but the officer beside him grabbed him by the hair. He shook his head at Richard.

Richard grew calmer. Besides, the car was moving too fast now. And he'd noticed that the officer's hand was on a gun holstered at the hip.

He sank passively back into the leather seat.

"Identification," said the officer.

Richard took his passport from inside his jacket. The officer read details from the passport aloud, and the driver relayed the details into the police radio.

The car sped by Marinsky Park and Arsenalna Metro Station. A voice came back over the radio. For a few minutes the two officer's and the voice on the radio were in conversation punctuated with light laughter.

When it was over, the tallest officer turned to Richard, smiled and said, "You try to be detective?"

Richard hesitated. He thought it was likely that the dots had been joined and the police knew about the interview with Maksym Olearchyk. How long before they connected him with the head-butting incident?

"You're making a mistake," he said. "The new girl ... Tamara. If Pavlo's not stopped, she could be next. I think he's the killer ... the Chort."

The car pulled up at a red light.

"You are dreaming," said the officer. "What do you try to make in Ukraine?"

He said something to the driver.

There was a short blast from the siren and the car jumped the red light. It accelerated to sixty miles per hour and was soon passing through an industrial zone.

Razor-wire fences. Incinerator chimneys. Trucks lined up at warehouse loading-unloading bays. Red forklifts buzzing about like beetles.

Further on, they passed a compound filled with earth-moving machines. Factory units under construction.

Another kilometre, then the landscape thinning-out to older premises. Long, low-rise, hellish-looking buildings with grime-caked windows and asbestos roofs.

"Where are we going? Can I have my passport back?"

The officer didn't answer.

thirty-one

Derelict factories with broken windows. Stacks and stacks of mouldering wooden pallets. A burnt-out car. Rusted and unidentifiable pieces of machinery scattered across a tract of wasteland.

"So where are we going?" said Richard, heart banging.

The officer shook his head.

"Nothing for you in Ukraine," he said.

The car slowed and then turned onto a rough track. Bumped over stones and ruts of dry mud, raising dust.

A hundred metres ahead, a warehouse stood alone amid broken tarmac and tall weeds.

No other people or vehicles anywhere in sight.

If this was supposed to scare him, it was working. His mouth had gone dry. Cold sweat trickled down his back.

The car stopped in front of the warehouse. It looked ancient. Certainly a long time disused. The entrance was dark and gaping. One of the corrugated-iron cladding panels was torn, curling outwards, as if rendered that way by a giant can-opener.

"Okay, we go," said the officer.

"You can't be serious?"

The officer got out, walked around the car and opened the door. Richard's eyes fell again to the gun at the officer's hip, then he swung his feet out and stood up.

Important not to show fear, a voice said somewhere in his head. Then he almost laughed aloud. *What a joke! They'd have to be morons if they couldn't sense his fear.*

He scanned the wasteland and wondered what his chances were if he ran.

Zero, he thought. *You're screwed.*

Shaky with fear and disbelief, he turned to the officer, expecting to be coerced into the warehouse. But the officer held up the passport, then skimmed it through the air. It landed among weeds and rubble.

"Nothing for you in Ukraine," he said.

He got into the front passenger seat of the car.

The car turned round and started back down the track, dust-devils eddying in its wake.

It rejoined the road and headed for the city.

After Richard had picked up his passport, he went into the warehouse. It was an empty shell. Narrow shafts of light angled in from holes in the sides and roof. The air was still and cool. He walked to the centre of the cracked concrete floor and looked around. The extremities were just discernible in the gloom.

He closed his eyes. Felt peaceful for a moment. Had the odd sensation that his consciousness was expanding to fill the cavernous space. Caught a smell of ashes and something like singed hair or fur. Thought he could feel hot breath on the back of his neck ...

He opened his eyes but was too afraid to move.

From out of the silence came a long, baritone growl.

He ran for the exit, windmilling his arms and spinning in every direction as he went.

Empty space. Empty space, and yet ...

He kept running. Over the broken tarmac and through the weeds and rubble and down the rutted track. Fear numbing the pain of his injuries. He ran and didn't look back. Didn't stop until he reached the road. Exhausted and sick and spooked out of his mind.

His thoughts cleared as he stood at the roadside.

He was beyond grief now. Beyond anger. He felt strong and detached. Felt like a conduit through which some other force was operating.

Again, he remembered the words from his own essay:

What's stranger ... is when we see the mechanism for what it is but still allow ourselves to be carried along by its power, in full knowledge (and maybe with a smile).
Dark paths are thrilling and seductive ...

In the west, sunlight gleamed on a cluster of high-rises and a tower-crane. He was a long way from the city, but he knew everything would be all right now.

He took off his suit jacket. The front of his shirt had a bloodstain in the shape of a long pointed beard. He turned his jacket inside-out, put it back on and reverse-buttoned it all the way up. With the collar and lapels turned out, it covered even more.

The effect was passable, if eccentric.

The first car stopped for him, readily morphed into a taxi and zoomed him back to the New Bratislava.

After a long shower in his cramped but clean *en suite*, he slept between the operating-theatre-green sheets.

At nightfall, he put on his black jeans, a long-sleeved tee-shirt, black roll-neck jumper and Doc Marten boots.

He found an anonymous backstreet restaurant and had a leisurely dinner with two small glasses of wine.

The size of the tip he left was partly in compensation for the steak-knife he slipped down the side of his boot.

The knife was only for self-defence, he kept reminding himself as he took the metro to Arsenalna, walked past Marinsky Park and started down the hill. He had no intention of using it unless necessary.

He could see the plan clearly in his thoughts. He wasn't sure why and how it would work, but he knew — *just knew* — that it would.

Minutes later, he went through the arched undercroft and into the area behind Café Oasis. Pavlo's Mercedes was absent. Good. He felt calm. Even took a moment to enjoy the night sky. Thought how wonderful it was that so many stars were visible. How — less than a kilometre from the centre — the light pollution in Kyiv was so low.

It was a bigger area than he remembered from when Pavlo had thrown him out following the assault on Nadya. Bigger and more public.

The five-storey tenement buildings spanned back for twelve or fifteen metres on both sides. In the semi dark, the black iron balconies and fire-escapes looked like weird sculptures.

A squeal and a flurry of movement drew his attention to the wheelie bins at the rear, and he saw a skinny cat with a wriggling creature between its teeth.

Further to the rear were more yards and, beyond the yards, more tenement buildings that overlooked. Music and television noises came from open windows. At least two residents were out on their balconies.

To his immediate right, the blind side-wall of Café Oasis featured only the familiar solid door. To his left, from the blind wall of the adjacent building sprouted random ironworks — remnants from the removal of disused gates, Richard speculated.

At the sound of the Café Oasis side-door opening, Richard retreated a few steps, then wished he hadn't ...

Olga appeared in her print-dress and apron and her bun of grey hair. Light washed out from the kitchen. In a second, she'd tossed a rubbish bag alongside the wall then closed the door again.

She was the whole reason he was here.

He walked to the door, intending to knock. Took some deep breaths. What was supposed to happen ... Olga or Tamara would answer his knock. He'd get both of them together again, in the kitchen, without Pavlo, and he'd muster all of his calm and charm, and he wouldn't blame Olga for changing her story about Nadya. Tamara would be more receptive to Richard's calmer approach. And one last time, he'd appeal to Olga's sense of humanity and request that they go to the police before Pavlo could kill again ... It was going to go well. It was going to ...

Headlights swept into the undercroft.

The Mercedes. Pavlo.

Too late to hide.

Pavlo parked up near the wheelie bins at the rear, got out, slammed the door and strode over.

Richard took the steak-knife from his boot.

But Pavlo was upon him. Kicking out. Pain seared all the way up Richard's arm — he felt pretty sure that several fingers were broken. The knife dropped from his hand. He reached for it again but Pavlo trapped it on the ground with a foot and sent it skimming away.

Then Richard was seized by a meaty hand around his throat. Pushed against the wall. Pinned there, struggling.

Maintaining the grip with his left hand, Pavlo drew back his right fist.

"Chort," Richard croaked.

Pavlo hesitated.

"*Shto?*"

"Chort. You. *Vi*. The Chort."

Richard felt the movement again of a dark mechanism deep within him. Engendering action without thought. Through the conduit. As if scripted.

He used Gaidak's close-quarters tactic. Brought his knee up as hard as he could into Pavlo's groin.

Pavlo grunted and released his grip. Stumbled away from Richard, anger supplanting the pain in his face. He lost his footing on the cobbles, skidded on the dropped steak-knife. He reeled backwards, flailing his arms as he tried to stay upright.

Richard threw himself forward. Rammed into Pavlo. Was oddly elated as Pavlo staggered back and stopped dead up against the opposite wall.

Then Richard was on him. Punching wildly.

Head blows. Body blows. Right. Left. Right. Ignoring the pain in his fractured fingers.

This is for Nadya ... this is for Nadya ... and this ... and this ... This is for all the other women ... and this is for Trixie. Trixie? Yes, why not? And this ...

Something was wrong.

Pavlo wasn't defending himself.

Wasn't fighting back.

Wasn't moving.

He just stood there like a scarecrow. Against the wall. Arms relaxed by his sides. Eyes wide and bright. Full of surprise, wonderment almost.

Richard backed off.

Pavlo's head jerked about in an unnatural way. Then he took two steps forward. Frowned. Looked as if he'd forgotten something vitally important. He hopped from foot to foot in a brief robotic jig.

Then he went rigid and keeled over, flat on his face, like a domino.

In a fanning jet, blood sprayed from a hole in the back his neck, the base of his skull.

Richard couldn't work it out. He knelt over Pavlo and the spraying blood caught him in the face. He looked up at the wall and saw, at head-height, the protruding shard of a piece of old ironwork, still dripping.

"No no no no no," he whispered.

With an effort, he turned Pavlo over.

There was a short gurgling in Pavlo's throat. He lifted a hand, and it came slowly back down, as if on a ratchet, as if he were stroking the air or playing musical notes.

His lips moved wordlessly.

Richard took out his mobile but the battery was flat.

Pavlo's body twitched then lay still.

His eyes glazed over. A pink bubble formed at the corner of his mouth, then popped.

From several streets away came the electric hum of a tram or trolley bus.

Richard sat back on his haunches.

What he'd thought was a shadow on the ground, he now realised was a shocking amount of pooling blood. Its coppery smell hung on the night air.

Anybody could see that Pavlo was dead.

Richard stood up and realised that his hands were shaking badly. Which was strange considering how calm he felt now. His mind was a place of clear cool streams and meadow flowers and jasmine-scented air.

He gazed up at the sky, and made out — beyond the scattering of bright stars — a silky sweep of fainter stars. An arm of the Milky Way.

He smiled.

The Russian word for *old* was *stari*.

He didn't know the Russian word for *star*, but he liked it that *old* was *stari*.

Is there anything older in the universe than the stars? Any older crime in human history than revenge?

thirty-two

Richard supposed he really should get out of here ...

Whether five minutes had passed or half an hour, he didn't know. From the tenements at the rear, TV noises and someone's laughter carried through open windows. Nobody was out on any balconies at the moment, but a few residents had been out earlier. Had anybody seen?

Should he muddy the crime scene?

Take Pavlo's wallet and dump it in a bin somewhere?

Make it look like a robbery?

Maybe not. He was already backing off beneath the undercroft. He wiped his hands and face as well as he could with parts of his clothes that weren't blood-soaked. At least everything he wore was black.

He walked quickly down the hill.

In the Maidan, the digital screen flickered and the Sunday rock-bands were packing up their gear.

He bought a blue-and-yellow baseball cap from a *babushka*, set it on his head and pulled it down low. He withdrew the equivalent of three-hundred pounds from a cash machine, stole into the hotel and took the lift to the sixth floor.

In his room, everything was as he'd left it.

He drank a glass of water thirstily, then paced the room in a state of high energy. He kept forgetting to breathe, or bursts of laughter would tumble out.

Not good, not good ...

He wasn't calm any longer. He was confused and panicky ... Losing the thread of things. He spread his travel documents over the bed, plugged his mobile into the wall socket and called the airline. Surprisingly, they could schedule the open-return portion of his air-ticket for tomorrow afternoon. In a daze, he confirmed it and jotted down reference numbers.

Pavlo's probably already been found ... How long before the police make the connections? They're not stupid. It could happen before morning. Or in an hour. It could be happening now.

He began stuffing things in his bag.

Assuming police intelligence was joined-up enough, the information he'd given to Maksym Olearchyk would lead them to the New Bratislava. If not here first, then to the KSE and Alexei Koval in the morning. As for Café Oasis, Richard had given his hotel contact details and mobile number to Olga and Tamara weeks ago.

No getting away with this. Everybody knew where he was ... He'd probably left forensic evidence all over the scene ... Give himself up then?

Fragments kept coming back: the pink bubbles on Pavlo's lips ... Richard's wild punches, until he'd realised he was punching a stuffed scarecrow hanging against the wall ... the metal bracket sticking out, dripping ... Pavlo's two-step jig before he keeled over ...

With a start, he came back to the present.

His hands had stopped moving.

What was wrong with him? He should be packing. The situation was so desperate that he couldn't risk staying here a moment longer.

He looked at his watch. 10.17 p.m. But it had stopped, its face broken. Must have been from when Pavlo kicked the knife out of his hand.

He took the watch off and dropped it on the floor.

The travel clock by the bed showed 11.38 p.m.

Move. Move! What was he waiting for?

His mind was spinning without direction.

The bedside phone rang. The reception desk? The police? It could just as easily be one of the sex-workers who seemed to have an arrangement with the hotel. He'd been propositioned by phone his first several nights at the New Bratislava and the odd time since. Alexei had laughed and said that it was normal for many hotels in Kyiv, but that you could opt out on check-in.

The phone stopped ringing.

And what would Alexei think of him now?

A while later, Richard realised that he was sitting on the edge of the bed staring at the blank TV screen.

He looked at the clock again. 1.25 a.m. How was it possible for time to move so fast while doing nothing?

Then he noticed that his hands were covered with blood. So much blood. It was even packed beneath his fingernails — a dark red crust, drying.

Where it had come from?

A bolt of black horror jagged through him.

Where had it come from? He'd killed somebody. He'd fucking killed a man, and for a moment there it had slipped his mind!

He took off his boots. Whipped off his jumper and tossed it to the floor. He was sweating like a pig anyway. The blue-and-yellow cap from the *babushka* came off at the same time. It was bloodied too.

Blood on the colours of the Ukrainian flag.

He stood up and sat down again.

Have to get a grip ...

He went to the door, looked both ways along the empty corridor, closed the door and leaned back against it. A shower ... Before going anywhere, he really should have a shower. It was a risk, but he was bloody and stank of sweat. A long hot shower and he'd feel much better. More able to face what was coming.

That was his plan now. Get cleaned up and put on whatever clothes were still usable.

Abandon the rest of his stuff here.

Travel light.

Just split.

Find an all-night club or bar.

Wait for daylight and then lose himself among the morning commuters and shoppers.

Early afternoon, get a taxi to Borispol Airport.

But the thought of leaving his hotel room caused him to quake. He didn't know if he could do it.

It was hell out there ...

To tread those acres of green-carpeted corridor, where the air-conditioning whispered malevolently ...

The truth was, he wanted to take his time in the shower and then stay in his room and be left alone while he worked a few things out.

Why not? Everybody should be allowed head-space to think things through. It had been an accident, after all ... Kind of ... No. You caused his death.

At the very least, you caused his death.

Richard sat on the bed again. Important not to get too stressed. Stress was bad for the health. The medical profession had been advising for decades that it can put undue strain on the heart and even lead to strokes.

He really should get in the shower.

Years ago — during his secondary-school teaching before he ever lectured at uni — he'd bought a CD called *Coping With Stress* by Dr Angelika Plenkt-Gomez. He used to lie on his bed and listen to the gentle, soothing, hypnotic female voice that took you through techniques of relaxation, breathing, visualisation.

Really should get in the shower.

Instead, he lay back on the bed and tried to conjure up the CD voice. Forced himself to breathe deeply and evenly. Flexed and relaxed the muscle groups of his feet, hands, legs, arms, stomach, face.

Focused on slowing down his thoughts.

Imagined himself lying on cushioning white sand in a tropical paradise.

From nowhere, the lyrics of a Martha and the Muffins song from about 1980 swam into his head:

The lure of 'Echo Beach', and how far away it was in time. Far, far away. Lulling him to sleep ...

"Rich," Trixie said to him in the dream, "remember that favourite Einstein quote of yours? Something about how the only reason for time is so everything doesn't happen at once. Okay? So he was right. Because everything *does* happen at once. All of history and all of the future are *now*. Our minds are so clever that we create the illusion of past, present and future. We create the illusion of structured time. And we can't escape from the illusory *now*. Except — under special circumstances — we *can*.

"I know you're in a lot of trouble over there. So, listen. I can help you. You've always been cynical about some of my beliefs, so it may not be easy for you to accept this. Once every thirty-seven years, one person on the planet is given a unique chance. It has something to do with a rare alignment between Venus, Saturn and Neptune.

"Listen carefully, Rich. When you wake up, all you have to do is change the settings on your travel clock. You have to do it as soon as you wake. Reset the hour, date and month. You can travel back to any time you want, as long as it's within the last year ..."

Daylight at the window.

The travel clock showed: 6.23 a.m. MON 11 APR.

Any sense of panic over drifting off and sleeping was dulled by the glue of slumber and the memory of the dream. He even reached for the clock to change the settings before waking-reality kicked in.

The full horror of the previous night flooded back as he sat up and saw blood smudged across the pillows and bedding. He was still wearing his tee-shirt and jeans. Now he stripped everything off.

There weren't many places on his body without either bruises or bloodstains. He looked at the bed again and laughed aloud at his thoughts. At least the operating-theatre-green sheets had come into their own.

In front of the wardrobe mirror, he examined his face. The mashed lip, the bruises around his left eye and cheek — they were all from yesterday's first visit to Café Oasis, when Pavlo had punched him and then propelled him across the café to crash into the tables and chairs.

Only yesterday? It felt like a week ago.

What now then?

Get out. Move. You can still make it.

But despite the urgency, he still didn't feel he could leave without a shower. He knew then that all rational thinking had gone la-la.

thirty-three

For fifteen minutes, he languished under the steaming water, shampooing his hair, soaping himself all over. Drying took a while because of having to dab around the many bruises.

A bloody handprint on the ceramic tiles jumped out at him. He thought about cleaning it off, then went into the main room and saw handprints and random bloody smudges in just about every direction he looked. The carpet, the walls, the bed, the cupboards.

He turned the pillows over, straightened the duvet.

Futile.

Get out. Get out now.

In another two minutes, he was wearing a blue shirt, brogue shoes and his Paul Smith suit with the tear across one knee. The wardrobe mirror showed him that even more bruises were ripening on his face.

He glanced at the baseball cap he'd bought from the *babushka* last night. Too bloody.

Then he spotted the orange scarf Alexei had given him. He wound it about his head and tied it under his chin. Aside from it looking ridiculous, if he bowed his head most of his face was hidden.

A deep breath, and he opened the door.

His heart leapt.

Striding purposefully down the corridor were five men in bottle-green military uniforms and caps.

Richard froze in the doorway.

Pointless going back inside. They'd seen him.

As they got nearer, he saw that they all wore medals and moved with a high-ranking haughty demeanour. The generals, or whatever they were, drew level then filed past. Only the fourth of the five paid any attention, fixing Richard with a brief quizzical stare, clearly taking in the orange headscarf arrangement and the bruising.

Richard slumped against the doorframe as the last of them went by. They continued to the end of the corridor, then they exchanged pleasantries and let themselves into their rooms like any other guests.

When the corridor was empty, Richard hurried to the lifts. Down in reception, he passed the desk and the maroon-jacketed porters and went straight out through the main door. Nobody would guess he was leaving for good; he didn't even have a bag with him.

Around Khreshchatyk and the Maidan, pedestrians were sparse and traffic was light. Most early morning commuters would be using the metro. A yellow bus was taking on passengers, and an army-style truck rumbled by blasting the gutters with a high-pressure water jet.

Feeling conspicuous and vulnerable, he withdrew another three-hundred pounds from a cash machine and added it to the thick fold already inside jacket.

For all he knew, his name could be with Interpol. His bank card could be blocked at any time.

He passed a group of three city cleaners washing down a tram shelter. One — a woman with a leathery face and inquisitive eyes — stopped what she was doing and stared at Richard.

For a paranoid moment, he convinced himself that the cleaners were undercover police. He walked faster and slipped around a corner, but kept looking back.

Too exposed out here.

He headed for the nearest metro steps.

For hours, he sat with his head pressed to a carriage window, registering everything and nothing. Up and down the Red Line. Again and again. Terminus to terminus. Acadeмmistechko in the north-west. Down through ten stations to Khreshchatyk. Then the more familiar stations of Arsenalna and Dnipro. Over the river. Hidropark. On and on. Livoberezhna. Darnitsya. Chernihivska. Lisova. End of the line. Back again.

Each station looked different in its own way. Then each station looked the same. Fluorescent light. Faded tiles. Old marble.

As commuters thinned out towards mid morning, he got off at Khreshchatyk and sat on a platform bench. Waited and watched as people embarked, disembarked, stood about. Metro trains came and went.

He panicked a little every time warm wind blew through the tunnel before each arrival. He had memory blanks. Time slips. Big gaps of nothing.

Some moments, he felt that his skin was screaming, that his body was about to burst into flame. At other moments, he felt numb and indifferent.

Then he remembered something ...

The airport. He had a flight to catch.

He pulled up the cuff of his jacket. Saw his bare wrist. Remembered that his watch was broken and dumped on the floor of the hotel room.

No mobile either. Where had that gone?

When the next train pulled in, he used the people who got off as cover. It had been a mistake even entering the metro system. He glimpsed the time on somebody's watch. 11.55 a.m. The flight was at 1.20.

All those hours melting away and now he was running late. Even by taxi, it was a forty-five-minute run to Borispol, and then there'd be check-in and customs ...

He followed everybody up the escalators and across the concourse to the security barriers. A last tug on his headscarf. Face down. Metro token at the ready. Softly singing the Martha and the Muffins song ...

Echo Beach ...

Out on the street, Richard climbed into the back of the first taxi. His guts were churning with paranoia. He kept seeing more and more street cleaners in their orange sleeveless jackets. Why were there so many? Or had he just not noticed before?

He didn't begin to trust the cheerful taxi driver until they'd left the city behind and were cruising along the freeway between flat tracts of birch forest. The spidery trees were coming into leaf, but were largely a canvas of dull brown, relieved in places by the green of firs.

It's taking too long, he thought. The speedometer needle was pinned to 90 kph, though he felt that he could get out and walk faster.

They arrived forty minutes before take-off. He could still make it easily. He paid the driver and ran to the entrance, then slowed to a walk as another cleaner gave him a sidelong look. She was kneeling on the ground swabbing off the marble of a low wall that supported the plate-glass windows. It had only been a quick look before she'd carried on cleaning. But now that Richard had seen her leathery face, he couldn't be sure that she wasn't the same cleaner from the tram stop many hours ago ...

Coming back to his senses, he went inside.

His eyes picked out the uniforms. Police officers in fur-collared jackets of dark-blue and hats with folded-up earflaps. Customs officers in petrol-blue, with caps and epaulettes and gold buttons.

So many officers — customs *and* police.

He made his way to the check-in desks, his hand hovering about his face in an attempt to hide the bruises. Hoping that he didn't look too much like a lunatic in the makeshift headscarf.

There was no queue. Last calls for the flight had probably gone out already. The girl at the check-in was all smiles. She didn't question his bruises or his lack of luggage. It all went smoothly. *Too smoothly* ...

For all he knew, the smiling girl was innocent, but she could just as easily be *on to him*. He read subterfuge in her every word and gesture. She could be working for the Ukrainian equivalent of Russia's FSB.

He thanked her and gripped his documents as he walked towards the customs gate.

It was no good though ...

He couldn't bring himself to go through. Security would be waiting for him in the departure lounge.

Maybe his paranoia about city cleaners and the check-in girl was unfounded. But the security services were on to him all right. They were preparing to move in and take him down. Weren't they?

Flights to London were being monitored. His air ticket and passport details would be on the screens in a control room at this moment.

He felt like a rat in a burning maze.

His limited moves were running out fast.

Circling steadily back to the exit, he thrust his shaking hands in his pockets before they betrayed his guilt.

Then he saw the newspapers on a news-stand.

The front page carried a large picture of a man's face, alongside the familiar four-paned window-picture of the victims. Maryna Petrenko. Bella Savchuk. Polina Boyko. One of the panes was still a greyed-out silhouette with a question mark in the middle.

Something about the four-paned picture was different, but he couldn't work it out.

The headline was a single word in Cyrillic. He'd seen it often enough to know that in English it was CHORT.

Richard felt giddy as he looked at the main picture.

It was a face he'd know anywhere.

But it wasn't Pavlo.

thirty-four

While the taxi headed back to the city, every five minutes or so he unfolded the newspaper and looked at the face.

Nikolai Gaidak.

Richard kept reliving the first encounter, months ago, on the metro platform. The humiliation of that smirking, liveried troll kissing his hand then spitting in his face. The fantasy of pushing the man into the path of the train ... If only he had. *If only* ...

The further humiliation in Bar Zavtra several weeks ago. The bigoted taunts and insults. Richard's thrown punch stopped by Gaidak inches from its target.

Far worse than any of that ...

He tried, but failed, to still the intrusive thoughts of that strutting, troll-like figure trailing Nadya through some ill-lit alley behind Arsenalna Station.

Those strong, fast little hands on her.

Once at Independence Square, he sought the backstreets.

He turned a corner and nearly collided with a heavily made-up woman who looked like a broken-down opera singer; a white poodle with a red bow on its head trotted behind her. In the next street, a man opened his door and fired a bucket of water towards the gutter. Richard skipped aside but the legs of his trousers got splashed a bit anyway. Another hundred metres and he found the sort of place he was looking for.

The Kievska Comfort Hotel was still fairly central, but tucked away and obscure — a dull brown building crumbling like a bad tooth amid a ragged mandible of paler tenements.

In a dim foyer, behind the scratched and fingerprint-smeared window of his corner booth, the myopic check-in clerk was immediately suspicious.

His English was good but he used it with reluctance and refused a room without seeing a passport. He kept eyeing Richard's bruised face.

Richard unwrapped the scarf from his head and draped it about his neck, hoping that a display of Orange Revolution solidarity might help.

He couldn't risk giving his real name, so he said all his documents were in his wife's bag and she'd be arriving from Sevastopol tomorrow.

"You want double room then?" said the clerk.

"Yes," said Richard, taking out and flashing a wedge of bank notes. "More expensive, right?"

"What time your wife come tomorrow?"

"Twelve o'clock. Midday."

"How long you want to stay?"

"A week ... maybe two."

"Okay. I give you one night to begin, Mr ... ?"

"It's Paul Smith," he said, improvising with the brand name of his suit.

When the money had been settled and the register completed, the clerk tossed a card-key on the counter.

"All information coming to me tomorrow," he said.

Richard made for the stairs. He wasn't expecting a working lift but then there was a *ding*, the rumble of the lift door, and the emergence of two laughing young men arm-in-arm. Richard smiled and took the stairs anyway.

The third-floor corridor had flaking mauve walls. The beige carpeting was springy and new.

Such was the Kievska Comfort. Card-keys and decay. Dilapidation and modernity.

In Room 305, plaster was missing from parts of the ceiling, the wooden laths exposed. A huge TV stood in one corner, a mustard-yellow armchair in the other. The room and *en suite* were shabby but clean.

Pavlo had it coming anyway ...

The thought kept surfacing, though he knew it was nonsense. No way would he be able to salve his guilt.

Is it possible though, he wondered, *to still evade capture? But how? Go on the run? Become a fugitive and live like a wild man in the forests?*

Annushka came to mind. Nadya had once said that Annushka was probably the daughter or the niece of an oligarch. Like Russia, Ukraine had a thriving underworld and a thriving black market economy. Maybe Annushka could put him in touch with the right people?

He still had access to thousands in his bank account, if it didn't get blocked. Money could buy anything. Maybe he could buy his freedom? Get false documents and skip the country? He pulled everything out of his bulging pockets and spread it over the bed. Annushka's number had been jotted on a scrap of paper. The scrap of paper was no more — dumped, lost, he didn't know where. But he was clear that he'd stored the number on the mobile. He was also now clear that the mobile was where he'd left it — on charge in his old room.

The fob-key to the New Bratislava room was there on the bed. He hadn't checked out. Could he sneak back in undetected and get the mobile?

With the orange scarf about his head again, he left the Kievska Comfort, smiling cheerfully at the myopic clerk on the way past.

Minutes later, he entered the Maidan from the streets behind the Trade Unions Building and set off along Khreshchatyk. He passed a blind flautist, a *babushka* selling roasted sunflower seeds, a man with a monkey dressed in a tiny red jacket and fez, another *babushka* griddling corn-on-the-cob over charcoal ... it smelled delicious but he kept moving.

Fifty metres from the New Bratislava, he stopped dead. Three police cars were outside. One uniform stood by the cars, another stood by the revolving doors of the entrance. The rest would be inside. There was a white van, too — it looked like a forensics unit.

Pavlo had it coming anyway ... No, his death was unnecessary and wrong. It was an accident though ... No, not really. You caused his death. It was as good as murder. I didn't mean for him to die ... You killed him.

Why had he imagined he could return to the room? It was late afternoon now. The blood and abandonment would have been discovered by one of the cleaning staff this morning, hours ago.

He turned and started briskly back in the opposite direction. His heart galloped and his mouth had gone dry. There was something else ...

A sleek vehicle in the corner of his vision. He turned to look, and the vehicle stopped. It was a black Land Cruiser with tinted windows.

Pavlo's friends ... It had to be.

Richard walked on steadily, glancing back. The Land Cruiser glided behind, keeping a distance of five metres.

The department store, Tsum, was on his left.

He ducked inside. Half walked and half ran through the open-plan departments — kitchenware, bedding, menswear — hoping for a rear exit.

As he passed a display of hats, he took off his improvised headscarf, draped it about his neck and tucked the ends down inside his jacket. He lifted a dark trilby from the display and slapped it on his head.

Hmm ... Good fit ... Lucky dip.

"Excuse me, sir," said a man in a brown smock. "The till is over there ..."

But Richard had spotted a rear exit.

He peeled a few notes from the fold inside his jacket and pushed them at the salesman.

"This is too much," said the man. "And you must still go to the till."

"I don't have time. Keep the change. Compliments to the store."

He slipped out onto a quieter street. Turned left, turned right, dodging between pedestrians and parked cars. Sprinted for fifty metres. Turned right again and leaned against a wall. Waited for his breathing to slow down. Peered around the corner. No store security. No police. No Land Cruiser. He waited again. Threaded his way through the backstreets and came out at the edge of the Maidan. Head bowed, he hurried to the nearest pedestrian underpass.

He knew where he was going next.

"Ruslana, right?" he said. "It's ... Paul Smith."

The young woman behind the counter at Bar Zavtra smiled politely but frowned as she took in his facial injuries. He tipped the trilby back on his head and explained that he'd fallen down the metro steps.

"I *think* I remember you," she said as she set the wheat beer in front of him.

He spread his newspaper on the counter.

"Gaidak, the killer. Three weeks ago, he was in here. I ... had a scuffle with him and I was asked to leave."

"Yes, the Chort," said Ruslana, glancing at the paper. She touched a hand to her face and said, "Oh ...Yes I *do* remember you. I am sorry, Mr Smith."

"It's fine. You can call me Richard."

"Not Paul?"

"Ah ... sorry. It's ... Paul Richard Smith. I prefer my middle name." He took a swallow of beer. "At least they've got him now, and I was hoping ... Could you tell me more about what the news story is saying?"

She summed it up for him: Gaidak was caught during the attempted abduction of a young woman he'd followed near the Maidan two nights ago. Overwhelming forensic evidence, including hair-lock trophies, had been found at his apartment.

Richard nodded.

The Chort article took up the first four pages. There was an article on the fifth page that he wanted Ruslana to translate, but didn't dare ask. It had a picture of Pavlo. Richard recognised the Cyrillic for Café Oasis. His own name wasn't in the text, but for all he knew there could be something to the effect that an Englishman was being sought to help with inquiries.

Pavlo hanging against the wall like a scarecrow ... Richard's wild punches ... a moment's glee ... then the realisation that something was wrong ... Pavlo coming forward like a zombie ... unhooking himself from the metal spike ... his grotesque two-step jig ... the fanning blood ...

"What else does it say about the Chort?" he asked.

"Oh, well ... the woman from the river," she said. "The police say they may never know who she was."

Richard stared at the floor.

Then he looked at the front page of the newspaper. Again there was something about the four-paned picture of the victims that wasn't right, but he couldn't think straight, wasn't able to place what bothered him.

He was out of time anyway.

Two police officers had entered Bar Zavtra.

Richard couldn't risk circling behind them to the exit just yet. But they were on their way to the counter, so he had to move. He gave some cash to Ruslana, picked up his beer and tried to appear casual as he made for the terrace overlooking the indoor shopping-centre.

When he was safely there, he chanced a look back and saw the officers talking to Ruslana.

Once, Ruslana even glanced towards the terrace.

Bar Zavtra's music system was playing Ella Fitzgerald. 'How Deep is the Ocean?' Her voice had to compete with the shopping-centre Muzak — some soulless atrocity that sounded like a panpipe rendition of Motorhead's 'The Ace of Spades'.

A group at one terrace table were noticing Richard because he hadn't sat down. He was hovering by the door to the main bar, staying away from the opening but unable to stop himself peering around the door jamb. The next time he looked, the officers were coming ...

"Mr Farr?" one called. "Mr Farr?"

Amid raised voices and alarm, Richard climbed over the safety rail and lowered himself down as far as he could. His hands gripped the edge of the terrace, his feet dangled in the air. There were shouts above him and more shouts from below.

But the shoppers had stood aside.

Left a space clear.

Into which he dropped.

Now — swimming around him — were the faces, the shopfronts, the stainless steel columns and surfaces, the clean splashing of the indoor fountain, the smells of perfume and pastries.

A woman came out of a jewellery shop wearing a little fur jacket — pure white with dark rings — like the pelt of a snow leopard. She smiled as she began to film Richard on her camera phone.

The officers were shouting from above.

There was a pain in his ankle, but he could still walk.

He could still run.

thirty-five

Back in his room at the Kievska Comfort Hotel — pretty sure but not certain that he'd given the police and anybody else the slip — he drew the curtains and peered through the gap. The urban backstreet was quiet with only the odd vehicle and pedestrian about. Lights were winking on as dusk fell.

He spread the contents of a plastic shopping-bag over the bed — brown rolls, cheese, two bottles of red wine. For the next half-hour, he ate and drank. Then he sat on the bed watching TV and opened the second bottle.

What would he do when the imaginary wife failed to show tomorrow? Was he even safe here overnight?

The police must know he'd moved on from the New Bratislava, even though he hadn't checked out.

How long before they made inquiries at other hotels, asking about suspicious foreigners?

And, of course, he couldn't go back to Bar Zavtra.

He got up and looked out of the window again.

The street was dark and quiet.

A pain in his hand was getting worse and he couldn't use two of the fingers. He tore a strip of cotton from a shirt and strapped the fingers together.

He lay on the bed with the remaining wine.

A documentary about the Ukrainian gas industry played on the TV. He watched it blankly, understanding nothing but the visuals. The TV ran on into other programmes as he drifted and finally slept.

When he woke, his travel clock was showing 8.03 a.m. A hangover did nothing to dampen the return of graphic images into his thoughts. Pavlo's death. The police. The black Land Cruiser.

He finished off the bread and cheese, took a shower, re-strapped his fingers with more cotton from the old shirt, and waited until ten o'clock before leaving.

"All information coming by midday," said the clerk.

"Yes, yes," said Richard.

He had the trilby with him but didn't put it on, and wished he'd left it behind. It would be part of the police description after yesterday's incident at Bar Zavtra. He found a *babushka* selling zip-up sports hoodies, bought one, and then gifted her the trilby to resell.

At Independence Square, he counted four police cars parked at random points as he skirted his way around.

It was an overcast day and he gravitated towards the cover of shadows or mingled with other pedestrians as he meandered his way to Passazh.

He walked slowly by the café and glanced in. As predictable as clockwork, Alexei was sitting at his usual table for his mid-morning coffee and vodka shot.

Despite the risks, Richard entered.

His face cowled by the hoodie, he sat at Alexei's table.

Soft laughter from Alexei, then:

"Ah, Richard ..."

A waiter appeared.

"Bring him coffee, please," said Alexei.

"You know everything, don't you?" said Richard.

"Perhaps. But, please ... Tell me."

When Richard's coffee arrived, he summarised events leading up to and concluding with Pavlo's death at the back of Café Oasis two nights ago.

"I believe you that it was a tragic accident," said Alexei at the end. "And there is not much to say. Your mistaken beliefs and foolish actions ... It is already known by police pathologists that blows were inflicted to Pavlo around the time of his death. You brought a knife with you, which you left at the scene. Whatever story you tell now — the truth or something other — your guilt and conviction are inevitable."

He unfolded his newspaper on the table.

"A few more days," he said, slapping the paper, "and everything would have looked different."

Richard stared at the newspaper.

Gaidak was on the front page again, along with the four-paned window picture of the victims. And now he saw what was different. It was the third position, not the fourth that was a silhouette with a question mark.

"They were political killings after all," said Alexei.

Richard frowned.

"What?" he said. "How? Why?"

"Gaidak lived near Darnitsya Metro Station. He was a doorman at Hotel Yalta, as you know. The murder sites were in a line that pointed the way to the city centre. Investigators know now that the body from the river — still unidentified — was the third victim, not the fourth. The fourth was Polina Boyko with the Tymoshenko-style hair. Gaidak was stalking a fifth woman close to the Maidan when he was arrested. She had Tymoshenko-style hair as well."

"So —"

"He was rehearsing, Richard, and all the while getting closer to his true target. Notebooks, documents and computer files have been found in his apartment. Details of Yulia Tymoshenko's calendar of events and public appearances over the coming weeks. He is an extremist. Old Soviet. Against the Orange Revolution. Detectives say he was planning to kill her on the 9th of May, which is Russia's biggest Victory Day celebrations — military parades in Red Square, *etcetera*. You know, the 1945 victory over Nazi Germany."

"I still don't get it ..." said Richard. "If the Kremlin wanted Tymoshenko dead —"

"No," said Alexei. "Not that. Gaidak was not a Russian agent. He was a lone wolf, acting towards his own sick, misogynistic and political ends."

"A lone wolf?"

"And now *you* are a lone wolf, Richard. Of course, detectives have been to the KSE. I had to give them all your details. What choice did I have?"

"You had no choice. And they knew anyway."

"And tomorrow ..." said Alexei. "I know from my contacts that tomorrow your face will be all over the media. So. Why did you come to me?"

"I was hoping ..." said Richard. "Hoping that you could put me back in touch with Annushka. I lost the mobile phone. Her number. I don't know, I thought maybe she might know ... *people*."

"People? Yes, I see. But Annushka flew to Washington last week with Omaha, the KSE's new tutor. A whirlwind marriage and off they went. He says they will come back, but ... well ... who knows?"

Richard laughed thinly.

"I should go," he said.

"Where will you go?" said Alexei. "I'm surprised that you've evaded capture until now."

Richard gazed around the café and out of the window.

"Nobody is coming," said Alexei.

"Don't you want to see me locked up?"

"No. I'd like to see you get away with it. Whether you deserve my help, I don't know."

Alexei's mobile phone beeped and he picked it up.

"Bear with me," he said. "Let me reply to this text."

When it was done and the phone back on the table, Richard stared at the lit-up panel that soon went dark.

"Who ..." he began.

Alexei smiled.

"An administrative detail at the KSE. That is all."

"Oleg?"

"No," said Alexei. "Oleg resigned. He partly managed a nightclub and now he is doing that full time. One of your old students, Galnya — she is now the KSE's administrator and she is excellent."

"Galnya? Yes, she —"

"Richard. You have my word of honour that I have always been sincere with you. Whatever it is you think Annushka's *people* could facilitate ..." He lowered his voice again. "I cannot soil my hands with any of this, of course. False documents. Safe passage out of Ukraine. Isn't that what you hope for? But you must understand that if I put you in touch with a friend of a friend of a friend, so to speak, then you cannot make any reference to my name going forward."

Pastries and more coffee arrived at the table. If Alexei had given a waiter the signal, Richard had missed it — *and that was the trouble really ...*

He looked out of the window and a lurching sensation filled his chest and guts. A black Land Cruiser slid sleekly by. Was it the same one that had kerb-crawled him yesterday? Pavlo's friends?

"Can I ask you a question, Alexei?" he said. "That time I saw you outside Café Oasis with Pavlo ... You went without me, to ask about Nadya. Or so you said. Did you really and truly never know him before that day?"

Alexei looked scandalised.

"*Really and truly?*" he said. "You are asking me t*hat*?"

Richard watched Alexei's face, trying to read him.

The phone beeped again.

Alexei began to reach for it, then stopped himself.

He's brilliantly clever, thought Richard. A master of compartmentalisation. A business executive. Director of studies. Teacher. Mentor. Guru. Multi-linguist. Wannabe politician. Orange Revolutionary. Confidant of lawyers and the courts. Family man. Each role occupying its designated layer in his psyche, with the neatness and precision of a *matryoshka* doll. What else? Friend? Betrayer? Was he offering safe passage? Or delivery into the hands of the police or Pavlo's avengers?

"Who's messaging you *now*?" said Richard.

"No," said Alexei. "I don't think you do deserve my help. Look at you! You cause the death of a Ukrainian man — and although I believe your story, I doubt the investigators or the legal authorities will — then you are running around and haunting the city like some kind of Raskolnikov. You come over here with your Western ways and your Russian grandfather —"

"My grandfather's long dead. Western ways? I thought you liked the West?"

"Do not patronise me, Richard. I cannot say that I am enamoured by the face of the West that *you* have shown me. Too unreliable. Too suspicious. Poor judgement and misguided incendiary action before all the facts are in. Can you deny it? And now the American, Omaha — *he* has flown the coop."

Richard broke eye-contact and drank some coffee.

Alexei laughed bitterly and said, "I see that inside your new ... um, *garment* ... you are still wearing the orange scarf I gave you. But is it, was it ever sincere? Or mere tokenism?"

"I know I let you down," said Richard. "If I could turn back the clock ... to a better time. The first time here in Passazh ... When you invited everybody here. Nadya too. I ... I was so happy. It was all so ... so ..."

"Innocent?" said Alexei. "But nothing can be turned back or undone. The time is now. The world is now. We face what we have to face — the hope and the terror, and we go forward in our limited life and time. In the wake of Ukraine's victory and the triumph of the people's politics, will the West allow us to join the hallowed institutions of NATO and the EU? Will they trust us?

Maybe I am innocent, too, by believing and hoping for these things?"

Two men came into the café and sat at a table at the back with a clear view of Alexei and Richard. Both wore leather jackets and had gelled hair.

Richard recognised one as Pavlo's brother, Roman — remembered meeting him at the family party in Café Oasis the first night back in the country.

The coffee machine hissed. There was a smash from behind the counter as an item of crockery was broken.

"Do you know those men?" asked Richard.

Alexei glanced over, then looked levelly at Richard.

"No I do not," he said. "But they have been to the KSE asking about you."

Richard stared at Alexei's phone, hesitated, then said, "You didn't ...?"

Alexei looked profoundly disappointed.

"What do *you* think?" he said.

Richard didn't know what to think, but he couldn't help himself. He grabbed the phone from the table. Alexei folded his arms. Richard saw that the last unanswered text message was from Galnya. He opened it, expecting it to be in Ukrainian but it was in English: *Thanx Alexei. Yes, Isabella say she come from Naples and begin teaching next week ...*

Richard placed the phone down.

"I'm sorry," he mumbled.

He looked into Alexei's face one last time, and understood everything.

The offer of help was no more. It couldn't happen. Not even because of Richard's suspicion and ingratitude, but because the narrow window of opportunity had closed. Alexei had fielded Pavlo's heavies at the KSE. But now they'd seen Richard and Alexei together.

If somehow Richard still slipped out of the country, Alexei would pay a heavy cost.

He finally understood. Knew that Alexei had always been sincere. Had tried to be and could have been the best friend Richard had ever known.

"I'm sorry, Alexei," he said again.

Then he got up and edged towards the door.

Roman and the other man stood.

Richard ran. Out of the door and to the front end of Passazh. Without looking back. Onto Khreshchatyk and down the underground steps. He ran through the passages and chambers. By the buskers and the toy-robot seller and the *babushki* with their flowers and groceries and cigarettes.

He turned into another passage, narrower and dimly lit — a passage he couldn't remember seeing before.

It was empty and dusty, and at its dead-end there was a wooden door in the wall.

The door had wrought-iron hinges and a big old latch. He expected it to be locked, but when he operated the latch and pushed against the door, it swung open.

thirty-six

Stone steps wound down a dark spiral well.

As he descended, he heard the sound of voices. The air about him was cool. He kept going. In another moment, the stairwell turned through a corner and opened out into a large chamber where ragged people squatted by fires, cooking and eating, and drinking from bottles. He could smell charred meat and something sweeter.

Eyes adapting, he saw that the stone walls of the large rounded chamber led nowhere else. Skylights and vents dotted the domed ceiling.

Richard threw back his hood and approached one of the fires. The huddled figures shifted to make room for him. From several of the people came brief eye-contact or a nod — otherwise his presence was accepted without comment or question.

He was about to say that he wouldn't be staying long, but he'd begun to shiver and readily moved closer to the fire. Some of the faces were bony, emaciated; others were haggard, wrinkled — all were dignified and ageless.

The person next to him offered food. He smiled his gratitude, took whatever it was and ate, tasting nothing. Another passed him a bottle and he drank deeply of something that was harsh but comforting.

"I won't stay long," he said.

A hand slapped him on the back in a comradely way.

From somewhere much deeper than the chamber, Richard fancied that he heard low groans, as of a large and proud animal in pain. He had a sense of water too — leviathan movements in a vast body of water.

"Is that ... ?" he said.

An old woman pushed a hunk of bread at him.

"Drink, eat," she said.

He took the bread and passed her the bottle.

Their welcome was a mystery.

He could have been one of their own, returning to the fold after a short time away.

Although he had no memory of falling asleep, he knew that he must have slept. He woke on the hard ground by the fire and sat up. People still ate and drank around him. Tendrils of wood-smoke hung and drifted, but inevitably threaded up to the grilles in the high ceiling.

He remembered the earlier meeting in Passazh, and some of Alexei's words came back to him:

The time is now. The world is now. We face what we have to face — the hope and the terror, and we go forward in our limited life and time.

Richard stood up.

"I'll go now," he said to the gathering. "But, thank you. *Dyakuyu*. Thank you, good people."

He slipped off the hoodie and held it out.

Somebody accepted it from him and put it on.

From inside his suit jacket, Richard took some notes and handed them over. The people shared the notes out and thanked him. He had no idea how much he'd given.

Then he went back up the steps to the heavy wooden door. Passed through it and along the passage, out to the main passages. Walked by the little shops slotted into the wall. By the vendors and the *babushki*.

"Richard? Richard!"

He stopped.

Stared.

Felt as if he'd fallen out of a plane without a parachute and was hurtling towards the ground.

It was Nadya.

"Richard," she said. "I ... You are *here*. You are hurt. What happened to your face?"

He couldn't breathe.

"Nadya," was all he could manage.

"I didn't think you were coming back," she said. "But what ... ? You make me afraid. What has happened? I waited at the post office ..."

Something like laughter rattled from his throat.

"Six weeks ago," he said.

She reached a hand towards him then stopped herself.

"Yes," she said. "Six weeks. I waited as we arranged ... I waited again at the same time the next day, and the next. I phoned your friend. He said your life was a big mess. That you probably wouldn't be back. That I should leave you alone, you already had enough problems. And Oleg, at the KSE, he said that you had been fired and you would *not* be back in Kyiv."

The shock of seeing her, the shock of everything — it had climaxed and exploded, leaving nothing behind but a feeling of turning to stone.

"Then Aunt Katerina was ill again and we went to the Black Sea. It was a difficult time. I had decided to ring your mobile phone, but ... by then I had lost the numbers you gave me. My aunt, she was very ill ... we cared for her all this time ... then she died. I only arrived back in Kyiv yesterday. But Richard ... who hurt you like this?"

"I tried to eat a table and chairs," he said.

Amid the numbness, his intellect ticked away coldly, processing information. Was it possible that she didn't know Pavlo was dead?

"I've been back for more than a month," he said flatly. "I kept looking for you at Café Oasis. Pavlo and Olga, they lied about you."

Nadya reached out a hand and rested it on his arm.

"Pavlo ..." she said. "After you left, Pavlo tried ... again ... you know. Then when I went to the Black Sea, I decided that I would not work at Café Oasis any longer. That I would never go back. I told you before that he helped my family ... Well, Pavlo came to the Black Sea, to Aunt Katerina's village. He pressured me very much. Wanting me to marry him."

"He didn't say I'd been looking for you?"

"I asked if you had been to the café but he said not. Anyway, I would not marry Pavlo, not even if I had not met you. I'd never marry him."

She didn't know. She might yet learn before tomorrow about Pavlo's death, but not all of the details. Not yet. What had Alexei said? *I know from my contacts that tomorrow your face will be all over the media.*

He turned away and began walking.

"No ... wait," she said, stepping in front of him and blocking the way. "I ... Maybe this is not a good time for you? Please wait a moment. You seem ... very different, Richard. If there is some problem. Did Pavlo cause these injuries? If you are not well ... You look tired ... and thin. Maybe we could ... go for a drink somewhere? Or to my family home in the south of Solom'yanskyi district ..."

He stared at her.

"Or maybe you need time?" she said.

She took a pen and a slim diary or address book from her handbag. On a blank page at the back, she scribbled something down, tore the page out and gave it to him.

He scanned the writing: her full name, Nadya Tsvetkova, a landline phone number and an address in Solom'yanskyi.

"I have thought about a lot of things, Richard ..."

He put the page in his pocket and tried to walk on again. She stopped him.

"It was a mistake not giving you my contact details before. I was wrong. But I was afraid. The years since London have been difficult. Strange. I was afraid ..."

He smiled.

Some experiences change you utterly. It's not possible to go back to being who you were before.

"Yes, I understand," he said. "What will you do with your life now, Nadya?"

"I really think ..." she said, smiling, "I think I would like to talk to Alexei at the KSE. Ask if maybe I could *try* to teach English. A few sessions a week at first maybe. It was months ago now, but he did mention training. Do you think he might still give me a chance?"

"Yes," he said. "I really do think so. I really do. I have to go now though. Something important to take care of."

"Of course ..." she said. "You ... have my details. I'd like it if you called me. To talk. Or to go somewhere ..."

He laid a hand on her shoulder briefly, then turned and walked away.

"I love you," she called after him.

A ripple of emotion, a faltering step, and then he kept walking without looking back.

epilogue

Richard sat at a customers' side-desk in the post office with the envelopes he'd bought at the counter.

He read through his hand-written document that began "Last Will & Testament of ..." and included the phrases "... all my worldly ..." and "... Nadya Tsvetkova only ...". He signed and dated both copies.

Into the first envelope, he put one copy and a note to Preeti requesting that she forward the will to a good solicitor. Into the second envelope, he put the other copy, all his remaining ready cash, and a lot more cash that he'd just withdrawn from a machine.

He addressed the first envelope to Preeti at the Marjoram Fields house in London, and the second envelope to Nadya at the Solom'yanskyi address she'd given him fifteen minutes earlier.

Then he went to a teller and posted both envelopes by registered post.

The Land Cruiser was still waiting for him outside.

It shadowed him as he crossed the square.

The sun was down below the buildings but it was still full daylight. A pleasant spring evening.

Since he hadn't been grabbed and hauled into the vehicle before he'd reached the other side, he mounted two steps and passed through the marbled entrance of a newly refurbished hotel.

Just inside the doorway was a tall, potted plant with large slotted leaves, of the variety *monstera deliciosa*.

Delicious Monster. He smiled. Trixie used to have one of those at the London flat. It didn't need much water, but it needed *some*. Left in Richard's custody, after

Trixie's drowning, the plant had suffered a long, dry, neglectful end. And he still felt guilty ...

In the soft lighting of the hotel foyer, muted classical music played and a fan turned lazily on the ceiling. The girl at the desk smiled a welcome through her reaction to Richard's facial bruises.

"I'd like a room," he said, producing his passport.

His right hand was swollen badly and two fingers were bound with the strip of fraying cloth. The girl stared at the hand for a second, then she picked up the passport.

"Oh ... it's Mr Farr? Is that correct pronunciation?"

"Yes, that's right. Richard Farr from England."

She kept looking at the passport. Then she glanced towards a glass-walled office at the end of the counter.

"Would you excuse me, sir?" she said.

"Yes, of course."

He watched her go to the office with his passport and consult a blonde woman who sat at a computer.

As he waited, he heard the hotel's entrance door open behind him. He turned to see Pavlo's brother Roman and the other man standing by the delicious monster. Roman gave Richard a civil nod, and Richard nodded in return.

The girl came back.

"Mr Farr," she said. "Yes, we can give you a room."

"That's good," he said. "Do you have anything on the tenth floor?"

She consulted a computer monitor.

"Yes, we have," she said. "Overlooking the Maidan."

"Perfect."

The girl gave him a nervous look.

"The manager ... she says ... um, if you don't mind leaving your passport here at the desk ... you can go straight up to your room and settle in. Um, and we can take care of formalities later?"

"Perfect," said Richard.

She looked relieved.

He accepted the card-key and crossed to the lift.

Room 1009 overlooked the Maidan beautifully.

The side-opening window only opened for six inches. It was then restricted by a metal safety-strap, but that was soon remedied with a smart blow from the back of a chair he raised and brought crashing down.

He swung the window wide and leaned out.

Two police cars were outside the entrance. More were speeding into the Maidan from Khreshchatyk.

A gentle knocking sounded on the door.

Not the police. No. It would be Roman.

Officers on the ground — and the gathering crowd — were looking up. Richard tucked the ends of his orange scarf more thoroughly inside his jacket, did the jacket up all the way, and climbed out onto the narrow ledge of corbelled stonework.

He didn't want or need a crowd.

Fortunately, the police were guiding everybody away.

More officers spilled out of arriving cars. Some helped to control the gathering, others entered the building.

Behind Richard, the knocking on the door grew louder and quickly graduated to banging and thumping.

But it was going to be all right.

A large semi-circular space had been cleared directly below where he stood ten floors up on his ledge.

It was a long way down.

Far enough ... Yes, far enough.

What do I believe? I believe that a person who walks a destructive path does so not because they don't have a choice, but because they in fact choose to walk a destructive path — consciously or unconsciously, alone or in collusion with a dazzling desirable other, even if sometimes that other is an innocent catalyst.

Teetering on the ledge, he thought back to the short, happy time he'd spent with Nadya. And he knew that he'd never been happier.

Behind him in the room, the door burst open.

He gazed out over Maidan Nezalezhnosti once more. Felt the breeze and the sunshine on his face. The independence monument swam in his vision. He raised his arms in a similar manner to the figure on top.

Then he closed his eyes and stepped off the world.

*

Author's Note: If you have enjoyed this novel, please consider leaving a star rating, brief review or comment on Amazon.

Printed in Great Britain
by Amazon